THIS LORD WOULD NEVER BE HER MASTER!

When Richard Glover, the Marquess of Chadwick, asked
Ginevra Bryant to be his wife, it was not a question but a
command. Ginevra's father, in desperate need of Chadwick's aid to save himself from ruin, told Ginevra she
must obey. The despair and fury of the London beauties
who had dreamed and schemed to wed this handsome,
powerful aristocrat told Ginevra how lucky she should
count herself. And Chadwick's tone when he voiced his
proposal was that of a man used to having his every desire obeyed.

Standing at the altar with Chadwick, Ginevra could not
find a way to say no. But though she had lost this first
battle, her war had only just begun—as this rebellious
bride vowed never to surrender her heart to this lord who
had never met a woman he could not conquer. . . .

THE
CHADWICK RING

The Chadwick Ring

by
Julia Jeffries

A SIGNET BOOK

SIGNET
Published by the Penguin Group
Penguin Books USA Inc., 375 Hudson Street,
New York, New York 10014, U.S.A.
Penguin Books Ltd, 27 Wrights Lane,
London W8 5TZ, England
Penguin Books Australia Ltd, Ringwood,
Victoria, Australia
Penguin Books Canada Ltd, 10 Alcorn Avenue,
Toronto, Ontario, Canada M4V 3B2
Penguin Books (N.Z.) Ltd, 182–190 Wairau Road,
Auckland 10, New Zealand

Penguin Books Ltd, Registered Offices:
Harmondsworth, Middlesex, England

Published by Signet, an imprint of Dutton Signet,
a division of Penguin Books USA Inc.

First Printing, February, 1982
11 10 9 8 7 6 5

 REGISTERED TRADEMARK—MARCA REGISTRADA

Printed in the United States of America

Publisher's Note

For Marshall, Daniel, and Gregory

Look, how this ring encompasseth thy finger,
Even so thy breast encloseth my poor heart.
—Shakespeare, *Richard III*

When Ginevra Bryant glanced up from her book and spotted the dark figure cantering along the drive to her father's house, she caught her breath and quickly retreated behind the sheltering branches of the beech tree. With her hand at her throat she peeked through the curtain of old limbs now thick with spring-green new leaves, and she wondered if she had been seen. The tall, lean man who handled his spirited stallion with such easy power showed no sign of noticing the girl cowering under the tree beside the garden wall. Still wary, Ginevra relaxed enough to admire the grace with which the rider swung down from the saddle and tossed the reins to the young groom who was racing across the drive to him, bare feet kicking up gravel as he skidded to a halt. A stone struck the horse in its sleek fetlock, and it shied, jerking the ribbons out of the boy's hands. Ginevra watched in amazement as the man barked out a single word and quieted the skittish animal. He caught the reins and handed them again to the groom, speaking to him in low, stern tones. Chastised, the boy bobbed his head respectfully and led the now-sedate horse toward the stables. The tall man peered after them until he was satisfied the boy could handle the stallion; then he turned and strode arrogantly up the steps to Bryant House, oblivious of the watching girl. Ginevra sank back against the trunk of the tree, limp with relief, heedless of the bark snagging the soft fabric of her grey muslin day dress. Her thudding heart resumed a more normal beat. He had not seen her. She was safe. She reached again for her book, and then she paused, her small fingers poised in midair. Why did she say she was "safe," as if he somehow

1

threatened her? He had never been discourteous to her, had never shown her anything other than a correct, if faintly disdainful, deference. But the simple fact remained: Ginevra had always been afraid of the Marquess of Chadwick.

He had always been there, as far back as she could recall, a dark blot on the otherwise perfect surface of the golden summer days she knew as a child at Dowerwood, the small but beautiful estate in Surrey where she and her mother spent the hot months while her father remained at Bryant House, near Reading, to supervise the harvest. Ginevra could still remember the first time Richard Glover, Lord Chadwick, paid a formal call on her mother, and she herself was summoned to the drawing room, a slight, dainty figure in a short pink dress with ruffled pantalettes peeking out beneath. She had curtsied to her mother before turning to the visitor, and when she saw him she gasped. She had never seen a man so tall before. Her own father was short and comfortably round, about the same height as his wife, and to Ginevra this towering stranger seemed almost supernatural. She forgot everything her mother had carefully taught her about the proper deportment before adults as she stared up, up at him, up the whipcord-lean body clad all in black except for his snowy ruffled shirt, up to the dark, craggy face with hooded eyes and wild raven curls. Ginevra had recently attended an Evangelical Sunday school in the company of one of the housemaids, and she vividly remembered an illustration from a lurid tract she was given there, a picture of a swarthy figure in black who lured the unsuspecting to lives of "unparalleled vice and infidelity," whatever that meant. Furtively she glanced at her mother, who watched the confrontation with tawny eyes full of anxiety, and ignoring the iron precept that a child must never speak to an adult unless spoken to first, Ginevra blurted to the man, "Are you the devil?"

She still remembered how it felt, standing before him trembling, her hands clenched into tight fists as she awaited the explosion that never came. Her mother collapsed back on the settee, mewling with mortification, but the marquess said nothing. He dropped to a squatting position in front of Ginevra and caught her chin with long fingers that swallowed up her face. For an endless moment he studied her defiant features, the quivering mouth, the wet eyes the same dark gold as her long plaits, and she in turn saw now that his eyes were not black like the rest of him, but were, astonishingly, a clear, piercing blue. When at last he spoke, his voice was deep and silky. "Well, Ginevra, do you think I am the devil?"

She blinked. "I do not know, my lord. You might be. You look like a picture I saw at Sunday school. That is why I asked."

He raised one eyebrow as he observed, "At this Sunday school you attended, did they not tell you that the devil is the Prince of Liars? If I say I am not he, how can you believe me?"

She considered this and at last shrugged helplessly. "I don't know. Are you a liar?"

Behind her she heard another agonized squeak from her mother, but the marquess ignored the woman as he slowly shook his head. "No, little Ginnie," he said softly but firmly, "I am many things, but I am not a liar. I promise I will never speak anything but the absolute truth to you." He stood erect again, lithe and powerful, and his eyes were hooded once more. With a dry chuckle he addressed Ginevra's mother. "Compose yourself, Lady Bryant. I assure you the chit has not offended me. I find your daughter delightful. I think"—he glanced down at Ginevra—"no, I am certain, that she will serve us very well." And with that enigmatic note he bowed elegantly and took his leave.

Ginevra did not see the marquess again that summer, but she did meet his two sons: Tom, who was just slightly older than Ginevra and with his black curls and blue eyes already a junior edition of his father, and Bysshe, the younger by three years, a frail youngster with lackluster brown hair and eyes, who was sulky and retiring except for those rare occasions when he burst into paroxysms of reckless activity. Ginevra was unimpressed that Tom was a viscount, heir to the adjoining Chadwick estates and the gloomy Tudor mansion called Queenshaven, or that even his sullen little brother was by courtesy the Lord Bysshe Glover. If anything, she felt sorry for the boys. They seemed to be growing up lonely and neglected, raised by servants, for their mother had died when Bysshe was an infant, and their awesome father was absent months at a time. In a childish effort to make up for all they lacked, Ginevra gathered the pair of them to her small heart, and during the summer months the three of them were inseparable, climbing trees, riding their ponies among the grazing sheep, lost in the happy days of innocence.

But when Ginevra was twelve, her childhood ended.

As she lounged on the moss under the old beech tree, her book forgotten in her hand, she remembered the day six years before when she had waited with her parents in the "best" parlor at Dowerwood, her hands folded primly in her lap as she sat rigid in a cherrywood armchair, immobile except for her curious, darting eyes. Contrary to custom, her father had left Bryant House in the care of a steward and had accompanied her and her mother to Surrey that summer. Now he shuffled restlessly in front of the fireplace and fidgeted with the embroidered silk screen. He glanced repeatedly at the pendulum clock on the mantel, comparing it to the watch he kept in the pocket of his long striped waistcoat, and sometimes he stared wistfully at the duelling foils mounted on the wall behind the clock, gazing at them as if he wished he were an undergraduate again with nothing more serious to worry about than developing a strong sword arm. Lady Bryant reclined languidly on the settee, wrapped in shawls despite the afternoon heat. Her greying hair, once the same burnished gold as Ginevra's, was tucked into a lace cap, and her dim eyes gazed unseeing at the papered wall hung with engravings framed in black brazilwood.

Suddenly Harrison, the butler, announced in stentorian tones, "The Marquess of Chadwick and Viscount Glover." Lord Chadwick strode into the room, imposing, intimidating, and radiating nervous energy. Ginevra gaped when Tom lagged along behind his father. The boy was impressive but clearly ill-at-ease in gleaming tasselled

Hessian boots and an intricately folded white stock, which seemed about to choke him. Still in short skirts herself, and unaware of her burgeoning womanhood, Ginevra was thunderstruck at the change that had come over her friend. Her bewilderment increased when, after civilities were exchanged by the adults, Tom rose at a signal from his father and cleared his throat ominously. "Ginnie," he began in an unnaturally deep rumble, "uh . . . I mean . . . Ginevra, I . . . I . . ." His voice suddenly shot up to a tremulous squeak. Ginevra watched sympathetically as Tom tried in vain to regain control of his voice, but he could not, and at last he lapsed into uncomfortable silence, flushed and quaking with humiliation. Ginevra lifted her hand to comfort him, but when she saw his father's cold blue eyes narrowed with disdain, her hand dropped back helplessly to her side.

Then the marquess spoke. "Miss Bryant," he said, and the form of address shook her almost as much as the obvious irritation in his deep voice, for until that moment no one had ever called her anything but Ginevra, "Miss Bryant, what my bird-witted son is trying so inadequately to do is ask if you will honor him by consenting to become his wife and future marchioness."

Ginevra stared up at him, mute with the fear he always inspired in her. In exasperation he repeated the question. "You mean . . . you mean . . . *marry?*" Ginevra choked. When the man nodded, she turned in confusion to Tom, but the boy was still struggling with his composure. Desperately she fled to the divan where her mother lay wan and colorless in her classical draperies, a recumbent caryatid. "Mama!" she pleaded.

Lady Bryant gently stroked her daughter's pale cheek. "It won't be for years yet, Ginnie darling," she reassured softly. "Although by law you and Tom could wed as soon as he turns fourteen, we all think it could be best if you wait until you are . . . oh, eighteen or thereabouts. By then you'll be better prepared for the high position you will aspire to as Tom's wife."

Ginevra tried to read the expression in her mother's tawny eyes. She could sense there were things being left unsaid. Finally she asked, "Is this what you want, Mama?"

Lady Bryant's lips turned up in a pale imitation of her once lovely smile. "It will be a brilliant match, Ginnie," she said. Her eyes sought out her husband standing gravely by the fireplace. She sighed, "At least this way I shall get to see my little one betrothed."

Ginevra turned to Tom again, Tom, her friend, her playmate, so suddenly and inexplicably changed. She demanded, "Can you really want to marry me?" Stiffly Tom inclined his dark head as far as his heavily starched neck-cloth would permit. Ginevra bit her lip. It was some kind of joke the adults were playing, it had to be—but they all seemed so deadly serious. Finally she said, "Very well, I will marry you, Tom," and she thought she heard a sigh of relief from her father. She watched Tom's blue eyes flicker in the direction of Lord Chadwick, and at his signal the boy took the girl's hand in his own and with simple and affecting dignity bent to brush his lips against her bloodless cheek.

Thus Tom and Ginevra were pledged, and it was several years before she realized that the scene in the parlor had been a charade, a dumb show performed to console her dying mother. The marquess wanted Dowerwood annexed to the Chadwick lands, and Sir Charles ensured an outstanding match for his daughter by making the estate her marriage portion. That the two children whose lives were being planned knew and liked each other was totally irrelevant.

In the autumn Tom and his brother Bysshe were packed off to school at Harrow, and Ginevra returned with her parents to Bryant House, unaware that she had spent her last summer at Dowerwood. By Michaelmas her mother was confined to her bed, and she died quietly in her husband's arms on Christmas Eve. Ginevra's grief was profound, but, jerked abruptly into womanhood, she had little time for tears.

During the next few years Ginevra worked hard, not only assuming her mother's duties as housekeeper and hostess but also overseeing the welfare of the Bryant tenants and their families. She began sewing her trousseau. In her spare time she continued her education by reading the books in her father's library.

When she was fourteen her father entertained a party of landowners, and although the task of seeing to their comfort fell heavily on her small shoulders, for once her father did not expect her to play hostess as well. While the men communed noisily in the main salon, Ginevra ate her meal from a tray in the library while she puzzled over the poems in a dusty volume she had found on one of the upper shelves, fallen behind the copy of Dr. Buchan's *Domestic Medicine or Family Physician* she had been seeking. She munched thoughtfully as she read, greatly admiring the skill of the poet yet confused by the disturbing images the words conjured up. Some of it was clear enough—"Naked she lay, claspt in my loving Arms"—but other lines were meaningless to her. Her smooth brow was furrowed when a deep voice inquired from just beside her, "Well, Miss Bryant, what are you looking so pensive about?"

With a stifled cry she jumped, gasping, "Oh, my lord, you startled me!"

"Forgive me," he said smoothly. "I did not mean to distress you. I only wanted to compliment you on the excellence of the dinner. I understand from your father that you prepared part of the meal yourself?"

Ginevra nodded. "Yes, thank you. I help Cook whenever I can. It's good practice for when . . . for when . . ." Her voice trailed off, and she blushed faintly.

"For when you and Tom are wed," he finished. "Tell me, my dear, do you look forward to your marriage?"

She glanced up, then, to see if he were teasing her, but his blue eyes seemed grave, and she tried to answer him seriously. She toyed nervously with one of her honey-colored curls as she sighed, "I don't really have time to think much about being married. The idea seems unreal. But I have years yet to learn to accept it."

"Yes, years," he murmured. "And in the meantime you will continue to sharpen your domestic skills. Your diligence is praiseworthy, although perhaps I should point

out that as Viscountess Glover it is unlikely that you will
be expected to do your own cooking." His winning smile
softened the ironic bite of his last words, and he continued with an air of polite curiosity, "What is that book you
read so studiously—the latest Minerva novel?"

Ginevra shook her head. "No, my lord, it's poetry,
something I found this afternoon. I like verse, but there's
not much available locally, and Papa never thinks to
bring me anything but romances back from his excursions
to London."

"Indeed. Why don't you read some of this absorbing
poetry to me? I should be interested to know what sort of
thing you enjoy."

Ginevra grinned sheepishly. "I am not proficient at
reading aloud, I fear. I expect my droning would only
make you drowsy. However, perhaps you could be so
kind as to explain this piece to me? Some of it simply
does not make sense. This, for example . . ." Her voice
took on a singsong note as she stumbled over the unfamiliar words:

> The nimble Tongue (Love's lesser Lightning) plaid
> Within my Mouth, and to my thoughts convey'd
> Swift Orders, that I should prepare to throw
> The All-dissolving Thunderbolt below.
> My flutt'ring Soul, sprung with the pointed Kiss,
> Hangs hov'ring—"

"My God!" he exclaimed, ripping the book from her
hands. "What *is* this?" Ginevra, stunned and speechless
with shock, could only gape as he leafed back to the title
page. One dark brow arched sharply upward, and he muttered, "Rochester. I might have known." He closed the
book with a snap and handed it back to her. "I suggest
you return this to wherever you found it without further
ado. I can see that I am going to have to advise your father to monitor your reading habits in future."

Appalled, Ginevra demanded, "But why? My father
doesn't care what I read!"

"That," said the marquess coldly, "is abundantly

clear." He gazed down at her tense, defiant face, and his expression softened somewhat. "Ginevra," he said, "I know you're just a little girl and can hardly be expected to understand the significance of books such as this. Perhaps it will help if I explain that while the Earl of Rochester was one of the greatest Restoration poets, he was also an unprincipled libertine whose short, misspent life would put even members of the Hellfire Club to the blush. His writings can scarce be considered a wholesome influence on a young mind. Do you understand?"

She cradled the book protectively against her budding breasts. "All I know is that you are giving me orders, and you have no right to."

His eyes narrowed, and he regarded her intently from beneath his almost effeminately long lashes. "Then know this," he said fiercely, the force of his words emphasized by the quiet pitch of his voice: "you will one day be a Glover, and the ladies of my family do not, I repeat, do *not* read obscene verse fit only for the eyes of a Covent Garden doxy!"

Ginevra's already rosy cheeks reddened even more. Her gold eyes widened and she gasped, "Oh, you . . . you . . . *odious* man!" She fled from the library, with his jeering laughter ringing after her.

She did not see Lord Chadwick again for three years—for which she was grateful—nor did she see Tom. Twice each year, on her birthday and at Christmas, Ginevra received letters from her fiancé, a series of formal, almost identical missives inquiring politely after her well-being. She replied in kind. Sometimes when she compared those stiff little notes to the passionate love letters penned by the heroines in the romantic novels her father brought her from his frequent trips to London, she wondered what chance she and Tom had for happiness in the cold-blooded arrangement their parents had made for them. She consoled herself with the knowledge that at least she and Tom were old family friends. That was more than many engaged couples could claim. She was sure that in time the regard they had for each other would ripen into a deep and enduring love, the kind of relationship her parents had had.

Ginevra looked forward to her seventeenth birthday eagerly, for Tom and his family were to visit, and at last the engagement was to be formally announced. She could even face the prospect of meeting the marquess again without dismay. Her anger had begun to abate even before the beautifully engraved volume of Blake's *Songs of Innocence* arrived from London by special courier, but it had been some time before she could remember the naive little girl she had been with a sort of wistful indulgence. Now she hoped to impress her future father-in-law with her new maturity, but mostly she wanted to see Tom again. She had an engagement present for him, a miniature of herself painted on ivory, looking poised and quite grown-up in the low-cut peach-colored gown she would wear to her party.

But Lord Chadwick arrived at Bryant House without Tom, accompanied only by a slender, gangling youth whom Ginevra identified with difficulty as young Bysshe, now taller than she was. Tom, the marquess said, was at Queenshaven, convalescing with a broken leg he had received trying to ride his father's stallion, something he had been strictly forbidden to do. Ginevra noticed Bysshe snort derisively, and she knew without asking that the younger boy must have ridden the horse successfully himself. When everyone insisted that Ginevra's first adult party should go on as scheduled, it was the marquess himself who placed the Chadwick betrothal ring on her finger. Ginevra could not help shivering at the hot light, quickly veiled, that flashed in his blue eyes as he studied her in her pink gown and murmured, "My son will be a fortunate man someday. . . ."

When Ginevra's birthday passed and the guests went away, she settled back into the life she had always known, suppressing the frustration she felt that she and her future husband had once again failed to meet. It wasn't important, she supposed, that she and Tom were now virtual strangers. After all, they were going to have a whole life together.

Then on a blustery night in March of 1816, three months before the long-awaited wedding, Tom and several underclassmen sneaked out of their quarters at Oxford and proceeded to a nearby gin shop, determined to get as drunk as possible before the proctors caught up with them. Urged on by his cronies, Tom stole the innkeeper's cart horse and tried to make it jump a five-bar gate. The horse sensibly refused the jump, and Tom was thrown and broke his neck.

Ginevra shivered, pulled back into the present by the freshening May breeze that cut through her thin dress. Lost in poignant memories, she had whiled away most of the afternoon, and now she had duties to perform. She must inform Cook that there would be one extra for dinner, and despite her aversion to Lord Chadwick, she would have to see that the best guestroom was prepared for him, since she presumed he would stay the night. It was unthinkable that he should journey all the way from Queenshaven and not lodge with them. Most likely his servant was still somewhere down the road with the luggage. Ginevra's lips twitched. She could not envision Lord Chadwick dawdling impatiently alongside a lumbering carriage when instead he might be galloping Giaour, his magnificent roan stallion, across the countryside. He was a man who raced through life—and always alone.

Ginevra rose from her seat under the beech tree, a slim, graceful figure dressed simply in soft grey. Her high-waisted muslin dress with long tight sleeves and a high neck was unadorned except for a simple ruffle of black lace at the collar and wrists. Although she grieved for Tom, she did not assume formal mourning when she learned of his death—after all, they had not seen each other for six years—but the somber clothes she did wear reflected the dark bewilderment of her mind: for as long as she could remember, her life had been ordered, predestined—and suddenly, without warning, all the plans came to naught. What was she going to do now?

Ginevra picked her way across the garden, skirting the daffodils dying back under the budding rose trees, and slipped through the gate that led around to the kitchen door of Bryant House. She was not ready to face Lord Chadwick just yet. She did not know what she could say to him to ease the loss of his son and heir. When her distraught father showed her the terse note the marquess sent—a few bleak lines inscribed in a hand as black and bold as the man himself—numb with shock, Ginevra had murmured conventionally, "At least he still has Bysshe to comfort him." But even while she uttered them she knew the words were meaningless. Tom had been the favorite, the beloved son—insofar as the marquess was capable of loving anyone. Little Bysshe, so unlike his father in looks, never lacked any material need, but he held no place in the man's heart.

As Ginevra passed into the kitchen, the soothing scents of the garden flowers were overwhelmed by the fragrant tang of fresh herbs wafting from the lamb sizzling on a spit before the large open fire. When the scullery maid tugged on the heavy chain that turned the wheel on one end of the spit, Ginevra heard a reluctant creak. She made a mental note to have one of the men oil the mechanism. Cook, a buxom grey-haired woman who had been ruler of the kitchen since before Ginevra's birth, was taking a colander down from one of the rows of shining utensils that hung on the walls of the spacious kitchen, but she set it aside and bustled over to the girl when she saw her. She smiled at her young mistress with the intimacy of lifelong acquaintance and said cheerfully, "Well, Miss Ginnie, and what can I be doing for you?"

Ginevra grinned and came straight to the point. "A disaster only you can prevent, I fear. As you know, Lord Chadwick has just arrived unexpectedly to see my father. What can we feed him?"

Cook rubbed her round cheek thoughtfully, leaving a smear of flour under a bright blue eye. "Poor man'll be hungry after his journey," she muttered, musing aloud, "what with losing his boy and all . . ." Ginevra's mouth quirked. To Cook food was the balm for all pains. The older woman pursed her lips and nodded sagely. "Don't you be worrying none, Miss Ginnie. My Ben caught some trout this morning, and there be chicken and lamb and fine, fresh strawberries. We'll fix his lordship as good a meal as he could get in London any day."

Ginevra patted the woman's plump arm. "Oh, Cook," she said with relief, "I can always depend on you. You prepare whatever you think best, and I'll go down to the cellar later to choose the wine." With a grateful smile she turned and went through the door that led to the main hallway. Wistfully Cook watched her go. Miss Ginnie was as kind and capable a mistress as one could wish, for all that she was still but a girl. It was tragic how her great marriage had come to nothing. Pray God that someday soon some fine gentleman would offer for her and she could at last know some of the happiness that had been lacking so far in her short life.

The hallway seemed chilly after the warm, redolent atmosphere of the kitchen, and Ginevra paused at the foot of the stairs, shivering. Should she make herself known to her father at once, or ought she first to go up and change her dress before she greeted their visitor? By lingering so long in the garden she was already remiss in her duties, she acknowledged ruefully, and no childish qualms could really excuse her discourtesy to the marquess. But on her skirt was a definite streak of damp, clinging earth, and she could not compound her ill manners by appearing before Lord Chadwick grubby as an urchin.

As Ginevra loitered in the hallway, toying with her dress, she heard angry voices coming from her father's study. She glanced up in surprise. She could not recollect the last time she had heard her father's voice raised. Since his wife's death Sir Charles had grown quieter, increasingly taciturn, until sometimes days went by without him uttering a dozen words to his daughter. Ginevra listened curiously. The two voices were distinct but muffled by the closed door, so that she could not make out the words. She heard her father's voice, high and querulous, the intonations of a man growing old before his time. Lord Chadwick's tones were much deeper, and she could not hear so much as feel them, like the distant rumble of thunder. Suddenly the marquess's voice rang out, piercing the closed door so that every word was clear: "No, Bryant, the boy is still too young."

Then Ginevra heard her father sputter, "But dammit, Chadwick, I cannot wait!"

Ginevra's heart faltered with sudden foreboding. Dear God, what was going on? What were the men plotting in the study—and for whom? Who was the boy who was too young—too young for what? She gathered her skirts in her hands and fled up the stairs to her bedroom.

Her chamber door opened just as she reached it, and Emma Jarvis, her maid and dearest companion, rushed out, looking harried. Emma was a tall, well-built woman twelve years Ginevra's senior, who had served the girl since she herself was little more than a girl. Her dark brown hair and pensive green eyes had captured the hearts of several of the men on the estate, but Emma ignored them all. Cook once hinted to Ginevra that Emma had had a sweetheart who fell to the press gangs and died at Trafalgar, and since then she dared care for no man.

Emma cried, "Oh, Miss Ginevra, there you are! I've been looking everywhere for you. Your father wants you in the study."

"Yes, I know," Ginevra sighed. "But first I must change my dress. I look like a mudlark. Find me something, will you? The brown bombazine, I think."

Emma made a face. "Not that awful thing, you know the color doesn't suit you at all. Why don't you wear the white muslin with yellow ribbons that you made for your trou—" She stopped abruptly.

Ginevra shook her head. "No, Emma, the evening is turning too cool for a light dress. Besides, it would be disrespectful to our guest to appear too gay when Tom died but two months ago. Now, help me into the bombazine and then we'll see if we can do anything with my hair."

A quarter of an hour later Ginevra tapped lightly on the door to the now-quiet study. At her father's command she entered. She kept her eyes trained on her father, but she was instantly and acutely aware of the man who stood tall and imperious before the fireplace, where a few embers warmed the dim, book-lined room. He was, as always, impeccably attired in riding breeches and gleaming boots, topped by a frilled silk shirt and an elegantly tailored coat of superfine, all of deepest black. Ginevra gritted her teeth. She ought to be wearing mourning, if not out of sorrow for Tom, then as a courtesy to his father. Fortunately, the marquess did not seem to notice.

She sketched a quick curtsy to her father and inquired, "You sent for me?"

Sir Charles grumbled irritably, "Yes, and you took your time coming!"

"Forgive me. I was out in the garden."

Her father shrugged. "No matter, you're here now. Do you remember Lord Chadwick?"

"Of course," Ginevra murmured as she turned and curtsied, lifting her eyes no higher than the tops of his boots. "How good to see you again, my lord."

From the slight movement of his legs Ginevra knew the marquess bowed in return. His deep voice was dry. "Miss Bryant. I spotted you when I arrived, but I hardly dared believe it was you, you are so grown up. You make me uncomfortably aware of the passing years. Tell me, do you still have a penchant for Sunday-school tracts?"

Ginevra's glance flew upward in astonishment to meet his. He never changed, she observed, flushing deeply. His eyes were that same unnerving, penetrating blue that always disconcerted her, and now they were alive with malicious amusement. With considerable effort Ginevra regained her composure enough to answer seriously, "I regret, my lord, that nowadays my domestic duties leave me little time for church."

"What a pity," Chadwick drawled. "In London a show of religion has become quite the thing among the *ton*. Many a man makes a point of staggering home from his club in time to lead the household in morning prayers."

Ginevra stared at him. She muttered under her breath, "Not you, I'll wager."

Chadwick heard her. His eyes sparked. "No, Miss Bryant, not I. I think you correctly analyzed my feelings in that regard the very first time we met."

Sir Charles followed this exchange with some confusion. "Daughter," he asked sternly, "are you being disrespectful to our guest?"

Before Ginevra could answer, Lord Chadwick interposed smoothly, "Of course she isn't being disrespectful, Bryant. She and I are merely recalling a conversation we enjoyed years ago."

Ginevra's father settled back against his desk, clearly bewildered. Chadwick continued to survey the girl with an air of cool calculation that made her increasingly uneasy. His glance lingered on her honey-gold hair, tied back with a brown ribbon into a thick knot almost too heavy for her slender neck. He dismissed her unattractive dress with a faint disdainful snort. Ginevra's first impulse was to conceal herself from those azure eyes raking her slight body, but instead she straightened her thin shoulders and forced herself to face him, meeting his insolent gaze with an air of self-possessed dignity she was far from feeling. She murmured, "I am sorry I was not here when you first arrived, my lord. Is there any way I may serve you?"

One black eyebrow arched quizzically, and Ginevra knew that Lord Chadwick was rigorously repressing whatever comment had first occurred to him. He reached into a pocket of his waistcoat and withdrew a small leather pouch, which he emptied into his palm. "I think it best if we come straight to the purpose of my call," he said. "I believe, Miss Bryant, that you are familiar with this. I should like to return it to you."

Ginevra stared at the heavy jewel-encrusted ring glittering in the man's large hand. Her delicate finger still bore marks on the place where the ring had resided for the past year, but she had never expected to see it again. She choked, "But . . . but I sent that back to you with the letter I wrote when . . . when Tom . . ."

"Yes," the marquess dismissed irritably, "your action was most commendable and circumspect, but now I'm returning the ring to you. I want you to keep it."

Ginevra retreated from his proffering hand. "But I can't keep it!" she cried, and she wondered why her father did not intervene. "It would be wrong! That's the Chadwick betrothal ring, to be worn only by the marchioness or the intended of the heir. You can't just give it to me."

Lord Chadwick made an impatient gesture, and the gems flashed in the firelight. "Obviously you don't understand," he said coldly. "It is in the guise of the Chadwick betrothal ring that I wish you to wear this." Ginevra stared at him, her golden eyes troubled. He continued implacably, "Miss Bryant, I am sure that you are old enough to realize that the alliance between you and my son was arranged primarily so that Dowerwood might eventually be annexed to my estate at Queenshaven, something I have long desired. I still do desire it."

Ginevra bit her lip, thinking hard. "Then . . . then are you saying, my lord, that now although Tom is dead, you still want Dowerwood, and therefore you . . . you wish me to marry your other son, Bysshe?"

The marquess scowled. "No, Miss Bryant. In truth I did suggest such a match to your father, but only if he would agree to delay until Bysshe is eighteen. The boy is not yet sixteen, younger than you and far too immature to assume the responsibilities of wedded life. I want him to finish his schooling first, perhaps see some of the world. After all, I can attest personally to the folly of an extremely youthful marriage. . . . However, your father does not agree with me."

Ginevra looked at Sir Charles. She felt a rising sense of irritation that the two men could so plot her life without consulting her. It was not as if she were still a child of twelve! Curiously she asked, "Why wouldn't you want me to marry Bysshe, Papa?"

He cleared his throat with difficulty. "Tr-try to understand," he stammered nervously. "I . . . I'm sure young Bysshe is a fine boy. But I cannot in good conscience consent to such a delay in the nuptials. If anything should happen to him before you are wed—pray God it does not!—you would be past twenty, still unmarried, and quite on the shelf. No, child, I would be remiss in my duty if I did not make your future secure *now*."

Ginevra stared at her father. Something was wrong. This sudden concern for her future rang false. Oftimes in the past she had wondered if her father even cared what became of her. He seemed only half-aware of her existence.

She turned to Lord Chadwick again, who was watching her narrowly. Squaring her shoulders, she said, "Papa. My lord. Since the two of you seem to have reached an impasse, I think perhaps it is time that *I* decided what steps are necessary to make my future secure."

The marquess nodded his head deeply in an insolent bow. "A most laudable aim, Miss Bryant, except that you are mistaken about its necessity. We have not yet reached an impasse. There is a solution, albeit a drastic one. I still want Dowerwood, and consequently I must take the sole alternative left me." He paused, and Ginevra stared up at him, her heart creeping into her throat as she tried to deny the notion forming in her mind. Even before Chadwick spoke again, Ginevra was slowly shaking her head, her amber eyes wide with horror. She took a step backward, half-turning as if to flee from him. The marquess smiled grimly. "Yes, Miss Bryant," he drawled, his deep voice heavy with irony, "I see you understand at last. I am asking you to do me the great honor and joy of consenting to become my wife."

❧ 2 ❧

Ginevra stared at Lord Chadwick. Her eyes were riveted to his long, narrow face, a sardonic mask carved from old oak, the lines radiating from his aquiline nose and thin lips deep and uncompromising. She had known him all her life but she had never really looked at him before. When she and Tom were children she had thought casually that her playmate favored his father, but now as she studied the marquess's features, the harsh planes of olive skin stretched tight over strong, high cheekbones and a stronger jaw, she searched in vain for some elusive resemblance to her lost friend. The boy's blue eyes had been gentle, but on his father those same eyes, set deep under straight black brows, shuttered by heavy lids, were piercing, hypnotic. Even their raven hair, at first glance so similar, showed the contrast between parent and child: Tom's ruffled curls had been as soft and innocent as the fur on a newborn lamb. Lord Chadwick's hair gave him the pagan look of a Roman idol before whom that lamb might be sacrificed.

Ginevra stood immobile, captive to the marquess's mesmeric gaze. Her hands clenched tightly over her breast, vainly pressing her pounding heart back into her body. She began to tremble as if she stood in a high wind. Tears stung behind her eyes, and her jaw ached with the effort to keep from blubbering out her fear like an infant. Lord Chadwick watched impassively as the tension built in her. He watched and waited.

Suddenly Ginevra shrilled, *"No!"* and tore away from him. She flew across the room to her father, who hovered anxiously beside his desk, and she flung herself into his arms, sobbing. But the protection she sought from him was not forthcoming. Flushed with embarrassment, Sir Charles pushed her away roughly and barked, "Compose yourself, Ginevra, this is the outside of enough!"

She stumbled backward, catching her slipper on the Turkey carpet, too stunned by her father's rejection to brace herself. Chadwick's large hands caught her from behind and steadied her before she fell, but instead of being grateful she flinched from his touch. Her liquid eyes blinked reproachfully at Sir Charles. She sniffed, "Papa, how can you even permit such a suggestion? Marry Tom's *father*? The idea is . . . it's disgusting!"

"Daughter!" Sir Charles gasped, aghast and humiliated by this unexpected rebellion from his usually tractable child. He crimsoned as he glanced uneasily at the marquess, who fortunately seemed unperturbed by Ginevra's words. He murmured, "Forgive us, my lord. Obviously I have been remiss in disciplining the graceless wench. I should have beaten her more when she was younger." He grasped Ginevra's shoulders bruisingly and shook her. "Girl, you will beg his lordship's pardon at once."

Ginevra gaped, stupefied. In all her life her father had never struck her or even spoken harshly to her—perhaps, she realized with wonder, because she had never crossed him in anything before. This sudden revelation of an alien side to her father's character shocked her almost as much as the outrageous match he proposed.

Mutely she continued to stare at her father as if he were a stranger, and in frustration he shook her again. Chadwick's face darkened as he watched her head snap back on her slender neck. His voice became dangerously soft. "Don't bully the girl, Bryant."

Sir Charles sputtered, "But, my lord, I must do something. She is insolent and unreasonable."

"No, she is just confused. In truth we did spring this proposal upon her without warning."

Sir Charles's grip tightened on her shoulders as he hastened to defend himself to Chadwick. "I am her father," he declared stiffly. "It is her duty to accept my decisions without question."

The marquess's eyes narrowed, moving from Sir Charles's flushed countenance to Ginevra's, paper-white. The man abruptly released his daughter, and she swayed slightly. Lord Chadwick said scathingly, "I'm sure that, given time, the chit will accept the wisdom of our plans, Bryant, but right now it will do no good to badger her. Allow us a few moments alone so that I may speak to her privately, to reassure her . . ."

Sir Charles glared at the other man with the sullen resentment of a schoolboy caned in front of his classmates. "Are you telling me what to do in my own home?" he blustered, trying hard to regain his composure. Chadwick, more than several years his junior, had the unnerving ability to make him feel as if he were in short pants again.

Chadwick looked down his long nose at him and the girl, who stood transfixed, still rigid with shock. He said soothingly, "Forgive me if I have offended you, Bryant. The situation is admittedly . . . awkward, and I thought I might be able to ease it some. Until now, I fear, both you and I have been somewhat lacking in . . . tact, don't you agree?"

"Yes, yes," Sir Charles mumbled at once, gratefully grabbing at the olive twig. "We men understand . . . naturally you wish to speak to . . . I'll fetch her maid . . ."

"By all means, fetch her maid," Chadwick said impatiently. "The proprieties must be observed. But first, allow us a few moments of privacy, I beg you."

Sir Charles hastily took his congé, acutely aware that he had not acquitted himself well.

Alone with the marquess, Ginevra studied the faded arabesques on the dull red rug she stood on. Her cheeks were stained with tears wrung out of her by her father's extraordinary behavior, and she refused to look up, lest Lord Chadwick see them. She thought she would endure the rack before she would cry in front of that cold, arrogant man.

The room was still, the silence broken only by the whisper of the low fire in the grate. When the marquess spoke, his voice was surprisingly gentle. "Does he often manhandle you in that fashion?"

Ginevra's small, firm chin trembled despite her efforts to control it. "No," she said hoarsely. "Never."

"I thought as much. Obviously your father is even more desperate than I suspected."

Her amber eyes flicked up in alarm. "Desperate? What do you mean?"

Chadwick's mouth tightened. He looked at the girl thoughtfully. In her brown dress she reminded him of a yearling doe at bay. He sighed, "Please sit down, Ginevra. You seem exhausted, and we have much to discuss, you and I."

She stiffened. She did not like him using her name; it sounded as strange as "Miss Bryant" had done all those years before. His deep voice gave the syllables a caressing, intimate quality she was anxious to deny. Now that her father in his bewildering mood had left the room, Ginevra's courage slowly returned, like blood seeping back into numbed limbs. She lifted her head and began primly, "My lord, I never gave you leave to—" The glint in Chadwick's blue eyes silenced her. She plopped unhappily onto one end of the settee and glanced sidelong at the tall man facing her.

He drawled, "My girl, I have known you far too long to need permission to call you Ginevra." After a moment he added dryly, "Of course, you may, if you wish, call me Richard."

Ginevra's nervousness was fast turning to indignation. The cheek of the man! She clenched her fists buried in the folds of her bombazine skirt, and peeking through her lashes she muttered acidly, "I think not, my lord. I would never be so familiar. I was always taught to respect my elders."

For a long moment the marquess stared at her, then astonishingly he gave a yelp of laughter. "Oh, little Ginnie," he cried, "I thought you were gone forever."

She blinked uncomfortably. "I don't know what you mean."

He sat down beside her. One arm rested lightly along the back of the settee, almost touching her shoulder, as he surveyed her coolly. Ginevra moved back a few inches, a bright spot of color washing each cheekbone. Chadwick's lips twisted. He said, "Ever since I first noticed you cowering behind the beech tree in the garden, I have been wondering what could have become of that impudent and utterly delightful little girl who once asked me if I were the devil. There seemed to be no trace of her in the somber, circumspect young woman you are now."

Ginevra was acutely aware of long fingers drumming on the top of the cushion, bare inches from her. She said, "Everyone has to grow up, my lord."

"A pity," he sighed. "I was very fond of that little girl—as I was also fond of a certain fledgling intellectual with a taste for highly improper poetry."

Ginevra flushed. "I wish you wouldn't remind me of that. I feel ashamed each time I think of that book. I realized you were quite correct in your estimate of it, once I became more mature."

Chadwick murmured, "Too mature, Ginevra? Are you really so grown up? Or are you merely older?"

"I don't understand you."

"I'm sure you don't." He caught one of her burnished curls and toyed with it.

Ginevra whispered huskily, "Please don't do that."

He dropped his hand. He observed, "You're a cross-grained little wench, Ginevra. You have the look of a woman, beautiful even in that impossible dress, and I know that for years you have performed the household duties of a woman, yet temperamentally you are still a green girl, as innocent and ignorant of . . . life as any schoolroom miss half your age." His voice became softer, more insinuating. "I think I shall have my work cut out for me, teaching you to be a wife."

Ginevra crimsoned. She stared mutely at her fingers, nervously pleating neat folds into the brown silk of her skirt. At last she choked, "I mean you no disrespect, my lord, but I have no wish to marry you."

He studied the top of her bent head, the thick, wavy hair that gleamed like antique gold against the drab fabric

of her dress. In a museum he had once seen intricately
carved bracelets of barbaric design, booty from the Spanish, who in their turn had plundered them from the Incas.
Even after three hundred years the bracelets retained the
deep luster, the compelling beauty that had made men kill
to possess them. And here shimmering before him was
that same gold, living. . . . He asked, "Is it the married
state itself that you fear?"

She whispered hoarsely, "No, my lord. I hope someday
to have a husband."

"Then why not me? In Town I am considered exceed-
ingly eligible. I have a great deal of money, my title is ancient, and I've never done anything too outrageously
scandalous—although I will concede that very little
outrages the *ton*."

Still Ginevra did not look up. When she spoke, her
voice was muffled and distorted, as if she had to force it
through her constricted throat. "Might not this marriage
be enough to . . . to outrage the *ton*? You are Tom's father. Surely that is reason enough to make talk of a union
between us . . . unseemly. Besides . . . you are too old."

Chadwick snorted and cocked one eyebrow. He said
dryly, "I am thirty-five, Ginevra—substantially older than
you, but hardly *too* old." He put a long finger under her
tremulous chin and tilted her head upright. "Disabuse
yourself of that notion at once, my girl, or I shall be
forced to take steps to prove to you how very wrong you
are."

As she gazed at him, Ginevra's amber eyes were over-
bright, her cheeks hectic. She stammered, "V-very well,
I'm sorry I said you were too old. But the fact remains
that you are the . . . the father of the boy I was once
pledged to. The very idea of us marrying is indecent. No
matter how much you want Dowerwood, I am shocked
that you could suggest such a match."

The marquess studied her defiant face. His cynical blue
eyes softened. He said gently, "But child, the idea was not
mine, it was your father's."

She gasped. "No. You are lying."

Chadwick's lips thinned. He said coldly, "I told you the

first time we ever met that I would not lie to you, and I meant it. Three weeks ago I was in London to confer with Castlereagh, and I received a communication from your father. He repeated his condolences on the loss of my son; then he pointed out that while Tom was dead, the union between our two families need not be."

Ginevra shook her head. "You must have misunderstood him. Papa would never be so callous, so insensitive."

"A man will be anything, if his need is great enough."

Ginevra bit her lip. "But what need could my father possibly have to make him so transgress the boundaries of decency as to—"

Abruptly Chadwick jumped to his feet. Startled by his action, Ginevra lapsed into silence as he stalked to the window, his hands jammed deep into his pockets. He pushed aside the heavy velvet draperies and stared blindly into the gathering twilight. When he spoke, his voice was harsh with irritation. "Ginevra, I grow excessively weary of your harping about 'decency.' I have made you an honorable proposal of marriage. You may not like the idea, and I admit that when I first called on your father I had no such notion in mind, but the fact remains: the offer has been made. It is now up to you to accept or reject it as you wish, but for God's sake, spare me your missish prattle about morality!"

Stung, Ginevra sank back against the cushions. Through her long lashes she gazed at his back, the wide shoulders lithe and powerful under his superbly tailored jacket, the muscular thighs, and long legs encased in gleaming boots. His every movement bespoke strength and grace. Ginevra shivered. She had seen him subdue an unruly horse with only a word, and even the most obstreperous of men would hesitate to cross him. Against the twelfth Marquess of Chadwick a mere girl would be utterly helpless.

Quietly Ginevra rose and crossed the room to his side. He was glowering into the darkness and did not look down at her. She gazed up at him, and her nerves knotted deep inside her. This man her husband? No. Never. He was too big, too . . . too virile, and he had the ruthless profile carved on Roman coins. Timidly she touched his sleeve. He scowled at her. "What now?"

She tried to smile and failed. "Again I . . . I must beg your forgiveness, my lord. I have been unbearably rude." She fell silent once more, hoping he would help her by saying something, anything. When he did not speak, she stumbled on: "I . . . I know that you have honored me greatly with your proposal, but I im-implore you, let me consult privately with my father before I give you an answer."

After a moment he shrugged. "Very well. When?"

Ginevra took a deep breath. "Tonight," she said. "After dinner I will speak to Papa, and then I will give you my answer." She stared at him, her wide amber eyes pleading mutely for his understanding.

He studied her face intently, and his harsh features relaxed. "Oh, little Ginnie," he sighed, reaching with long fingers to trace the dainty line of her cheekbone, "if only you and I had—"

The doorknob turned, and Chadwick dropped his hand.

Emma came in. Her alert green eyes noticed the tension in the air, but she bobbed a quick curtsy and said neutrally, "Miss Ginevra, your father told me I was to attend you."

Ginevra exhaled with a shudder and retreated from the window. "Thank you, Emma, but I am finished in here now." She bowed formally to the marquess. "My lord, if you will excuse me, I will send a footman to show you to your room, and I shall see you again at dinner."

Chadwick nodded. "Miss Bryant," he murmured, and Ginevra wondered if she was imagining the faint mockery in his voice.

After the meal Ginevra left the men to their port and retired to the drawing room, where she and Emma worked quietly at their sewing. Emma was piecing a small quilt, patchwork after the American fashion, a gift for the cook's daughter, who expected her first child soon. Beside her Ginevra worked apathetically, stitching an intricate pattern of yellow roses in silk on a piece of fine white cambric. The fabric was destined for the yoke of a new nightdress, part of her trousseau, and since Tom's death she had lost all interest in it, continuing only because she had already invested too much time in the piece to discard it. Now she laid the embroidery in her lap and stared blindly at it as an unwelcome and disturbing picture slowly formed in her mind: herself chastely adorned in that demure white gown, her dark gold hair tumbling loose over her shoulders, as she waited, waited, for Lord Chadwick to come to her. . . . Her hand trembled, and the silk floss tangled almost magically into a knot Gordius himself would have admired. Ginevra regarded it with disgust and pushed her sewing aside.

Emma glanced up from her own work and noted with concern, "You seemed very agitated tonight. Is there any way I may help you?"

Ginevra shook her head. "No, Emma. I am caught in a coil like that thread there, and I fear there is no escape. I'll know better after I've spoken to my father."

Emma studied the girl's pale face and said kindly, "Perhaps something to drink would soothe you. May I bring you some tea? Ratafia, if you prefer?"

Ginevra shook her head again. "No, thank you, but I should like that book I was reading, the one by Mary Wollstonecraft. Do you know where I left it?"

"I believe I last saw it on the stand beside your bed. Shall I fetch it for you?"

"Please." Ginevra watched her maid leave the room, and she wondered just how much of the situation Emma was aware of. Probably a great deal. Servants had the uncanny knack of knowing everything. Emma might even know what had caused Sir Charles to force Ginevra into this awkward and impossible situation in the first place.

Ginevra's ruminations were interrupted when Lord Chadwick came into the room. Unlike Ginevra, he had changed for dinner, and the unrelieved black of his evening clothes only emphasized his height and the excellence of his tailor. The coat was styled along the vaguely military lines fashionable since the onset of the French wars, and Ginevra recalled that when Lord Chadwick was very young, he had been for a time an officer in the Navy, serving under Parker and the great Nelson himself, until he was wounded at the Battle of Copenhagen and invalided from the service. She wondered if he ever regretted leaving the Navy. He was probably a good officer. He had the air of a natural leader.

Chadwick coughed, and Ginevra suddenly realized that she had been staring. Blushing furiously, she tried to hide her discomfiture by asking, "Was your meal satisfactory, my lord? Is there any other way I may serve you?"

"Thank you, Miss Bryant, no. Everything was excellent. I hope you will extend my compliments to your cook—unless I have you to thank this time?" She shook her head, and he added in a low voice, "Your father wishes to speak to you now, Ginevra. In his study."

Ginevra sighed and rose reluctantly from her chair. She smiled bleakly at the marquess. "Thank you, I'll go at once." Her voice trembled slightly. "Please make yourself at home. If you should desire anything, you have only to ring for it." Like a sad little wraith she slipped from the room.

The study was almost dark, lit only by the fitful glow of the fire in the hearth. Sir Charles sat hunched behind his desk, leaning on his elbows, his nose mashed against the steeple formed by his stubby fingertips. Lost in thought, he gazed sightlessly at the pewter standish in front of him. Ginevra once again waited in the center of the room, determined not to incite her father's anger. Head bowed low, folded hands working nervously at her waist, she had unconsciously assumed the position a petitioning tenant might use when begging a favor, a favor he expected to be denied. Sir Charles glanced up and recognized the stance, and it irritated him. He gestured to a chair. "Sit down, child, I'm not going to beat you." Silently Ginevra took the seat offered, her eyes large and resentful. He sighed impatiently. "All right, I admit I was harsh with you earlier. Now, stop gawking at me in that doleful manner."

"I'm sorry."

Silence hung between them. Sir Charles asked tersely, "Ginevra, have I been a good father?"

"I have always thought so, Papa."

"Do you believe I would deliberately plot your unhappiness?"

"No, Papa." She studied her fingers entwined demurely in her lap.

Suddenly Sir Charles banged his fist on the desk. The inkwell bounced. "Then, confound it, girl," he cried, "why are you defying me now?"

Ginevra's wan face colored. "I'm sorry," she repeated, leaning forward to add with a flash of spirit, "but I do not wish to marry Lord Chadwick." She subsided into the chair again and gazed at her father.

Sir Charles regarded her wearily. He had been under a great deal of strain lately, and it made him uneasy to watch the chit so quiet and solemn, peeking up through her lashes like a wounded fawn. Dammit all, he was not some kind of felon! He had gone to considerable difficulty, risking a humiliating rebuff, to arrange an excellent, even a brilliant match for her, one that far exceded the usual expectations of the daughter of an unremarkable country baronet. And now, instead of showing him the proper gratitude, Ginevra stared at him with those eyes like sovereigns and waited for him to justify his actions. He had always been too soft with her, that was it. Distraught over his wife's untimely death, he had tried to console himself with the diversions readily available in London to any man with a little money, and he ignored the girl who reminded him so painfully of his lost love. He had allowed her too much freedom, let her read unsuitable books. The possible consequences of his neglect seemed unimportant when her future was already settled with young Tom Glover, but now his laxity as a parent was returning to plague him. The girl had to marry well—and quickly!—and she calmly declared that she did not want to. God! What would he do if she remained mulish, if her recalcitrant behavior offended Lord Chadwick? Dowerwood or no, the Bryants still stood to gain far more from any union than did the marquess's family. . . . Sir

Charles stiffened with determination. He was going to post the banns and be done with it. Ginevra would marry Chadwick even if he, her father, was reduced to ranting like a hack actor playing old Capulet in a Drury Lane production: "Fettle your fine joints 'gainst Thursday next, to go to church, or I will drag thee on a hurdle thither."

He essayed a different tactic. "My child," he intoned, "the world is not an easy place for a lone woman, and if anything should happen to me, you would be quite alone. You have no brother or uncle to care for you, and indeed, upon my death my title and Bryant House will pass away from our family to a distant cousin I have never met, whose generosity toward you might be questionable. Dowerwood is not part of the entail, but even if I gave it to you, you are not equipped to manage it. Consequently, it is my most pressing duty as your father to arrange a good marriage for you, so that you will always be safe, under the loving protection and guidance of a husband."

Ginevra mumbled, "Yes, I know that." *And it's not fair,* she added silently.

"Then surely you realize that a match with Chadwick would be advantageous far beyond my wildest aspirations for you." He chuckled uncomfortably. "Why, think, child, you would even outrank your old Papa."

Ginevra shrugged. "I don't care."

"What!" Sir Charles exploded. "Not care about being a marchioness? In God's name, why not? You ought to be on your knees with prayers of gratitude! You were eager enough to unite with the Glovers before."

"It was different before," Ginevra cried, wounded by his callousness. "I was going to marry Tom."

Her father stared at her, shaking his head in exasperation. "Oh, Ginevra," he clucked, "don't tell me you fancied you had a *tendre* for the lad? How could you? You hadn't seen him in six years. He probably changed beyond all recognition."

Ginevra pleaded helplessly, "But he was my friend, Papa. Surely that wouldn't have changed." She toyed with the stiff fabric of her skirt, fast becoming very wrinkled under her nervous fingers. She was distressed by the justice of her father's words. All the doubts she had felt in the past returned to haunt her. Of course her fiancé would have changed. She had known an amiable boy of twelve, but the Tom Glover who died while on a drunken spree was eighteen, older than his own father had been when he was born, and perhaps already as much a rake and libertine as the older man ever was. . . . Something died inside Ginevra. The union with Tom would have been as loveless as most such arrangements were. Despite her puerile protestations of lifelong friendship, she would have been marrying a stranger.

When Ginevra looked up, her father could see the resignation in her tawny eyes. She had taken his words to heart at last. Oddly, her capitulation gave him some relief, but no joy: there was little pleasure in crushing dreams. He felt a pang at the weariness evident in her voice when she said humbly, "Forgive me for being so obstinate, Papa. You are right, of course, marriage with any of the Chadwick family would be a great honor. I am indeed fortunate that his lordship is agreeable." She hesitated, perking up slightly. "But . . . but couldn't you relent and let me marry Bysshe Glover instead? He's the heir now, as lofty a match as Tom was. I know he is still at Harrow, but he is not so much younger than I that our marriage would be impossible, especially if we wait. In three years I'll only be twenty-one, not *truly* a hopeless spinster as you seem to fear. Perhaps Bysshe and I could even spend some time together beforehand, to get to know each other. It would mean so much to—"

Sir Charles interrupted flatly, "No, Ginevra. You must marry Lord Chadwick himself, and as soon as possible. If you don't . . ." His voice died away, and he colored with embarrassment.

Ginevra observed her father curiously. He looked unwell, she thought; almost old. Something was troubling him gravely. She repeated, "If I don't, what?"

Sir Charles wanted to bluster indignantly that the girl had no right to question him—but he did not. With a twinge of guilt he acknowledged to himself that his own bungling had placed her in a damned awkward position.

She would marry Lord Chadwick, he would see to that. The man was rich, titled, extremely eligible, a prize catch. And yet . . . and yet, only in the dark recesses of his soul dared Sir Charles admit that the marquess was not the sort of man he truly wanted to wed his daughter. Ginevra was a sweet and loving child, and for all his grace of manner, Chadwick displayed a cynicism, a deeply ingrained bitterness, that augured ill for anyone who cared for him.

Ginevra asked again, "Papa, what will happen if I don't marry Lord Chadwick?"

Her father rasped, "I will lose everything." Ginevra stared at him, incredulous. He amplified, "I am in debt, child. The credit sharks are after me."

Ginevra frowned thoughtfully, full of remorse. This possibility had never occurred to her. "Oh, Papa, I'm sorry, I should have realized! But the harvests have been so plentiful that I never dreamed . . . These must be difficult days for you, with all your responsibilities. I know from reading the *Gazette* that since the end of the war corn prices have plummeted. Why, they say already that many small farmers have been forced to—"

Assailed with compunction at her unwarranted sympathy, Sir Charles said sharply, "My money worries have nothing to do with economics, Ginevra, and I wish to point out that it ill becomes a young woman to pretend knowledge of so unfeminine a subject." He rubbed his temples, vainly attempting to stave off the headache settling behind his eyes. How could he explain to her the pressures that had driven him to London, there to fall victim to the wiles of ivory-turners and the meretricious delights of the muslin company? He had tried frantically to soothe the anguish caused by the loss of his wife, and he succeeded only in hurting the child she had left in his care.

As penance he now confessed bluntly, "Ginevra, for years I have borrowed money on the strength of your upcoming marriage to Tom Glover, putting off the creditors with assurances that someday my daughter would be a rich woman. Time has run out. They will not wait even a few months longer, much less two or three years until young Bysshe is old enough to marry. If you do not wed as scheduled, I shall undoubtedly go to the Fleet Prison, and you and those who serve us will be evicted from our property. The Bryant name will be disgraced, and we shall probably starve like the other poor homeless wretches wandering the countryside these days."

Ginevra shuddered. She was conscious of the element of bathos in her father's plea, for she knew that she and he, well-educated and of gentle birth, would manage some way, no matter what happened—she could always become a governess!—but if there was a genuine danger of losing the estate to the moneylenders, what would become of the tenants, the servants who had devoted their entire lives to the comfort of the Bryant family? How would they survive? Now that the war was over, the country was in a depression. Farmworkers who only four years before had barely subsisted on twelve shillings a week now tried to live on less than ten. Thousands were unemployed.

She gazed at the flickering fire in the hearth as she asked quietly, "Are you saying then that everything will be well if I marry Lord Chadwick?"

Sir Charles nodded. "The Glovers have always been as proud as Lucifer. Family is all-important to them. The man would never let his wife's kin come to grief."

Ginevra sighed, still not looking at her father. She wondered if she would ever be able to look at him again. But despite his betrayal, she knew where her duty lay. "Then I really have no choice, do I?"

Lord Chadwick was lounging negligently on the settee, leafing through a small volume, when Ginevra returned alone to the drawing room. For a moment she stood in the doorway, watching the way the candlelight played on his dark curls. Her husband . . . She shivered. He glanced up, and with one fluid, unbroken movement he uncrossed his long legs and stood erect, waiting until she perched nervously on the opposite end of the sofa before he sat down again. When Ginevra remained mute, he passed the book to her and noted in his deep voice, "Your maid brought this in while you were closeted with

your father. I can see he is still lax about your reading
material, or does he really believe that *A Vindication of
the Rights of Woman* is suitable for a girl of your tender
years?"

Ginevra bridled at his superior tone. "As I told you
once, I read whatever I like, and I like Mary Wollstonecraft. She was a great woman."

"A notorious one, you mean," he drawled. "She was
the mother of two bastards, and now her daughters seem
bent on emulating her. Their affairs with Byron and Shel-
ley have become so flagrant that they have shocked even
the *ton*, no mean accomplishment. The whole ménage is
expected to flee for the Continent momentarily."

Ginevra's knuckles whitened as she gripped the slim
book, blushing at his mockery. She stammered, "I . . . I
am not certain that . . . that what you say detracts from
the sense of her words. I have learned much from her."

"Indeed? You mean you wish to learn a trade, venture
out into the world and compete with men without allowance for your feminine frailty? What occupation would
you pursue, Ginevra? Something physical, a stonecutter,
perhaps, or do you think you would prefer—"

"Stop it!" Ginevra cried, tears springing into her eyes
at his sarcasm. "You have no right—"

"I have every right," he said implacably, "and I think
perhaps that after we are married I shall have to monitor
your reading habits." He saw the sudden stricken look in
her wet eyes. "For we are going to be married, aren't
we?"

"Yes, my lord," she choked, looking away.

He caught her chin between his fingertips and turned
her face back toward his. Her small jaw trembled in his
hand, and her golden lashes vibrated against her cheeks.
Chadwick's stern expression softened slightly. "Is the idea
so very appalling, little Ginnie?"

She gnawed at her lip. "It will take some getting used
to, my lord."

His fingers dropped away from her face, and he caught
her left hand. "Then here," he said roughly, "perhaps this
will help accustom you to your fate." As he shoved the

heavy betrothal ring over her knuckle to the place where it had rested for more than a year, he rasped, "Don't ever try to take off the ring again, Ginevra. It signifies that you are mine, and what I have, I keep."

Ginevra outstretched her fingers to stare at the gems flashing coldly in the firelight. The ornate gold hoop, a Chadwick heirloom for over a century, was a posy ring whose stones—lapiz lazuli, opal, verd antique, emerald, malachite—spelled out the simple but poignant plea: *Love Me.* The band and its message seemed to weigh down Ginevra's slender hand. She thought: In all the time I wore it for Tom, it never felt the way it does now, like a shackle. . . .

She was not aware that she had spoken aloud until Chadwick exclaimed irritably, "Ginevra, this so-called shackle that you despise is one that a considerable number of women have sought from me."

Ginevra glared at him. "I'm sure they have," she snapped, her spirit reviving, "and I'll wager that by rights you owed it to most of them, too!"

When she realized what she had said, her cheeks reddened furiously, and she bowed her head, waiting for him to retaliate. But once again the marquess surprised her. Instead of striking back for her rash words, he studied her flushed face and asked seriously, "Tell me, child, do you resent the life I've led?"

Slowly she shook her head. "No, my lord. I . . . I take many things amiss, but not that. Your past life is nothing to me."

"How very tolerant of you," he drawled. He took her hand in his and began to toy with the ring, tracing the carving with his fingernail, as he asked, "Ginevra, will you explain to me, please, what it is exactly that troubles you about our marriage? Do you object to me personally? If so, I think that, given time, I could change your opinion of me." His voice became somber. "Or is it because I am Tom's father? True, that cannot be altered, but my poor boy is gone now and will not be hurt by anything we might do." He smiled again and kissed her fingertips one by one. The touch of his lips startled her, shooting hot tremors along her arm. When he turned her hand over and pressed a kiss into her palm, she gasped.

He was teasing her, charming her, and when he repeated his question, she wrinkled her pale brow and answered reluctantly, lest she spoil their momentary rapport. She said thoughtfully, "I think what disturbs me most about our marriage is the way I have been used in this arrangement, as . . . as security for a bad debt. I know I am not the first girl to ransom her family's good name in this manner, yet I feel demeaned by it."

Chadwick shook his head. "No, Ginevra," he said urgently, "you must not think that way. You are not responsible for your father's malfeasance. I assure you that I regard you with the utmost respect."

Ginevra studied the marquess's face. He was a very handsome man, she conceded with a sigh, and when he was in this unfamiliar, almost tender mood, he seemed younger and well-nigh irresistible. No wonder the London ladies doted on him.

She ventured, "My lord, may I ask a question of you?"

"Of course, Ginevra. Anything."

"I was wondering . . ." She hesitated before proceeding awkwardly, "We both know why I have accepted your proposal, but . . . but why did you extend it in the first place? This I do not understand at all. You have admitted that you could have your pick of any woman you want, so why marry me? I do not believe that Dowerwood is so important to you. You are a wealthy man, and the prospect of acquiring one small property, no matter how lovely, can hardly be enough to sway you. Therefore, what do you gain by marrying me?"

Chadwick stared at Ginevra, and a shuttered look fell over him. The merry, teasing light died out of his blue eyes, leaving them dark and impenetrable, and he dropped her hand. Ginevra sensed his withdrawal, and she shrank back, hurt and bewildered by his abrupt change of mood. Ridicule dripped from Chadwick's voice as he ran his eyes insolently over her slight figure and jeered in an undertone, "What shall I get? Are you so utterly innocent that you don't know? I find that hard to believe." He watched the color drain from her face, and he mocked, "Of course you know, Ginevra, you've known all along. I'll get you. Don't you think that will be enough?"

that brought the week to a close. I had expected to be
bored. No exactly but... there's no point in going
over that. Of course you know I didn't understand all
that I got out. Don't you think that all of this might
be pointless.

❧ 3 ❧

Ginevra huddled in the window seat, saying good-bye to
her home. She was clad only in her chemise and white
silk stockings, but the half-open draperies shielded her
from prying eyes as she gazed down at the garden glowing
in the sparkling morning light. Through the open window
she could smell the rich, heady scent of musk roses wafting upward on the warm June breeze. She sighed wistfully. She had always loved the way her bedroom
overlooked the garden. In high summer the chamber was
redolent with the essence of the flowers, and she used to
lie awake in the perfumed darkness, weaving her girlish
fantasies of adventure and love everlasting. . . . Now she
had spent her last night in this room, it was hers no longer. The wardrobe was empty, its door ajar, and the
dressing table looked strangely alien wiped bare of the
girlish bric-a-brac she had collected over the years: a
seashell from Bournemouth; a desiccated camellia tied
with white ribbon, relic from the wedding of the vicar's
daughter. . . . Her possessions had been carefully packed
into chests and bandboxes and even now were waiting
downstairs in the boxroom, to be loaded after the ceremony onto the baggage coach Lord Chadwick sent. All that
remained of Ginevra's in the room where she had spent
most of her life were her daffodil-colored going-away outfit spread on the bed—and the wedding gown itself.

Behind her Emma said gently, "Miss Ginevra, it's time
to dress."

Reluctantly the girl rose from her perch at the window
and went to the maid, who was removing the gown reverently from its wrappings. When she raised her arms to

38

help Emma slip the dress over her head, the slide of cool silk against her bare skin made Ginevra feel as if she were donning a mantle of ice. While Emma fastened the row of tiny buttons up the back, Ginevra regarded her reflection dispassionately in the long mirror. It was a beautiful dress, she admitted, certainly no one could deny that. Her father, giddy with relief that his financial worries were over at last, had sent to a fashionable London dressmaker, demanding that she spare no expense in providing his daughter with a bridal outfit that would "rival that of Princess Charlotte herself." The couturiere responded admirably, not so much because of Sir Charles's orders as because she realized the advantages inherent in dressing the future Marchioness of Chadwick, and the resultant gown was a miracle of restrained elegance, rich without overwhelming the young bride it adorned. It was made of white silk patent net over an underslip of ivory *mousseline de soie,* with a very high waist and a low square-cut neckline that revealed the soft swell of her breasts. The bodice and hem were heavily embroidered with ivory silk and seed pearls, and the pattern was repeated more lightly on the short puffed sleeves. "*C'est un petit rêve d'une robe,*" Madame Annette—née Annie Brodie of Ipswich—declared, and Ginevra agreed: it was a dream of a dress—for a nightmare.

Emma's skillful fingers had shaped Ginevra's dark gold curls into a heavy coiled chignon at her nape, and her bare throat seemed very pale and defenseless, its vulnerability emphasized by the ivory miniature of her mother that she wore on a white velvet ribbon, her only ornament except for the Chadwick ring. Silently Ginevra watched in the cheval glass as Emma stood behind her and pinned an ankle-length veil of Brussels lace onto her hair with a fragrant coronet of orange blossoms and white roses. When she drew the veil down over her eyes, her vision became obscured by the tiny flowers powdering the lace. It's like looking through snowflakes. Ginevra shivered. A snowstorm in June. No wonder I feel so cold.

Emma handed Ginevra her long white gloves and her prayerbook, and Ginevra noticed that tucked inside the

front leaf of the book was a spring of rosemary. She regarded it quizzically. Emma said, "Cook sent that up for
you, Miss Ginevra. It's for luck. She said we mustn't
neglect the old ways."

Ginevra smiled then, her first real smile in days. "That
was kind of Cook. I'll have to go down and thank her."

Emma shook her head. "There isn't time now. But
we'll all be there at the church. She'll see it then."

"Of course." Ginevra turned away. At the door she
halted suddenly and stammered, "Emma, I . . . I don't
think I can . . ."

Even through the veil the other woman could see that
Ginevra's honey-colored eyes were shimmering. Swiftly
she gathered the girl to her bosom. "Hush, Ginnie, hush,"
she crooned as she searched her mind frantically for
words that would still the trembling of the slim body in
her arms. "Everything will be well, you'll see. Think . . .
think how proud your dear mother would be, to see her
daughter looking so beautiful and about to be married to
a fine lord."

For a moment Emma wondered if she had said the
wrong thing, but then Ginevra pulled away from her and
said stiltedly, "Of course, you're quite right. This is what
she longed for." She straightened her shoulders and lifted
her chin with a defiant, almost regal air—an effect she
promptly spoiled by sniffing inelegantly. Her eyes widened
and she squealed in distress, "Oh, Emma, quickly, where
is my handkerchief? My nose is . . . is going to . . ."
Clumsy seconds ensued while Emma tried to breach the
barrier of the long veil to pass Ginevra a scrap of embroidered linen. By the time disaster was narrowly averted, both women were giggling mirthfully, and Emma
offered up a silent prayer of thanks that Ginevra's lachry-
mose mood had passed. With an encouraging smile she
ushered the girl out of the room to meet her waiting father.

The village church was small and undistinguished, but
its squat exterior of weathered native limestone was
softened and given dignity by the magnificent twin willow

trees that grew on either side of the entrance. As Ginevra's father handed her down from the carriage, she surveyed the mossy facade with affection. Although in recent years she had had little time to attend services, she loved the old church. Her .mother was buried in the churchyard alongside the almost forgotten baby brother who had lived just long enough to be christened, and Ginevra knew that she would miss the comforting presence of those graves when she worshiped in London. She supposed that she and Lord Chadwick would occasionally go to church in Town, probably some grand cathedral like St. Paul's. He did say that religion was currently fashionable among the aristocracy.

Ginevra was touched to note that the yard was full of people of all ages, decked out in varying degrees of "Sunday best," and most of them sported white flowers in their buttonholes, bridal favors in her honor. They were the villagers, many of them her father's tenants, and she had been their mistress since she was twelve years old. She had played with their children when she was little, and later while still only a child she had taken over her ailing mother's duties of nurturing and caring for them in time of sickness or want. At least one of the toddlers skipping among the gravestones was a baby Ginevra had helped deliver when the midwife was ill. Now they had come to pay tribute to their Miss Ginevra as she made a great marriage to a rich and powerful lord, and they shook their heads in wonder to think that the little girl with yellow pigtails who had once had the run of their cottages was now about to become a marchioness, next best thing to a duchess.

When Ginevra and her father reached the door of the church, the congregation was already assembled. The sexton gave a signal, and the vicar's wife began pumping out the processional hymn on the wheezy reed organ whose dissonance had been the bane of the parish for decades. As Ginevra lingered in the vestibule, anticipating the moment when she and her father would start down the aisle, she wondered suddenly what Lord Chadwick's first wedding had been like. She knew so little about him, about his life before he disrupted her own. Probably then a great choir had sung anthems by Bach or Handel, and his lady had come to him preceded by a dozen bridesmaids. Ginevra had no attendants. Her closest friend was Emma, but she was sensible that the older woman would have been mortified by any suggestion that she be maid of honor. So Emma stood at the back of the church with the other servants, smiling tenderly, while Ginevra clung to her father's arm and slowly made her way to the altar and the stranger who waited there for her.

White patterns of lace floated before her eyes, shimmering as she walked, blurring her vision and imparting a fantastic aura to the scene. Two men loomed before her: the vicar in his snowy surplice, and Lord Chadwick, dark and impeccable in a grey tailcoat, a single perfect ruby ornamenting his intricately tied cravat. Ginevra thought dazedly: This isn't happening, it's a dream, a chimera. Soon Emma will waken me, and I'll be in my own room again, all these apparitions will vanish . . .

But the familiar voice of the vicar cut through the comforting mist, and Ginevra's father mumbled something and slipped away from her, patting her arm awkwardly as he retreated. Lean, strong fingers grasped her hand and guided her forward to kneel at the altar. She would not look up at him. As they settled onto the worn cushions that had served generations of parish couples, she kept her eyes trained on his hands, the long and powerful digits that curled firmly around her small ones, directing her movements as easily as he would control those of a skittish filly. Somewhere over her head she heard his deep voice respond clearly to the vicar's exhortations. In turn she murmured her own replies softly, tonelessly, and when the time came, she slipped the white glove from her left hand and let him take her pale, work-roughened fingers in his brown ones again. "With this ring . . ." she heard Lord Chadwick say, and he touched the tip of her thumb with a wide gold band that was warm with his body heat. "In the name of the Father . . ." He moved it to her index finger. ". . . and of the Son . . ." Middle finger. ". . . and of the Holy Ghost." Now he was slipping the band down over the knuckle of her ring finger, to the place where it would remain forever. "Amen," he said, and his hand tightened possessively over hers.

He rose from his knees in one lithe movement, drawing her up after him. She still kept her eyes resolutely downcast until she heard him mutter in a commanding undertone, "Look at me, Ginevra." Slowly, shyly, she peeked up through her lashes, and as she did he lifted the lace veil away from her face, and she could see him clearly for the first time. The sheltering mist vanished from her mind as if burned away by the fire leaping in his eyes, and their gazes locked, jewel-bright, blue and gold. She stood mesmerized, unconscious of anything but the man towering over her, until one corner of his stern mouth twitched and he murmured, "Well, little Ginnie?" And sliding his large hands around her slender neck so that his fingertips caressed her nape and his thumbs traced the delicate line of her jaw, he bent to kiss her.

To her surprise his mouth was firm yet gentle, urging rather than demanding her response, and as her lips began to move under his in this, her first kiss, she quivered, stunned by the unsuspected sensations he was arousing in her. By the time he raised his head she was breathless, her face flushed with wonder, and, oddly reluctant to break contact, quite involuntarily she reached up her hand to stroke the hard line of his mouth. Someone in the congregation suddenly sobbed with pent-up emotion. Chadwick, wryly aware of the enrapt eyes concentrated on them, caught Ginevra's fingertips in his own and kissed them lightly before tucking her arm under his. "Later, my love," he whispered as the reedy organ gasped out the opening chord of the recessional, and Ginevra's astonished delight at the endearment was tempered by the knowledge that his voice sounded amused and somehow triumphant.

When the Chadwick coach finally climbed out of the lambent Kennet Valley and crossed southward into the shady forests of Hampshire, Ginevra gratefully pulled back the russet leather curtain from the window to allow the cool breeze to fill the interior of the carriage and play over her flushed cheeks. She peered out the window behind to see if she could catch a glimpse of the baggage coach that followed with Emma, the marquess's valet, and the luggage. When she did not see it, she settled against the cushion with a sigh, and beside her her husband asked solicitously, "Are you weary, my dear?"

She turned to smile from beneath the stiff brim of her hat. "I am a little tired, my lord, but mostly I am overwarm."

"Of course you are," he agreed, although he seemed personally unaffected by the heat. "This afternoon is exceptionally sultry. Why don't you remove that very fetching bonnet and rest awhile? We still have two or more hours to travel before we reach Queenshaven." Even as he spoke he began loosening the jaunty yellow bow tied just under Ginevra's left ear, and with a moue of relief she massaged her nape and smoothed the damp honey-toned tendrils that had escaped from her heavy chignon. Before he set it on the seat opposite them, Lord Chadwick perused the bonnet, a confection of lacy woven straw and sun-colored ribbons. "My compliments to your milliner," he said with the air of a connoisseur. "Is this French? Never tell me it was crafted by some village seamstress!"

Ginevra shrugged. "No, of course not. It came from London. Papa contracted with a woman called Madame Annette to provide my wedding dress and trousseau. I don't know anything about her, but Papa says her designs are quite the thing among the *ton*."

"Papa has extravagant tastes," Chadwick muttered under his breath, thinking of the sizable accounts he himself had settled with Annette over the years. Her establishment in the Burlington Arcade was a favored shopping place for certain fashionable ladies who had come under his protection in the past. Ah, well, the couturiere was a shrewd businesswoman who realized she was valued as much for her discretion as for her style. He continued aloud, "Your father chose your dressmaker well, Ginevra. You looked . . . quite breathtaking in your gown this morning." He watched a hint of pink wash her cheekbones, like the blush on a cream-colored rose petal. "I hope your wedding was everything you desired."

Acutely aware of his gaze, Ginevra schooled her expressive features with an effort and answered too quickly, "Of course it was, my lord." She twisted around on the seat and peered through the window at a flock of freshly shorn sheep browsing in a clearing beside the road. Curly lambs frolicked among the older animals, who looked naked and defenseless deprived of their heavy winter coats. One fat ewe lifted her head and stared stupidly at the passing coach.

"Ginevra," the marquess said, and reluctantly she turned to him. "I detect a certain reserve in your enthusiasm," he chided, his blue eyes probing her face. "Tell me, my dear, for I do sincerely want this day to be all you ever dreamed of."

Ginevra lowered her lashes and frowned down at her rings, toying with them as if to ease the unaccustomed weight. She pondered her reply. "I was not . . . disappointed with the wedding ceremony," she said at last, deliberately overlooking the fact that throughout most of the service she had felt like a puppet, a lay figure acting out a part for someone else. Only the kiss had been real. "And . . . and I did enjoy the breakfast afterward. Cook quite surpassed herself, I've never seen such a feast before. But . . ." Her voice died away, and she bit the soft underside of her lip.

"But what?"

She heard the steel in his words, and with a deep breath she continued, "My lord, while I appreciate that you must prefer the comforts of Queenshaven to the lesser facilities available to you at Bryant House, I should have liked very much to delay a day or so before beginning the journey to Surrey. I . . . I always looked forward to celebrating my bridal in the country style, with dancing and games and a charivari that would continue until dawn." She halted abruptly as she saw a pained expression flicker across his dark features. Lud, she thought, what a peagoose I am! Her new husband was far too sophisticated a man to find pleasure in the old customs she loved, heritage of her rural upbringing. If he danced, it would be a waltz at Almack's, never a romp on the green, and God help anyone who suggested that he allow the wedding party to lead him to her chamber and fling their stockings across the bed. "Forgive me," she murmured stiffly, "I spoke without thinking. I should have realized that to a person of your exalted station, such rustic amusements would seem unbearably tedious."

As Chadwick listened to her snappish words, the kindly light faded from his eyes. When he spoke, his voice was cold and heavy with sarcasm. "I do not like being called a snob," he said disdainfully, "and I collect I must remind you—*my lady*—that for these past four hours your station has been quite as exalted as my own."

Ginevra flushed again. "Forgive me, I . . . I . . ."

Chadwick waved away her stammered apologies impatiently. "Leave it, and try to rest. We accomplish nothing by talking while you are tired and fretful."

Ginevra shrank back into her corner and closed her eyes, not so much to rest as to hide the teardrops trembling on her lashes. What had come over her? He had been so kind, for a moment they had been conversing almost as . . . as friends, and then she ruined everything with her outrageous remarks. Of course he was angry. To accuse a man of Lord Chadwick's stature and accomplishments of anything so petty as snobbery was not only unjust, it was stupid and offensive. He'd probably never speak to her again.

Thus she was surprised when she heard the marquess say quietly, "My dear, I'm sorry that your wedding day has not been as festive as you wished. I know when one is very young, there is a certain appeal to all the traditional trappings and celebration, the noise and the bawdy jokes. But I beg you to remember, I am not quite so young as you—and I have had all that before."

Ginevra's eyes flicked open. She asked carefully, "Is that why you had no friends, no family, at the wedding? I was greatly surprised when not even your son was there."

Chadwick shrugged. "Although I did inform Bysshe

that I was remarrying, I preferred him to remain at Harrow until the end of the term. He missed several weeks of study in March when his brother . . . At any rate, I have arranged special tutoring for him, and it will be another month or more before he leaves school for Queenshaven. If you wish, he may join us briefly in town in the fall."

Ginevra protested, distressed by the cavalier manner in which her husband dismissed the presence of his younger son, his only son now. "But, my lord—"

He said, "The subject is not for discussion."

"Yes, my lord."

After a moment Chadwick noted, "I did invite my mother to the wedding, but she felt the journey would overtax her. However, I have strict orders to present you to her as soon as we reach London." He observed the expression on Ginevra's face. "What's wrong? Didn't you know I had a mother?"

She shook her head. "No one ever mentioned her. I suppose I assumed she was dead."

"Oh, no, she's very much alive, although her health is not as robust as it once was. Probably the reason you have not heard her mentioned is that until two years ago she was resident in France, under house arrest, as it were, like the other British subjects unfortunate enough to be caught in France when the First Consul decided he had had enough of the Treaty of Amiens. She was in enforced exile for over twelve years."

"How awful!" Ginevra cried.

"Not really. She was quite comfortable. She lived in the château of some distant cousins of hers, members of the *ancien régime* who were . . . adaptable enough to keep their heads during the Terror. At first I had some wild, half-formed notion of journeying to France clandestinely to 'rescue' her, but before I could work out my plans, she wrote to advise me that she had married her jailer."

"She did *what*?"

Chadwick smiled grimly. "A remarkable woman, my mother. Instead of suffering during her exile, she acquired another title. She is not only the Dowager Marchioness of

Chadwick, but also the Comtesse d'Alembert, and twice
as rich as before."

"And you resent that?" Ginevra asked.

Chadwick looked surprised. "Resent what, that she was
able to manage so well under difficult conditions? No, of
course not. I'm glad she and her comte—he died some
three years ago—were happy together. But I was very
young then, not much older than you, and I suppose it
hurt to think that she didn't need me."

It still hurts, Ginevra thought, but she kept silent. She
tried to envision Chadwick's mother and failed. She suspected that the lady had a personality quite as strong as
that of her son, and the thought of meeting her was unset-
tling.

They rode on in silence for several miles, and then the
marquess said, "As you grow older, Ginevra, you will find
that life is not always as uncomplicated as you think now.
Appearances can be deceptive, and people are often vin-
dictive and unkind. That was one reason I invited none of
my acquaintances to our nuptials." He brushed long fingers over the lapels of his grey coat of half-mourning.
"Also there would be certain social restrictions imposed
on a large ceremony so soon after . . ." He sighed. "You
must not think I regret you in any way. I did hope to
spare you the kind of people who would have descended
upon us like a flock of magpies had they guessed what we
were about. Unfortunately, you will of necessity meet
most of them soon enough, and I might as well warn you
now that not all of them will be . . . courteous." He
paused before adding dryly, "Certain mamas of eligible
daughters have been hanging out for me for some time,
and they will not take kindly to the knowledge that you
have conspired to filch me from their avid clutches."

Ginevra gasped, "But . . . but I . . ."

Chadwick's expression warmed. "Oh, child, don't you
know when you are being teased?"

She turned away stiffly and peered out the window of
the coach again, determined to admire the lush green undulating hills. The road was smoother here, built over the
remains of the old Roman highway from Silchester to

Basingstoke. Behind her she heard her husband say, "I do fear that your adjustment to London society will be difficult, and I wish I could delay your return there until you have had time to gain confidence as my wife." At the touch of his hand on her shoulder, she reluctantly looked at him again. He seemed unusually serious. "Were the choice mine, I should have liked to go abroad for our honeymoon and introduce you to some of the world you have yet to see. Barring that, I would prefer more than the bare week we may spend at Queenshaven." He smiled ironically. "Perhaps in future we shall have time to travel, but for the moment I must remain at Castlereagh's beck and call. The situation in Europe is explosive, and he seems to think I can be of some small service." He observed her obvious puzzlement. "Didn't you know I dabble in diplomacy?"

Ginevra shook her head. "I know so little about you."

He studied her pale, intent face. He smoothed back an errant curl from her forehead, and his blue eyes lit up as he murmured, "We shall change that soon enough, little Ginnie," and brushed his lips lightly across hers.

Lulled by the gentle rocking motion of the well-sprung carriage, Ginevra dozed through the rest of the journey. When her husband roused her, she mumbled groggily, "Where . . . where are we?" and sat up, her gold eyes cloudy with bewilderment. Her cheeks colored as she realized she had been sleeping with her head on his shoulder.

Chadwick smiled at her confusion. "We are approaching Queenshaven. Don't you recognize the countryside?"

"It's been so long," she said as she looked out the window. She could see that the low chalk hills of the South Downs were behind them now, and they were traversing the heavily wooded plain of the Weald. She surveyed the countryside with the increasing delight of acquaintance renewed. She pointed to a side road just ahead which wound off into the forest. "Isn't that the turn to Dowerwood?" Chadwick nodded, and she craned her neck to gaze hungrily down the road, following in her mind's eye the familiar route leading to the small but lovely estate where she had spent her childhood summers. Her face was glowing when she declared, "I was so happy there."

Chadwick said, "I pray you will be equally happy at Queenshaven."

Ginevra blinked. "Yes, yes, of course," she muttered, subsiding into the corner. She cursed herself for her foolishness. Dowerwood was not her home. Her residence in Surrey would not be the house she had loved as a child; rather she was to be mistress of Queenshaven, the impressive but gloomy Tudor mansion begun by a long-dead Glover to honor young Catherine Howard, the fifth wife of Henry VIII, who fell to the headsman's ax before the building was completed.

The marquess watched the emotions play across the girl's face, and he said quietly, "I fear you would find Dowerwood sadly changed from your memories of it. Your father had to dismiss most of the staff, and with only a caretaker in charge, the estate has fallen into disrepair. Would you like to ride over there one day this week? We could assess the damage and perhaps make a start of amending it."

"I should like that very much," Ginevra replied, "but I don't ride."

"Not at all? Surely I hold in my mind an image of a little girl with long honey-colored plaits, her skirts askew, who galloped a fat pony through a flock of sheep?"

Ginevra stared at him, then laughed merrily. "Oh, dear, I had forgotten that. What a bumble-broth it was! Tom—no, I think it was Bysshe, it sounds more like him—dared me, you know. He said no girl could ride bareback, so of course I had to accept the challenge. I couldn't control the pony, and I was terrified the sheep wouldn't scatter, but somehow I managed to stay on. When my mother found out, she gave me a very stern lecture on why I was too old for such disgraceful escapades, but Papa soothed her by promising to get me a sidesaddle so that I could learn to ride like a lady." Her laughter faded. "He never did. That was . . . that was the last summer we spent at Dowerwood."

After a pause Chadwick said briskly, "Well, you shall

have your saddle now—and a horse as well. There is a little chestnut mare, sired by Giaour, my stallion, but her dam was a docile creature. She is spirited but . . . governable, and I think she would suit you very well." He glanced at Ginevra. "That is, of course, if you wish me to teach you to ride?"

"I'd enjoy that. Thank you."

"Good. We'll see to it in a day or two."

The carriage passed the stone gatehouse and lumbered up the long drive to Queenshaven. Ginevra picked up her bonnet. "I'd better get ready," she said lightly, to mask her increasing agitation.

Chadwick patted her hand. "Compose yourself, my dear. No one is going to—" He stopped abruptly, staring out the window, and his hand tightened cruelly over hers. He swore viciously.

"My lord!" Ginevra yelped in pain, and he released her bruised fingers.

"Forgive me, I did not mean to hurt you." He spoke absently, still scowling in the direction of the main entrance. "It appears we have . . . guests."

"Guests?" Ginevra echoed. "Today?" She peeked over his shoulder and saw a trim curricle with yellow lacquered wheels pulled up in front of the steps. A small man in a smart livery stood beside the vehicle, talking to a servant who wore the distinctive grey-and-red uniform of the Chadwick household. He gesticulated with every other word, but the Queenshaven footman remained impassive. The small man jerked around at the sound of the carriage pulling to a halt behind him.

Chadwick's face was thunderous. Shyly Ginevra asked, "Is that someone you know?"

The marquess said, "Yes. His name is Ferris. He waits upon . . . an acquaintance of mine."

"But what is he doing here?"

"God knows." Chadwick reached for the door handle. "Remain here, and I'll get rid of him."

Impulsively she touched Chadwick's arm, suddenly certain that the stranger meant them no good. "Please be careful."

"Of Ferris?" he asked. "Ferris is not the problem."
Just for a second his long fingers curled protectively over
hers; then he descended from the coach.

Ginevra watched from behind the russet window curtain as Lord Chadwick strode across the drive to the man
waiting by the curricle. He dismissed his own servant with
a nod; then he demanded, "Well, Ferris, to what do I owe
this intrusion?"

Ferris smiled uneasily. "My lord, I . . . I bring a
message from my mistress."

"Indeed." He waited impatiently. "Well, hand it over."

Ferris mumbled, "The message is not written, my lord.
Madame de Villeneuve asked me to deliver it personally."
He hesitated, glancing sidelong at the wedding coach;
then he blurted, "Madame instructed me to tell you
most humbly that she regrets the incident at Vauxhall
Gardens Tuesday last and she hopes that you will forgive
her her ill temper and will not allow it to affect your
. . . your relationship."

The marquess regarded him enigmatically. "A most
. . . intimate message to be carried by a third party. I
wonder why Amalie did not choose to write it."

Even Ginevra could have advised Ferris that when the
marquess's voice became quiet, too quiet, it was prudent
to avoid taxing him further, but she no longer monitored
the men's conversation. She had sunk back against the
squabs, her face as colorless as the bleached straw of her
bonnet. Amalie de Villeneuve—who was she? No, no,
better not to ask. She didn't want to know. She didn't
want to think about this London lady who pursued Lord
Chadwick, who wanted him not for a debutante daughter
but for herself. Who had already had him.

Ginevra felt sick. Ever since that world-shattering moment earlier in the day when her husband kissed her, she
had moved in a daze, flattered by his attention, hypnotized by his charm. He enticed her with every glance
from those compelling blue eyes, and she succumbed, forgetting completely the sort of man he was. He was a rake,
a libertine, a practitioner of the seductive arts since before
she was born. Against him a green girl like herself was ut-

terly defenseless. She shivered with disgust at the incipient
tenderness she had left for him, the childish hope that
they might be "friends." How could she overlook the fact
that he had married her to acquire a piece of property?
He cared nothing for her personally. He hadn't bothered
to invite anyone to the ceremony, and he intended to
spend no more than the minimum acceptable time alone
with her in the country. With his deceitful tongue he wove
poignant images of a man forced to curtail his honeymoon
out of duty to his sovereign, but in truth he was probably
anxious to return to London to the arms of his mistress,
the one he had flaunted publicly not a week before the
wedding.

Chadwick's voice, thick with cynical amusement, pene-
trated Ginevra's brown study. "Why do I have the suspi-
cion that Amalie sent you to spy upon my bride?"

The small man stammered, "My lord, forgive me, I
. . . I beg y-you! Madame was most insistent, and I . . .
I dared not contravene her. When she becomes angry—"

"Yes, I know what Amalie is like," Chadwick said
dryly. "I do not blame you for fearing her, but I am
afraid I cannot let you accede to her orders. My wife is
not to be ogled like an animal in a zoo. I think you had
better be on your way, Ferris."

"M-my lord—"

"Ferris, I said go!" The marquess's voice was cold and
implacable. "If Amalie is cross with you, tell her I said to
remember who pays your salary—and her rent."

The man snapped to a salute. "Yes, my lord!" He
jumped into the curricle and whipped the horses to a gal-
lop, spraying gravel as the light vehicle careened down
the driveway.

Chadwick returned to the carriage. He smiled and said,
"Forgive the delay, my dear. I know you must be anxious
to go inside."

Ginevra blinked. Was this all there was to be, a casual
dismissal and nothing more? He must know she had heard
some of his conversation with the other man. Would he
not offer some explanation of why his name was coupled

with that of another woman even after the banns had been called?

Chadwick said, "Ginevra, are you coming?"

She looked down, and her eyes were caught by the flash of sunlight on her rings. Of course there would be no explanation—for there would be no inquiry. She was Lord Chadwick's wife now, and wives did not ask such questions. If a man pursued his lightskirts even after marriage, his wife must pretend ignorance of his activities. She was expected to console herself with the protection of his name and perhaps even be grateful that other women diverted his unwelcome attentions from her person. She looked up again. "Of course, my lord, I am ready when you are." She laid her small hand in Chadwick's, and as he assisted her down from the coach, he glanced at her sharply, wondering why she suddenly seemed so much older.

When she glanced back over her shoulder, the yellow curricle was just disappearing down the drive, and the footman returned to stand stolidly by the front door. Chadwick gave Ginevra his arm and escorted her into the welcome coolness of the vast and obscure entry hall. He patted her hand as he turned to address the manservant. "Her ladyship is tired from the journey, and I think we'll postpone any tour of the house until tomorrow. Tell Mrs. Timmons to show her to her apartment and send up someone to attend her there until the coach with her own abigail arrives." The footman quickly left in search of the housekeeper, and Chadwick made as if to go.

"But . . . but, my lord . . ." Ginevra stammered, suddenly clinging to him as the one familiar object in this strange new world.

He smiled down at her, his dark face lined with fatigue or anxiety, she wasn't sure which. "Go on, little Ginnie," he urged softly. "Rest awhile. I'll tell Mrs. Timmons to have our supper sent up to your room later, and we'll talk then." He raised her hand to his lips; then he turned and strode away, his heels echoing on the stone floor.

"Good night, Miss Gin . . . my lady."

The dull thud of the sitting-room door as it shut behind Emma echoed through Ginevra, a reverberation of her own unease. She dug her fingers into the dark velvet upholstery of the Queen Anne wing chair whose back she leaned against, clinging to it in an effort to prevent herself from running after the maid, begging her not to abandon her to the man who would come soon, soon. . . . Ginevra sighed. She could not recall Emma now. She must face what was to come alone.

She sank into the chair, and the gossamer silk of her white negligee fluffed up over her knees, weightless as thistledown. She smoothed down the fabric nervously while she glanced around. She did not like this tenebrous room. The light from candles in a massive floor sconce was absorbed by the dark furnishings. The only bright spots anywhere were the reflections on the silver covers of the supper dishes spread on a low table beside her. A draft caused the yellow flames to flicker, casting distorted, oscillant shadows on the obscure hangings, the drab furniture, the portrait of some dour female Glover over the mantel. It was Lord Chadwick's fault that she was in this awful place, she thought resentfully. Like Pluto carrying Persephone off to the underworld, he had abducted her from her bower of sunlight and flowers to bring her to this dreary, lifeless chamber that looked as if it had not seen daylight in a century. Oh, certainly the antique furniture was of excellent quality, the very best, and the practical side of Ginevra's mind did note with mild satisfaction that under the housekeeper's direction the room had been meticulously aired and dusted. But it was all so dark, so gloomy and ominous, and she hated it, she hated it. She wanted to go home.

Tired and agitated, Ginevra bowed her head in despair. Her thick gold tresses tumbled loose over her shoulders, flowing in gleaming waves almost to her waist. Home. Now home was wherever her husband chose it to be, whether Queenshaven or London. She pondered the choice, trying to cheer herself. Queenshaven she detested, but London might not be so dreadful. She had never been there, her father had never permitted her to accompany him on his business trips, but she was sure the city had much to commend it. She could frequent the parks, the lending libraries, and perhaps Lord Chadwick would occasionally take her to a theatre on the Tottenham Court Road or to a concert in Vauxhall Gardens. . . .

Vauxhall. Where he liked to go with his mistress.

Ginevra shuddered. For hours she had curbed her thoughts, refused to contemplate the exchange she had overheard between the marquess and the intruder, but now her imagination was loose, racing unrestrained over parlous paths she had tried to avoid. Her husband had a mistress, some Frenchwoman, probably the latest of a long line. Exactly how many women had there been altogether in his life? How many compliant females had basked in the hot glow of his blue eyes, quivered under his caressing fingers? Scores, hundreds? He was a father at seventeen, a widower before he came of age, and God alone knew the number who had succumbed to his practiced charms since then. To his credit, not all the running was on his part, he was a man women would never ignore. His looks guaranteed that, if not his title and wealth. When he called on her father, Ginevra noticed how one of the Bryant housemaids, a buxom wench not long in service, eyed him appreciatively. Ginevra reluctantly conceded that as far as she knew, the marquess had not accepted the girl's blatant invitation. Most men would have done, and not only when the girl was willing. A merchant from Leeds who once visited Sir Charles ordered tea to be brought to his room at midnight, and nine months later Ginevra helped deliver the result of that late summons. A young farmer married the unfortunate mother in time to save her from public disgrace, but Ginevra resented the way the man responsible had escaped. When she complained to her father, he seemed unconcerned even though the incident took place under his roof. These things happened, he shrugged, it was the way of the world. A lady like Ginevra would do well to pretend ignorance of such matters.

But how could she pretend ignorance when any moment now her husband, a virtual stranger to her, was going to walk into her bedroom and demand her submission?

As if in answer to her thoughts, Ginevra heard the connecting door from Lord Chadwick's suite open, followed by the sound of his footsteps striding purposefully across her bedroom to the sitting room where she waited, rigid with apprehension. In the doorway he paused.

Ginevra brushed a burnished lock of hair from her eyes and glanced up nervously. He was staring at her. In the dimness his eyes were shadowed and inscrutable, his austere features only faintly limned by the wavering candlelight. He had not changed his clothes, but his jacket and waistcoat were gone, and his ruffled white shirt was partially unbuttoned, revealing the triangle of dark hair on his chest. Ginevra quickly averted her eyes from that disturbing, intimate sight. Her cheeks grew hot. She pretended great interest in the silver tea service as she waited for him to speak. He did not. At last she stammered without looking up, "G-good evening, my lord."

"Good evening, Ginevra." His voice was low and surprisingly husky. He settled onto the couch across the table from her, never taking his eyes off her. In the dark room she seemed ethereal, illuminated. She intensified her scrutiny of the teapot. The silence became unbearable. She quavered, "W-would you care for some tea?"

He smiled. "Yes, thank you. One sugar, no milk." Ginevra glanced up just long enough to give the cup to him. When she folded her trembling hands diffidently in her lap, he asked, "Are you not having any?"

She shook her head. "Oh, no, I couldn't. I . . . I don't want anything right now." She stared at her white knuckles.

Chadwick set his tea aside untasted. "I'm not thirsty either." He studied her pale face, the downcast eyes with golden lashes fluttering long and silky against ivory skin. He sounded not unsympathetic as he murmured, "Poor little Ginnie, are you very nervous?" She nodded jerkily. He said, "There's no need to be afraid. I won't hurt you." She quaked silently. He stood up and held out his hand. "Come here, Ginevra," he said softly.

She looked at him then, her amber eyes travelling up the long, strong length of him until they met and were held, hypnotized, by the dark intensity of his blue gaze. Slowly, almost against her will, her hand reached out to join his. His grip was gentle but irresistible, and he pulled her from her chair. When she stood, her negligee floated down around her, clinging like wisps of mist, and her skin gleamed pearllike through the sheer silk. He caught his breath. His hands encircled her slender waist, and he drew her toward him until her small breasts brushed the front of his shirt. She was still staring at him, entranced, when he bent his head to kiss her.

It was a light kiss, his warm lips just grazing hers in a fleeting caress, and she blinked with disappointment when he drew away. He sensed her chagrin and smiled complacently. Stepping back, but with one arm still around her, he asked with the neutral air of a concerned host, "Are you settled into your new quarters? I hope they meet with your approval."

Yet a little dazed from that kiss, she took a moment to adjust to his abrupt change of mood. "Ev-everything is quite . . . comfortable," she said at last.

"How diplomatic," he drawled, his tone lightening. He gave her waist a squeeze. "I'm sorry, my dear, when I ordered this suite prepared for you I forgot what a horror it is, positively Gothic. I don't think the rooms have been redecorated since my grandmother's day. Now I know why my mother has always preferred the London house! Ah, well, your first domestic duty as my lady can be to engage a decorator to do everything over. Mrs. Timmons can give you the names. Do you think you'll like that?"

"It might be fun," Ginevra ventured shyly, glancing around and envisioning the grim chamber stripped of its depressing hangings and made light and airy with tones of white, gold, and apricot. "Yes," she repeated more firmly, "it would be fun."

"Good," Lord Chadwick said. "I like amusing you."

Ginevra paused, frowning, as she caught the nuance of something he had said. Astonished at her own temerity, she questioned, "Did . . . did your wife not use this suite?"

Instantly her husband's face became shuttered. "No," he said flatly. "My father was still alive then, and he and my mother used this wing. On those rare occasions when Maria honored us with her presence, she stayed in rooms in another part of the house altogether."

"I . . . I see."

"No, I don't think you do." Chadwick's tone sharpened. "Ginevra, those days are long past. You are my wife now. You would do well to ignore matters that do not concern you."

Ginevra bridled with irritation. He sounded just like her father! Driven by an impulse she would have been incapable of explaining, she demanded fiercely, "Do those matters include Amalie de Villeneuve?"

The arm clasping her waist became hard and cold, a fetter of iron. Lord Chadwick said, "No, she can be of no importance to you."

Even in the poor light Ginevra's face glowed with outrage. She tore herself from his grasp and stuttered indignantly, "How c-can you say that? I . . . I am your wife!"

His eyes narrowed, and he bowed mockingly. "As you say. I have endowed you with my name, my title, and all my worldly goods. What more do you want?"

What more? Ginevra thought wildly, pivoting away from him, her gown afloat. She crossed her arms in a childish attitude of defiance, hurt and confused. Was she being unreasonable to expect fidelity from her husband, fidelity and respect and . . . and love? Did such qualities exist in real marriage, or were they just fantasies contrived by the writers of purple romances? Did no one love? She had always thought her parents shared an ideal relationship, full of tenderness and warmth. Was she wrong about that too? The things she had learned recently about her father made her wonder if any man could be trusted. Small wonder he had had no qualms about forcing her to marry Lord Chadwick, condemning her to be used at the man's convenience and then discarded. Oh, God, she didn't think she could stand it! She drooped her head and began to tremble.

The marquess watched the small, quivering figure in silence, his face unreadable. He sighed, "Oh, Ginevra, you are so very young . . . Now, in addition, you are tired and overwrought." He wove his fingers through the gleaming mass of her hair and began to massage her nape. "Come, love," he urged softly, "you need to rest. You'll feel better after you sleep." He felt the tense muscles in her neck relax reluctantly under his soothing caress. Brushing aside the sheer silk of her gown, he teased her shoulder with his lips. When the tip of his tongue trailed lightly over her skin, she jerked convulsively. He murmured, "You must rest, little Ginnie. Come to bed."

"W-with you?"

"Of course with me."

Ginevra hesitated. "No," she said.

Chadwick's stroking fingers stilled. "I beg your pardon?"

She lifted her head and repeated firmly, "I said no, I don't want to go to bed with you."

He grasped her shoulders and slowly turned her around to face him. Ginevra met his gaze, her gold eyes rebellious but wary. He said evenly, "Perhaps you'd better explain yourself."

"What's there to . . . to explain?" she retorted, stumbling over the words. "I've told you, I don't want to share your bed. I don't want to become one of your . . . your women."

"My women?" he roared, his grip tightening. "You are my wife!"

She sniffled, "Only because my father made me marry you. Only be-because you wanted Dowerwood. Well, now you have Dowerwood." Her voice dropped to a husky murmur. "But you don't need to have me as well."

He stared down at her, his face white under the tan. "Is that how you see it?" he asked, his tone deceptively silky. "And just exactly what makes you think you know anything about my needs?"

Ginevra blushed but continued resolutely, "I . . . I am sure there are others who . . . who would suit you much better than I could. I don't care, as long as . . . as long as you leave me alone."

His blue eyes raked her, stripping away her meager defenses. "Why, you little . . . How dare you speak to me that way?" His fingers dug viciously into her shoulders. "You are my wife. This morning you vowed to serve and obey me. Do you know what that means, the form that service takes? If you have any doubts, madam wife, perhaps I'd better show you now." He swung her into his arms and stalked across the room.

He carried her high, her face buried against his shoulder, muffled in the linen frills of his open shirt, and she lay stunned, stupefied, until he kicked the bedroom door shut behind him. The sharp explosion of sound went through her like an electric shock, and squealing wildly, she began to fight. She thrashed and flailed frantically, pummeling his bare chest with her fists as he carried her with inexorable purpose toward the curtained darkness of the Glovers' ancestral bed.

He threw her down across the turned-back coverlet, and her hair sprayed in a golden shower over the cool lavender-scented sheets. Even as she tried to twist away from him his body descended onto hers, the hard length of him pinning her to the mattress, making her hotly aware of his arousal. He caught her wrists in a merciless grip, and she squirmed impotently as his cruel gaze swept over her. Her frenzied movements disarranged her negligee and exposed her breasts to his hungry eyes. She could feel him inhale raggedly at the sight, and she sobbed, "No . . . no, my lord!"

"Yes . . . yes, my lady," he mocked, and swooping down, he stopped her pleas with his mouth.

The lips that had brushed hers so gently only moments before were hard now, brutal, crushing the breath from her and bruising her tender lips against her clenched teeth. When she attempted to turn her face away, he released her wrists and wove his fingers into her bright tresses, holding her head immobile. She pushed against him without effect, and her fingers caught in the rough hair on his chest. Even in her panic the intimate feel of his skin was so unexpectedly pleasant that she gasped.

The gasp was her undoing. When her lips parted, his tongue invaded her mouth relentlessly, making no concession for her youth and inexperience, ravishing her innocence. Fiery waves began to flow through Ginevra's veins, stirred by his devastating assault. She was becoming dizzy, faint, losing all powers of resistance. When one of his hands unwound from her hair and slid down to cup the delicate weight of her young breast, she knew with anguish that she was lost. Her own body was turning traitor, succumbing to his expertise as a lover. He was taking her, taking her, and she could fight no more. He would use her as callously as he had used his first wife and that Frenchwoman and all the other women in between—and his skill was such that he might even make her enjoy his touch—but when he was finished he would discard her. He cared nothing for her, she was just an object, a convenient receptacle for his pleasure—and she thought she would die from the shame of it.

Ginevra began to cry.

Scalding tears of despair welled up in her golden eyes and splashed onto her cheeks as she twisted her face back and forth, and the salt stung her raw lips. Her breast shook with silent sobs under his caressing hands, and at the tremor he raised his head to stare at her.

His eyes were obsidian as they raked her bloodless features, the quivering mouth swollen from his attack. He caught his breath and became a leaden weight pressing her into the bed. Finally he choked in a voice so low she might have imagined she heard it, "Damn you, Ginevra, damn you to hell."

He lifted himself away from her and towered beside the bed, panting hard and watching with pitiless scorn as she tried with shaking fingers to remedy her dishabille. He rasped, "You needn't fear that a glimpse of your naked body is going to inflame me past all self-control. I have many faults, but raping children is not one of them." He spun on his heel and stalked toward his door.

Bewildered, Ginevra stammered, "M-my lord?"

"What now, for God's sake?" His voice was harsh, and he did not look at her.

She whispered lamely, "I'm sorry." She saw him stiffen. She asked, "What do we do now?"

He shrugged, but his fists were clenched at his sides. He said coldly, "I am going back to London. As for you, you can remain here until . . . until you grow up. I would prefer that my friends there do not discover that I have taken to wife a green girl utterly inadequate for the role of Marchioness of Chadwick." He moved impatiently toward his bedroom door.

Ginevra cringed under his burning contempt, but she steeled herself to ask one last timorous question. "Wh-when you are in London, will . . . will you see Amalie de Villeneuve?"

For a moment she thought he would not answer her, but at the doorway he paused. When he turned, his blue eyes were frosty, his smile wolfish. "As I told you earlier," he said, his deep voice heavy with disdain, "Madame de Villeneuve—and my relationship with her—are none of your concern whatsoever." Then he was gone.

❧ 4 ❧

Sunlight streamed across the bed, and soft scented breezes played over the rich hangings, dispelling the lingering aura of musty velvet and melted candle wax. With eyes shadowed by her sleepless night, Ginevra read for the second time the brief note her husband had left her. Her fingers trembled as she carefully replaced the single sheet of cream-colored paper in the envelope and tucked the flap into place. She stared at the bold black handwriting slashing the face of the envelope. The Lady Richard Glover, Marchioness of Chadwick. Remembering his last hateful words of the night before, she was sure that he had addressed the letter that way, with her new and obviously undeserved title, to mock her. And why not? she thought tiredly. Her behavior merited his contempt; it already had her own. She was a coward. During the night she had listened with thudding heart while he stalked back and forth in his room like a caged animal, restless and incensed, and each time his hard footsteps hesitated just on the other side of her door she had held her breath painfully as she waited for him to twist the knob. When he did not, she berated herself for lacking the courage to go to him instead. Finally his movements had stilled, and the ominous silence had been broken by a new sound coming from outside the house, in the direction of the stables: the receding thunder of a powerful stallion as it galloped down the long drive into the warm Surrey night.

Ginevra toyed with the letter. She picked at the red wax of the broken seal until crumbs littered the sheets like drops of blood, and she thought about the virgin stain that should have embellished her marriage bed. No doubt the housemaids who changed the linens would note its absence; probably by nightfall the rumor would be rife belowstairs that the marquess had found his bride unchaste and had abandoned her in his disgust. She winced at the irony of that thought and set the letter on the nightstand.

Two paces back from the bed Emma stood and watched her young mistress impassively. She noted the frown marring Ginevra's pale face and said in a voice devoid of expression, "My lady, may I say how sorry I am—we all are—that his lordship was called away so suddenly? Of course everyone feels honored to serve a gentleman holding such an important position in the diplomatic corps, yet it seems unfair that he should be forced to curtail his honeymoon . . ."

Ginevra looked blankly at her maid. "Is that the reason you think he left?"

Emma's green eyes were frank and cool and revealed none of the heat with which she had already quelled burgeoning gossip among the staff. "I believe it is the explanation that his lordship asked Hobbs, his valet, to relay to the household."

"I see," Ginevra muttered, relaxing against her pillow. She was filled with reluctant gratitude for the lie. Her husband had covered himself plausibly, with a minimum of embarrassment for either of them; after all, a summons from Whitehall was one that no one could ignore, even on his wedding night. Once the initial rumors subsided, the inhabitants of Queenshaven would accept the marquess's continued absence stoically. They might even commiserate his neglected young bride.

Ginevra's amber eyes flickered to the note lying on the stand. Perhaps the more romantic members of the household would imagine that Lord Chadwick had paused in the midst of his hurried leave-taking to pen tender words of consolation before he departed. She alone knew that his letter was a brutally terse outline of the financial arrangements she would need to be aware of in his absence. The lines had been written in an angry scrawl, beginning with an abrupt "Madam" and signed as coldly "Chadwick." Every period looked as if he had stabbed the paper

with his quill. No affectionate missive this, and yet . . .
and yet, what other man, so livid with frustration and
rage that he deserted his nuptial bed, would still delay
long enough to ensure that his recalcitrant bride was informed of the allowance he had established for her?
Ginevra sank deeper into the bedclothes, staring at the
heavy rings glittering on her finger. Her throat clogged
with the galling taste of self-reproach. She had not wanted
this marriage, but regardless of her reluctance she had the
very morning before pledged in the sight of God and in
the face of that company to live with the marquess as his
wife. Had she not been henhearted, had she not offended
him with her missishness, they might have come to terms
with the awkward situation. But now she had sent him
riding off into the welcoming arms of his mistress, and she
did not know what to do.

Emma interrupted Ginevra's troubled thoughts. "My
lady—"

The girl gritted, "Don't call me that!"

Emma's carefully neutral mask slipped slightly at the
unprecedented sound of her lady's raised voice. "Miss
Ginevra?"

Ginevra blushed. Extending her hand in a gesture of
supplication, she pleaded, "Forgive me for snapping at
you, Emma, but I . . . I just can't stand the thought of
you becoming so formal with me. I don't think I could endure that, not after everything else that has happened.

"No, miss." Emma's eyes moved over the chaotically
jumbled bedclothes, and she recalled the tearstains that
had been visible on Ginevra's cheeks when she first drew
back the heavy drapes to admit the morning sun. She
fought the impulse to pull the girl into her arms and comfort her. "Shall I ring for breakfast now?" When Ginevra
shook her head, Emma went on resolutely, "In that case,
may I suggest a hot bath? I've taken the liberty of ordering one for you. I thought it might ease any . . . discomfort you may be suffering this morning."

Ginevra glanced sharply at Emma. She colored furiously as the significance of those tactful words sank in. In
a low, hoarse voice she whispered, "Yes, I would like to

bathe. I'm still very stiff from yesterday's journey. But there is no need for you to concern yourself with . . . with other things." She drooped her head, and her dark gold hair flowed over her shoulders to curl at her breast as she murmured, "I am no more Lord Chadwick's wife now than I was at this hour yesterday."

Emma's mask fell away completely. "Not at all?" she gasped. "But . . . but his lordship . . ."

Ginevra lifted her lashes and regarded her friend ironically. "Don't look so shocked, Emma. I assure you there is nothing wrong with my husband's manhood. The fault is entirely mine. It appears I am more like my father than I suspected. I seem to acquire obligations that I am incapable of fulfilling."

She twisted her hands together tightly until the knuckles blanched and the fragile bones creaked in protest. Slowly she unplaited her slender fingers and splayed them on the sheet, studying them impersonally as the blush of color returned. Her hands were small and well-shaped, but they were not a "lady's" hands, pale and smooth and soft. Ginevra's nails were not delicate ovals, but were cut short and blunt, for cleanliness, because at Bryant House she had never known when she might be called to bind up a wound or ténd a sick child. Countless needlepricks had roughened the pads of her fingertips, and across the back of her left hand a straight brown scar recalled the time when she had burned herself while helping Cook manipulate the roasting spit. Despite the rich rings, they were not really the kind of hands to wear jewels, not the kind of hands that Frenchwomen no doubt had, hands to stroke and inflame a man's lean, hard body. Ginevra's were the hands of a woman who worked, as she had worked in her father's house since she was twelve years old. From childhood she had been mistress there—and now she was mistress of Queenshaven, and as such, she had obligations not only to her husband but also to the household. Even if the marquess never came to her again, there remained many duties for her to perform.

Ginevra straightened her slight shoulders and brushed her curls back from her face. She swung her head around so that the gleaming mass of her hair streamed down her back in a golden torrent. As she looked up at Emma, who was watching her with tender concern, Ginevra said, her voice low and firm, "I've changed my mind about breakfast. Please ring for it. The bath, as well. And kindly inform the housekeeper that after I am dressed I shall wish to meet the staff. It's time we became acquainted."

Behind the satin hangings of the bed, the air was sultry with the honey-and-ammonia odor of sex and the cloying scent of patchouli. As the Marquess of Chadwick stared upward into the shadows cast by the wavering candlelight, he grimaced with distaste and wondered how much of that betraying perfume clung to his own skin. His elegantly starched cravat that now lay in a limp wad on the Aubusson carpet already reeked of brandy; by the time he dressed and made his way back to his own house, his clothes were going to stink like the rags of a whore in a Haymarket stew.

Now that the spasm of anger and lust had been slaked, Chadwick was impatient to return home, where the long-suffering Hobbs, still aching from his unexpected journey back from Surrey, would rise from his own bed to ensure that his master had a hot bath and fresh linen awaiting him. Good Christian soul that he was, he would tend the marquess's needs silently but with a speaking air of reproach, as if to remind him that he was too old for such unruly behavior.

Chadwick shifted his weight restlessly, and the woman beside him wriggled closer in her sleep. She was warm and velvety against his own cool hardness, and where their naked bodies touched, her lush flesh was slightly damp. When he stirred again she flung one arm across his broad chest possessively, as if to restrain him, in a gesture he found strangely irritating. Her long carmine fingernails dug into the heavy muscles of his shoulder, and the glittering bracelet on her wrist caught at the dark hair on his chest. He must have made some sound of protest, because her liquid black eyes opened suddenly and blinked at him, still hazy with sleep. *"Cheri, qu'as-tu?"* she murmured drowsily.

"It's that damned bracelet, Amalie," he grumbled, dismissing a trinket whose value could have supported a rural village for a year. "You're scratching me with it. You know I hate for you to wear jewelry to bed."

She gurgled with amusement and sat up beside him, her legs just touching his arm, and the coverlet fell away from her tawny body. *"Pardon,* Richard. I only do it to show you how much I like my present." Like a pagan priestess she extended her arms so that the bracelet caught the light, the gems a sparkling contrast to her matte skin, the rubies gleaming with a fire that was reflected in her hair. She had the most exotic coloring the marquess had ever seen: black eyes, golden skin, and hair like a flame. When he first met her he had assumed that her hair was dyed, albeit skillfully, with the same henna she used to tint her nails—but that was before she came under his protection and he became intimately acquainted with the dark auburn triangle between her thighs. Sometimes he had mused about the possible heritage that could have produced such a barbaric combination. Amalie denied being anything but pure French, the daughter of a Creole planter, raised in the West Indies not far from the island where Marie-Joséphine-Rose Tascher de la Pagerie began her own life, before she scaled the heights as the Empress Josephine. While Amalie did concede that one of her ancestors could have been a Spanish sailor, shipwrecked during a hurricane and nursed back to health and potency by the mistress of the plantation, Chadwick was more inclined to think that her ebony eyes and warm-hued skin resulted from the master's coupling with one of the housemaids.

Aware of Chadwick's appraising glance, Amalie unfastened the offending bracelet and leaned over him, deliberately dragging her full breasts across his chest as she dropped the gems onto the nightstand. When he did not respond to her provocation, her dark eyes narrowed thoughtfully, but she said nothing. Slowly she sat on her heels again, parting her knees slightly to make him aware of the musky recesses of her femininity. With a languid stretching movement she dropped her hands to the bed behind her, lolled her head backward, and arched her body upward until she was a golden bow, tense and vibrant, as if she quivered with desire. Chadwick recognized the posture at once—Leda offering herself to the swan— and he had to admit that she did it well, with all the grace and style that were said to have marked Emma Lyon's "attitudes," a diverting spectacle much appreciated among the *ton* in the days before that lady married Lord Hamilton and caught the eye of the great Nelson. But it was the very studied air of Amalie's gesture that served to dampen any ardor that her deliberately erotic movements might have stirred. He knew her too well now. Although he had never pretended any affection for her, when she first came to him he had been amused and aroused by her apparently unbridled ardor. Only gradually did he become aware of the calculation behind her every action; only as their affair had progressed did he realize that the governing passion of Amalie's life was greed.

The marquess trailed his long fingers up her thigh and patted the auburn triangle with a dismissive gesture. "I must go now," he said, and he slid out of bed.

Amalie collapsed into a disgruntled heap. She stared resentfully at Chadwick's lean naked body. Once she had been so sure of him, so confident of her power, and now he was obviously unmoved. She asked petulantly, "Why must you be in such a hurry? Why can't you stay the night?"

The marquess frowned at the proprietary note in her voice. He dressed quickly, and he tucked his shirt into his trousers and reached for his waistcoat before he answered, "I think not, Amalie. I would prefer that my carriage did not stand all night at your curb."

Amalie shrugged. "*Et pourquoi pas?* It wouldn't be the first time."

"No, but as yet my presence in Town is not generally known, and I wish to keep it that way." He picked up his rumpled cravat and draped it around his neck, wrinkling his nose at the unmistakable smell of liquor. He had been

deep in his cups earlier in the evening, but now his head
was clear, and he was more than a little ashamed of his
behavior. When he flung himself out of his London house
and ordered his driver to take him across town to Amalie,
he had been intent only on easing the frustration and rage
that had fermented inside him for two days, ever since
Ginevra rejected him. Now he regarded his conduct with
distaste, the sort of gutter antics he had put behind him
years before. If only to maintain his self-respect, he ought
to act more temperately, with a modicum of discretion.
His alliance with Amalie was of too long a standing for
him to use and discard her like some two-penny jade. He
owed her more consideration than that; she had always
been a compliant, if expensive, mistress, and as far as he
knew she had even been faithful to him, which was more
than he expected, perhaps more than he deserved.

As he tied his cravat into some semblance of a knot, he
watched Amalie step down from the bed, naked as a
wood nymph. She retrieved the bracelet and clasped it
around her wrist again before she padded across the room
to her dressing table. A diaphanous silk negligee the color
of new grass lay slung across the stool. She slipped on the
robe and sat down to brush her hair, frowning sulkily at
the mirror. Where her heavy swath of hair fell down her
back, the fresh green color of the silk made her tresses
glow as if burning. Chadwick sighed. Amalie was a very
inviting and seductive woman, and their relationship had
always been thoroughly satisfactory physically. In addition, it was convenient and comfortable, virtues he found
increasingly attractive. She had been there when he
wanted her, and beyond her passion for jewels, which he
had no aversion to indulging, she had made no demands
of him. Until recently.

Although he had for some months noticed with irritation Amalie's growing self-assured and possessive attitude
toward him, still he had been stunned by her violent, very
public reaction when he told her he was being married.
He had planned the evening carefully: a lavish meal followed by a concert and fireworks at Vauxhall; when she
was in a good mood, he would assure her that her lease

and accounts were to remain open long enough for her to find a new patron; and then as a final gesture of their amicable parting he would present her with the magnificent ruby bracelet. But the evening had ended with fireworks of a kind Handel never orchestrated: instead of meekly accepting Chadwick's decision, Amalie had shrieked and railed like a betrayed wife.

Chadwick stared at his mistress, as the explanation suddenly occurred to him, the motivation for her shrewish temper and her unconscionable intrusion upon his wedding day: Amalie had been so sure of him that she had dared to imagine he might marry *her*. The very insolence of the thought took his breath away. Oh, certainly, almost every year some member of the aristocracy scandalized the *ton* by wedding his demirep, and of course many of those women who pretended to be high sticklers were in fact little better than married whores, but such would never be the case for a Marchioness of Chadwick, and he could not understand how Amalie had come to think otherwise.

Indeed, until recently he had little thought to marry again. His first marriage had been such a misalliance that he was in no hurry to repeat the experience. It had been the shock of the death of his son, so like him and yet a stranger, that had made him think seriously about reestablishing some sort of family life. He already had his mother and Bysshe who depended on him, and indeed the idea of finding some suitable young woman to grace his table and share his bed, perhaps give him more children, was not unappealing. He had taken time away from his political duties to survey the latest bevy of debutantes at Almack's, but while his mere presence in that hallowed hall raised the hopes of sundry doting mothers, not one of the simpering misses paraded for his perusal had aroused any feeling in him other than boredom. His reaction had puzzled him, for certainly some of the girls were attractive, one or two even beautiful, and still another few showed promise of wit. He had not understood his indifference until the day he rode to Reading in answer to Sir

Charles's curious letter, and he spotted a girl with eyes like gold guineas cowering behind a beech tree. . . .

Chadwick's hard mouth quirked wryly as he shrugged his coat over his broad shoulders. How arrogant he had been, how supremely confident that he could order his own life! He would dismiss his mistress with a minimum of fuss, and then he would overcome his young bride's very natural reluctance and with skill and consideration initiate her into the mysteries of womanhood. Instead his mistress declined to be dismissed, and his wife retreated from him as if from Beelzebub. Of course he hadn't helped matters any, allowing himself to become so hipped by the presence of the hapless Ferris that he had lashed out at Ginevra and then stormed back to London. He had embarked on a binge unequalled since those long-ago days when his first wife died, and he had come to his senses only as he plunged himself feverishly into the familiar darkness of Amalie's body. And all the time his mind had protested, *Ginevra, Ginevra* . . .

Amalie turned away from her mirror and looked at the marquess, trying to assess his strange mood. Her voice was carefully humble as she asked quietly, "Richard, are you still angry with me about last Tuesday? Is that why you will not stay with me? I tried to explain . . ." She gave a laugh that was just short of convincing. "I'm sorry I made a fuss, but you should have been frank with me, *mon chou*. Did you think I would not understand? How could I not? The French invented the *mariage de convenance*. I can see that you might decide to remarry if some girl's *dot* were tempting enough, but of course it need make no difference between us."

Standing by the door, Chadwick regarded the woman perched on her vanity stool. He looked at her—not sadly, but perhaps with a twinge of regret for all those times their bodies had merged in an act of love that had no love in it. He knew the contours and textures of her flesh as well as he knew his own, and he knew enough about the workings of her mind to be aware that she must resent being supplanted by a much younger woman. Had there been any tenderness between them, he might have pitied her. But despite her hurt pride, he knew also that Amalie would weather his departure. At thirty-two she was still a striking and desirable woman, one who would have no trouble finding someone else to offer her a *carte blanche*. Even if she did not, he had always been very generous with her; no doubt in typical French fashion she had prudently stored away a tidy sum against the day when her smooth flesh wrinkled and those voluptuous breasts sagged. He said gently, "I'm afraid you don't quite understand, Amalie. After tonight I shall not be seeing you again."

Amalie's black eyes widened, and the warm gold surface of her skin showed ashen through the translucent negligee. "I don't believe you," she said hoarsely, jumping up from her stool. "*Ce n'est pas possible.* You can't leave me!"

"But I can," Chadwick answered, "and I must. Don't pretend to be surprised. I told you only a week ago that I intended to terminate our relationship."

She shook her head fiercely, her hair reflecting highlights as ruddy as the gems on her wrist. "*Non. Non.* You told me some flummery about settling down with a bride, but now, bare days after your wedding, you come to me again, with gifts and—"

"I had planned to give you the bracelet the other night," he interrupted. "It was meant to be a . . . token in honor of my engagement."

Amalie's expression hardened. She gestured toward the tangle of scented sheets. "And what was *that* supposed to be, a wedding present?"

He took a deep breath. "No, Amalie, *that* was a mistake. I should not have come here. I wronged you, and I wronged my wife." He stared at the great bed where he and Amalie had pleasured each other more times than he could count. He wondered why the memory suddenly seemed so unpalatable. His blue eyes darkened as he remembered Ginevra lying across the cool, fresh linen of another bed, her hair sprayed out in a golden nimbus, her young breasts innocent and inviting beneath him. . . .

Amalie's harsh, racuous laugh ripped his reveries.

"Your wife!" she jeered scornfully. "What kind of wife sends her husband into another woman's arms two days after the wedding? Was she frightened, is that it? Poor Richard, did she shy away from your embraces, scream and then run home to her *maman*?" In her fury Amalie's eyes became as opaque as jet. "How could you?" she growled. "How could you throw me over for some milk-faced virgin?"

Chadwick stared at his mistress. He had never seen her like this, and he thought curiously that in her rage no one would ever call her beautiful. Her features twisted and distorted until they were a grotesque caricature of themselves, like a pagan mask. In her vivid silk robe, with her nipples and navel clearly visible through the sheer fabric, she looked like an idol for some unsavory fertility cult. He thought of Ginevra again and knew that he did not want to discuss her with this woman. He turned away from Amalie and made a pretense of searching for his hat.

She grabbed his arm. Her long red fingernails dug into the sleeve that Weston had cut with such loving care, and she pleaded, "Tell me, Richard, I must know. Tell me what hold this girl has over you that you would give up me for her."

Chadwick shook her off. "Leave it, Amalie," he said sternly, impatiently. "My wife is no concern of yours." His voice trailed off as he recalled similar words he had spoken only two nights before. He continued more soothingly, "Be satisfied that I have instructed my man of business to cover your accounts for another quarter. With three months at your disposal you ought to be able to secure a new protector who will suit you. Perhaps you should aim higher this time. I hear that one of the royal dukes is looking for—"

"No!" Amalie cried. "I will not let you discard me like an old shoe. You belong to me!"

From his superior height he stared down at her, and his blue eyes glazed with ice. "You mistake yourself, madam," he said. "I belong to no woman." He scooped up his beaver hat and stalked out of the room.

Amalie did not follow him. She collapsed against the

doorframe and listened intently to his heavy footsteps marking his progress through the elegant *appartement meublé* whose lease he paid; she heard him utter a terse good night to the sleepy maid, whose salary he also paid (Ferris had been dismissed out of hand). The front door slammed, and from the window opening onto the street she heard Chadwick bark out orders to his startled coachman, drowsing on his high perch. When the jingle of the bridle and the hollow clop of the horses' hooves on the cobbled pavement faded into the distance, Amalie gazed down at the jewels on her wrist, basking in their cold fire. "So, my lord, you claim you belong to no woman," she murmured, letting out her breath with a hiss. "*Eh bien, nous verrons.* We shall see." Her free hand twisted the sharp links of the braclet until it cut into her wrist as if it were a garrote around a slim white throat.

Ginevra set the empty basket down by her feet and sank back wearily against the cushions as the barouche pulled away from the shabby little cottage. A few yards down the road two women bobbed respectfully as the carriage passed, and they watched its progress with curious eyes. Ginevra glanced at Emma and noted ruefully, "I don't think I shall ever become accustomed to being curtsied to."

"It's your due," her friend said unanswerably.

The folding top of the vehicle protected Ginevra's bent head from the harsh rays of the noonday sun, but even in the half-shade her gold eyes were pensive. She tucked a strand of hair back beneath her fashionable bonnet and picked idly at the fine blue sarsenet of her day dress, in her mind contrasting the thin silk with the coarse, worn cotton that had garbed the woman whose house they had just left. Ginevra noticed that after several days of enforced idleness her fingers were smoothing again, and she remembered the way her hostess's hands, so red and dry that the skin cracked, had bled at the knuckles when she offered her straw-colored tea in a chipped cup. Ginevra said, "It hardly seems fair. I've done little or nothing, yet everyone acts so pathetically grateful."

Emma said, "You're the new mistress of Queenshaven, and you've shown the tenants that you are interested in their welfare. You've visited them, you've inquired after their sick. That's all they really want."

"Well, I'm not sure it's all I want. I'm not used to playing Lady Bountiful, handing out food baskets and patting babies on the head. I ought to be doing something of value."

Emma chided, "Now that they've met you, I'm sure the people will feel free to come to you if they really need your help. I don't know what else you think you could have done in the short time you've been at Queenshaven. Truly, for all the years your mother lived at Bryant House, I doubt that she could have been a more conscientious mistress than you have proved to be in these last four days."

Ginevra nodded, smiling. "Thank you, Emma. I do try to follow her example. Queenshaven is much like ho . . . my father's house, only bigger." She stared across the undulating fields of green, separated by neat hedgerows that stretched into the distance until they abutted with the dense woods that marked the boundary between Queenshaven and Dowerwood. Sleek cattle grazed near the wood, and Ginevra wondered if Lord Chadwick planned to fell those trees now that he owned her old home, to merge the two estates into one vast expanse of rich pastureland. When she was a little girl, Ginevra's summer world had all been on the far side of those trees, and to her immature mind the marquess's estate had been something immeasurably large, like the ocean, too huge and awesome to be comprehended. Yet now she found herself mistress of both properties.

Perhaps it was ironic that she had never regarded her future in those terms, the terms that had been so important to her parents. Even when she was engaged to Tom she had never considered at any length that she was destined someday to be the great lady of Queenshaven, the Marchioness of Chadwick. She had seen her future with her young fiancé as a continuation of their childhood, happy and innocent as the poems in that volume of Blake

that the marquess had given her. She wrinkled her nose as
she tried to remember what had become of that book; she
had not seen it in months. She shrugged. It was gone forever, like the days to which it referred.

Ginevra sighed wryly. When she had thought with trepidation of her future as the marquess's wife, the one thing
she had never imagined it would be was boring, nor had
she dreamed that she might someday miss the chores, the
endless decisions she had faced when she ran her father's
house. Mrs. Timmons, the Queenshaven housekeeper, appeared to be in no great hurry to delegate her long-standing authority to a mere chit of a girl, and to date
Ginevra's only household duties had been to approve the
menu and to preside in solitary splendor at table, gazing
down the long, lonely expanse of gleaming mahogany to
the empty chair that was used only by the master of the
house.

Perhaps that was the most baffling thing of all about
her new status: she missed her husband. She couldn't
imagine why—she did not even like the man!—yet during
meals she found herself glancing surreptitiously at the
massive carved chair opposite her, as if at any moment
she might peek up through her lashes and meet his sardonic gaze. And at night . . . at night she would lie
awake, twisting with an ache she could not define, staring
at the wall that separated their adjoining chambers, her
thoughts piercing it to envision Chadwick's hard, lean
body stretched across his own bed, vibrant with nervous
energy even in repose. Would he wear a nightshirt of fine
lawn as her father did, or . . . or would he sleep naked?
Ginevra blushed at the tantalizing images conjured up by
her fevered brain. Her fingers curled into her palms as she
remembered the feel of his warm brown skin, the musky
man-scent of him. Did he lie there in the dark thinking of
her, picturing her in her wispy white gown, her slender
form pinned beneath his? . . .

Each night Ginevra would have to bite her lip to keep
from crying out in pain when she remembered that her
husband did not lie in that bed at all, that he slept some-

where in London, in another bed, perhaps in other arms, and she had sent him there.

She clenched her fists as she gazed deliberately at the bright countryside, blotting out unwelcome thoughts. She did not want to return to Queenshaven, not right away. For a few hours she wished to forget her bewildering new life and pretend she was a child again, before she took on so many responsibilities, before her body began to assert itself in ways that puzzled and upset her. She leaned forward and caught the coachman's attention. He pulled the barouche to a halt and swivelled around on his perch to listen respectfully to her instructions. She said, "I want you to go back to the last fork and take the other turning. Drive us to Dowerwood."

The driver frowned and touched the tall hat that covered his grizzled hair. "Begging your pardon, milady, but there's precious little to see at Dowerwood these days. The house is boarded shut, and there's just the Harrisons living in the old caretaker's cottage."

Ginevra brightened at the familiar name. "Harrison! That must be the butler and his wife. They were there when I was a girl."

The man shook his head. "No, ma'am, the only people at Dowerwood are old Mrs. Harrison and her grandson. Himself died at Lammastide four years ago. They say he never got over the loss of his boy, the young lad's father, who was killed on the Peninsula fighting Boney."

"Damned French," Emma murmured.

Ginevra cast a startled glance at her friend before sinking back against the squabs. She thought for a moment about the butler with his ramrod-straight posture and booming voice. "I'm sorry. I didn't know." She looked questioningly at Emma, who shook her head. After a moment Ginevra continued briskly, "Well, no matter. We will still go to Dowerwood and pay our respects to Mrs. Harrison." She relaxed as the driver skillfully brought the carriage about and began to retrace their route to the fork half a mile back. As they drove toward that dense barrier of oak and walnut trees, Ginevra mused to Emma, "It's funny, the things we remember from childhood. I think even now I could pick out Harrison's voice in a crowd of people. As for his wife, she was our cook. I could not tell you what color eyes she had, or whether she was fat or thin, but I can still taste the gingerbread she used to make whenever Tom and Bysshe rode over for tea." She was silent for a moment; then suddenly she burst out, "Oh, Emma, why do things have to change?"

Emma patted her hand reassuringly.

Ginevra tensed again as the barouche slipped beneath the overhanging trees of the shady forest. What would she see at Dowerwood? The marquess, the coachman, everyone had tried to prepare her for the worst, and she wasn't sure she could face it. She had always loved the old *cottage ornée* with its pastiche-Gothic spikes and spires and the heavily draped ivy that made the rooms dark and cool even in high summer. Now would she find the plaster fretwork crumbling, the iron filigree rusted and hanging loose from the eaves?

Slowly the carriage bounced and scraped along the deeply rutted drive now clogged with grass and thistle. Several times the driver had to crack his whip over the heads of the horses to make them pick their way through the mud puddles left by the previous night's rain. When the carriage finally pulled to a halt in front of the boarded-over front door, Ginevra stared at the house in dismay, all her worst fears confirmed.

Dowerwood, her precious Dowerwood, stood shuttered and closed, abandoned, the mouldering remains of a once thriving residence, as derelict as her dreams.

She pressed her hand to her lips to stifle a sob, and the coachman asked diffidently, "Are you going to be all right, milady? I'm sorry, but I told you how it would be."

"Yes, you did," Ginevra said hollowly, staring at the barred entrance marked with the outline of the knocker that had once hung there, "and I'm grateful for your concern. Now, why don't you get down and take a walk or something, relax. I'm sure you must be very weary of driving."

The coachman smiled his gratitude. "Thank you, milady. I'd be that glad to stretch my legs a bit." He climbed down from his seat and tugged the brim of his hat in a deferential salute before he loped off into the woods.

Ginevra turned to Emma and said, "I'd like you to go around to the caretaker's house—take that path and it will lead you directly to it—and see if you can locate Mrs. Harrison."

Emma regarded her mistress uncertainly. "Are you sure? I hate to . . ."

Ginevra shook her head. "I'm quite all right, believe me. I . . . I would simply like to tarry here awhile, look things over. You go on ahead. Perhaps you can inquire whether Mrs. Harrison can find some kind of refreshment for the driver. He must be hot and thirsty."

Reluctantly Emma left the carriage and followed the overgrown walkway Ginevra had indicated. Watching her companion absently, Ginevra admired the graceful way she lifted her long green skirt so that the hem would not be stained by the wet, wild grass. She let out her breath in a windy sigh. Emma was a lovely and loving woman, and it seemed a pity that she appeared destined to spend her entire life attending one lone girl, when she ought to have a husband and children of her own. Ginevra acknowledged that Emma might remain single by choice. If the rumor were true, as she had heard, that Emma had loved a young sailor who died fighting the French, then perhaps her friend had decided that it was better to cherish a memory than to risk having new dreams blasted.

Ginevra hopped down from the barouche, wincing as a sharp stone bruised her foot through her thin-soled slipper. She pulled her skirt back far enough to peer down at her small feet in their ridiculously unserviceable shoes. The white kidskin slippers with the long ribbons that tied around her ankles were part of her trousseau, the sort of footgear that a radiant young bride should wear in elegant salons when she received her first visitors into her new home. Certainly the shoes had never been intended to be worn while slogging through mud to a farmworker's cottage. She ought to have borrowed some sabots from one of the dairy maids.

Ginevra tugged off her blue straw bonnet and stared at it. It was also beautiful and utterly impractical, as were all the new clothes her father had ordered for her. Madame Annette, the couturiere, obviously was accustomed only to deal with ladies of leisure. Ginevra's dressing room was crammed with delicate frivolities of silk and satin, gowns to grace a ballroom, lingerie so sheer that she felt the veriest Cyprian when she glimpsed herself in the mirror as she dressed. She found it hard to believe that only weeks before she had had no clothes beyond the sturdy garments she fashioned herself.

She tossed the bonnet onto the carriage seat and shook her head so hard that her dark gold curls pulled loose from their confining hairpins and tumbled wild and free over her shoulders. She knew she looked the complete hoyden with her hair in her face, she knew she would have to restrain her tresses in some semblance of order beneath her hat before the driver returned, but just for a minute she wanted to be free of restriction. She wanted to close her eyes and remember again for one perfect moment what it had felt like to scramble about in short skirts, with her hair streaming down her back.

She shut her lids tightly and let the faint breeze stir the wispy tendrils that brushed across her face. When she was a child, on a warm summer day like today she would gobble her breakfast in the nursery, go to her mother's room to say good morning, and then she would rush downstairs and burst through the green baize door into the kitchen. Already the spicy aroma of Mrs. Harrison's special gingerbread would be wafting with heady richness from the stone oven in the wall beside the open fire. If she was very lucky, the cook would have saved her one last spoonful of the batter to lick while she sat on the back steps and waited for the boys to ride over from Queenshaven.

Ginevra sniffed. Her eyes blinked open in surprise as

she caught the smell of . . . something . . . drifting toward her from the boarded-up manor house. She inhaled again, puzzling, wondering if her vivid imagination had conjured up the scent: not gingerbread, that would have been too much, but definitely the smell of cooking food. Slowly she made her way to the back of the house, passing through the overgrown kitchen garden, pushing aside the feathery fernlike bushes that had once been her mother's treasured asparagus bed. As she approached the back entrance, she noticed for the first time the thin trail of smoke that issued from the kitchen chimney. Now she could identify the smell as some sort of meat-and-vegetable mixture, a soup perhaps, but one that lacked the full-bodied essence she remembered from her childhood days in Mrs. Harrison's kitchen.

When she timidly pushed open the creaking door at the top of the steps, she noticed at once how dark and dismal the kitchen seemed, a far cry from the immaculate room she had known in years past. The windows were encrusted with dirt and cobwebs, and the only illumination came from a small fire in the grate, where a tall rawboned woman with grey hair tucked beneath a voluminous mobcap bent over a kettle. Ginevra cleared her throat. "Mrs. Harrison?" she asked tentatively.

The woman turned, startled, blinking against the bright light pouring through the open door. She clutched her long wooden spoon against her sunken chest as if it were a shield. "Who are you?" she demanded. "What do you want?"

Ginevra stepped closer. "Mrs. Harrison, it's me, Ginevra Bry . . . Glover. Don't you remember me?"

The woman squinted "Miss Ginnie?" she echoed uncertainly. When the girl nodded, the woman let out her breath with a sob. "Miss Ginnie! God be praised!" She pulled the girl against her, and Ginevra noticed that her faded blue eyes were awash with tears. Mrs. Harrison hugged her convulsively; then she stepped back to study her. "You've grown to be a beautiful woman, just like your mother," she marvelled, "and you didn't forget an

old woman, even though you're married to a great lord."
She hesitated and looked stricken. "Forgive me, miss . . .
my lady. I . . . I didn't mean to be so familiar." She bent
in an awkward curtsy.

"Mrs. Harrison," Ginevra chided, pulling her upright,
"don't be like that! How can I play the great lady to you,
when you've wiped my dirty nose more times than I can
count?"

The woman relaxed, and her mouth widened into a
gap-toothed grin. She cackled, "Not only your dirty nose,
missy!" She stared at Ginevra again and nodded as if an-
swering an unspoken question. "I knew you'd come," she
declared. "My Jamie wanted to set out for Queenshaven
on his own, but I said there was no need. When I heard
you were staying there, I knew you'd come to Dowerwood
as quick as you could. I told him I needed him right
here."

"Jamie—he's your grandson?"

"Oh, yes, Miss Ginnie. Jamie's a fine lad, strong and
quick, a joy for an old woman's heart. He's only six years
old, but if I'd sent him to Queenshaven for help, he'd
have made it right enough, for all that it's such a long
way by foot. But I didn't have to send him out, because I
knew you'd come."

Ginevra grasped the woman's bony shoulders. "Of
course I've come, Mrs. Harrison, and I'll help you any
way I can. Now, tell me what's wrong. Are you ill?"

She shook her grey head and frowned. "Oh, no, it's not
me, miss. Jamie and I, we're both in good health, thanks
be to God."

"Then what's the problem?"

Mrs. Harrison said, "It's the young lord, Master
Bysshe."

Ginevra stared. "Bysshe is here?" she asked hollowly.

"Yes, miss. He showed up two nights ago, drenched
with rain, riding some half-dead nag. He said he'd run
away from school but didn't want to tell his father yet,
him being on his honeymoon and all. I told him he could
stay for just a little while but that I thought as how he
ought to go up to Queenshaven as soon as possible. But

before I could get him to go on home to face up to his lordship, he fell sick. Terrible sick." Mrs. Harrison gazed at Ginevra with wide, hopeless eyes. "Oh, Miss Ginnie," she wailed, "I think it's scarlet fever!"

❧ 5 ❧

Ginevra demanded, "Where is he?"

The woman stammered, "He's . . . he's in the master bedroom upstairs. I swept and aired it for him. I . . . I couldn't expect him to stay with Jamie and me, our cottage isn't grand enough for—"

Ginevra rushed past her and flew up the stairs, her long hair streaming behind her. She had no eye for the devastation wrought on the house by six years of disuse, the mildewed wallpaper, the obvious signs of mice. She ran down the hallway, past rooms filled with furniture shrouded under holland covers, past a grandfather clock where a fat brown spider crawled along the immobile pendulum. At the end of the corridor she burst through the open door into the chamber where, as a child, she used to visit her mother each morning and again just before tea.

A small boy perched on a stool beside the bed, guarding a basin and a pitcher of tepid water, but it was the figure in the bed that captured Ginevra's attention, a youth who tossed restlessly in his sleep. His long sandy hair fell over his flushed face while his boy-into-man's body twitched beneath its sweat-stained nightshirt. "Bysshe, Bysshe," she murmured helplessly, watching his swollen red tongue lick at his pale, parched lips as he gasped for air. She did not need to touch him to know that he burned with fever.

The little boy dampened a napkin in the basin and with great care dabbed it at Bysshe's lips. Ginevra smiled involuntarily at his stern concentration, and she said, "You must be Jamie. Did your grandmother show you how to do that?"

The boy jumped up, startled, his eyes wide and questioning. "Are you Ginnie?" he asked.

Ginevra blinked. "Yes. How did you know?"

Jamie tilted his head toward Bysshe. "He called for you. I wanted to go fetch you at the big house, but Gran said she needed me to help her here." He grinned with relief. "I'm glad you've come. Gran has been worried."

He began to moisten the cloth once more, and Ginevra said, "Here, let me do it." She sat on the stool and proceeded to bathe Bysshe's hot, dry face. Some of the buttons of his nightshirt were undone, and beneath the fine sprinkling of new hair on his chest she could see that the trunk of his body was covered with a bright red rash. Scarlet fever. She knew the signs from an epidemic that had begun among the pupils of a dame-school near Bryant House and had then passed to almost every tenant family on the surrounding farms. She had been up for days, nursing the sick, and she knew that there was very little that could be done except to make the patient comfortable—that, and pray that the disease would not become virulent and settle in the ears, or worse, the heart. She glanced at Jamie and quailed as she thought of the risk Mrs. Harrison was taking with her grandson. "It's good of you to want to help," she said carefully, "but aren't you afraid of becoming ill yourself?"

He regarded her with a look oddly dignified for his six years. "No. Gran says I already had the fever when I was little."

Ginevra nodded. Sometimes infants weathered the disease better than anyone else. "That's good. So did I." After a moment she continued, "Jamie, I want you to do something for me. Outside the house you'll find a lady in a green dress. Her name is Emma. Please tell her that I need her. Then go see if your grandmother wants you. I think she has your lunch ready."

When the little boy had scampered away, Ginevra returned her attention to Bysshe. She unfastened the remaining buttons of his nightshirt and pulled the soft fabric away from his shoulders. With smooth, soothing strokes she sponged his hot, reddened skin, and she observed with dismay that the water seemed to evaporate almost immediately. As she dipped the napkin into the last of the lukewarm liquid, she wondered fleetingly if she could sell her soul for some chips of ice; at the moment it seemed a fair exchange.

As she bathed Bysshe, Ginevra thought again how unlike her husband his younger son was. With his fair coloring, short nose, and childishly round face, the boy must resemble his father's first wife; she could see no sign of the marquess in him. When she tried to turn his soft chin so that she could reach beneath his thick, unruly straight hair, Ginevra noticed with surprise that Bysshe wore something around his neck, some medallion or piece of jewelry. Whatever the ornament was, his throes had caused it to fall beneath him, and the ribbon was cutting into his throat, irritating the rash. She slid one arm under his back to lift him, no easy task now that he had grown so, and with her other hand she pulled the long ribbon free. The pendant, she discovered with a frown, was a large gold locket. She wondered if it contained a picture of his long-dead mother, and curiosity made her unfasten the catch. When she opened the engraved leaves, she found herself gazing at an exquisite miniature painted on ivory, the portrait of a young girl in the first blush of maturity, her honey-colored hair falling artlessly over her bare shoulders, just brushing the rise of her breasts revealed by her low-cut pink gown.

It was not Maria Glover. Ginevra now recognized the locket as the keepsake she had sent to Tom when their betrothal was officially announced.

She bit her lip, puzzled and pensive. In the traumatic days following Tom's death, she had forgotten all about the miniature, even when she sent her ring back to Lord Chadwick. She wondered how Bysshe had come to wear it. Why should he want to? As she pondered, the boy's lids suddenly flew open and he stared up at her with fever-bright brown eyes. His face twisted into a troubled scowl, and he lifted one hand weakly to stroke her cheek.

The effort seemed too much for him; his arm fell back to his side. "Ginnie," he croaked, "this time . . . this time you're not a dream."

Ginevra's eyebrows rose sharply, but she answered quietly, "No, Bysshe, I'm not a dream."

He sighed hoarsely and relaxed. "I knew . . . you'd come to me," he murmured, swallowing painfully. "I knew the old woman was . . . wrong. You wouldn't . . . you couldn't be . . . with . . . with *him*." His eyes drooped shut and he drifted back into an uneasy sleep.

When Emma and Mrs. Harrison appeared at the doorway, Emma picked up the near-empty pitcher and vanished back into the kitchen to draw fresh water. Mrs. Harrison stood twisting her apron nervously. She asked, "Was I wrong to let him stay here, Miss Ginnie? He told me there was some kind of quarantine laid on his school and if he went back there he'd have to stay all summer. Should I have made him go back? It wasn't my place, and he didn't seem to think there was any danger, and . . . and sometimes it does get lonely here, with just Jamie for company."

Ginevra shook her head impatiently. "No, of course you weren't wrong, Mrs. Harrison. If anyone was at fault, it was Bysshe, for leaving Harrow, although I expect he will fare better here, away from everybody, than he would in a crowded infirmary."

"He didn't seem sick at all when he first arrived," the woman continued. "He was happy and laughing. He said he hated school and it felt good just to get away, even if it did mean riding through a downpour. But . . ." Here she hesitated and regarded Ginevra uncertainly. "The strangest thing happened, I hardly know how to credit it. It must have been some kind of awful mistake. Master Bysshe, he was teasing and joking—it did me good to hear my Jamie laughing at his pranks—then he made some remark about not being anxious to make the acquaintance of his new stepmother, her being a—begging your pardon, miss—a London tart." She colored furiously at Ginevra's astonished glance. "I know he didn't mean anything by it—boys do have the strangest notion of what's funny—but I lit right into him. I told him I didn't care if he was a viscount now that his brother was gone, he had no cause to speak that way about a decent woman, especially not since she was an old friend of his. When he asked me who I meant, I said to him, 'Why, Miss Ginnie, of course,' and for the longest time he just stared at me as if I was addlepated. Then he stormed out into the rain again, and when he came back two hours later, he was feverish."

Ginevra blanched as she listened to this recital. When Mrs. Harrison finished, for a long moment the only sound in the musty room was the rasp of Bysshe's labored breathing. Ginevra looked down at him and choked, "My God, he didn't know."

"No, miss," the woman said impassively.

Ginevra inhaled deeply, too shocked to feel anything beyond an icy numbness. She gazed at the youth lying on the bed. He had grown since she last saw him, he must be close to six feet tall now, but even the loose nightshirt could not disguise the adolescent thinness of his body. Bysshe, her old friend—her new stepson. Why hadn't Lord Chadwick told him? Was it because he suspected that his son was no more prepared to accept the altered relationship than Ginevra was? She sighed, "Thank you for telling me," and she dipped the napkin into the basin again.

She was still at Bysshe's side two days later. Emma and the coachman had returned to Queenshaven to fetch the servants and supplies necessary to make Dowerwood habitable during Bysshe's convalescence, but Ginevra did not stir from the room, even to sleep. She drowsed in an armchair and prayed for his fever to break. When it gave no sign of doing so, and more ominously, when Bysshe began to complain that his ear pained him, Ginevra asked Mrs. Harrison to send someone to the nearest town to find a physician.

The woman shook her head in disgust. "He'll not come, miss. He hates to leave the gin shops, even to tend those who need him. And believe me, the young master would be better off without the kind of treatment that one would give him. A real toper, he is."

Ginevra said wearily, "We have to try. All I can do is give Bysshe sponge baths and dose him with laudanum if the pain gets too bad. Surely even a bad doctor could do more for him than that."

But as soon as the man appeared, Ginevra regretted calling him. He was old and cadaverous, dressed in a rusty black frock coat that reeked of ragwater and strong snuff and other foul odors Ginevra preferred not to identify. As Mrs. Harrison had predicted, he was drunk and unclean and surly because he had been summoned to a "run-down old farm." The nails of his palsied hands were filthy, and they ran roughly over Bysshe in the most cursory of examinations, terrifying the boy in his weakened state. When the man took from his ancient medical bag a knife to bleed Bysshe for his fever, Ginevra saw with disgust that the blade was still stained with dried blood from his last patient. "Stop!" she ordered, just as he moved to slit the vein. "I don't want you to touch him."

He turned on her with a resentful glare. "If you won't let me go about my business, why did you drag me here?"

"There must be some way to treat him without bleeding him. He's already very weak."

"Interfering female," the man muttered querulously. "Bleeding and purging, that's the cure for everything. I ought to know: I've been a doctor these thirty years and more. I served on the staff of St. Bartholomew's Hospital. Do you think I'll let some silly chit order me about?"

Behind him Mrs. Harrison snapped, "Mind your tongue, you . . . you swill-bellied old cabbage head. Who do you think you're talking to?"

The physician regarded her balefully; then he turned his bleary eye on Ginevra, noting her stained dress and disheveled hair. He shrugged insolently. "Who's she? Some young lightskirt, no doubt, hiding away from her keeper. Everyone knows the quality ain't been near this place in years." He grabbed Bysshe's arm again. "Now, let me get on with this, since you've dragged me all this way. You ought to be grateful I've come, a man with my qualifications."

Once again Ginevra stayed his hand. "I want you to leave him alone," she said quietly but firmly, and unconsciously she straightened her shoulders with a creditable imitation of her husband's supercilious air. "You'll be paid for your time, never fear. I shall see that you are recompensed as befits a man of your remarkable . . . credentials." She paused. "St. Bartholomew's Hospital, did you say? I believe my father told me about it once. Forgive me if I'm wrong, but is that not the place where patients are required to deposit a burial fee of some nineteen shillings, refundable in the unlikely event that they recover?"

The man's visage paled, then reddened fiercely. "Just who do you think you are, to talk to me that way?"

Ginevra smiled coolly, and she was wryly aware of making use of her new rank for the first time. "I am the Marchioness of Chadwick," she said, "and I serve notice to you now, before witnesses, that in future, should you dare to practice your quackery on any of my people, whether here or at Queenshaven, I will have you hounded from the district like the mountebank you are." She nodded curtly and turned away. As soon as the door slammed behind the departing physician, she began to tremble.

From the bed Bysshe regarded her with glassy eyes and chuckled weakly, "You tell him, Ginnie." Then he tugged at his earlobe.

After Ginevra had once again forced the bitter tincture of opium down the boy's swollen throat, she asked Mrs. Harrison, "How does it happen that an incompetent sot like that is able to maintain a practice?"

The woman sighed in resignation. "The war, milady. We had a good doctor—young he was, and quick—but he died in Belgium, and there was no one to take his place, except . . . well, you see what we ended with." Her faded eyes strayed to the sleeping youth. "I don't know what's going to become of him if we don't get someone soon who can help him."

Ginevra nodded, following her gaze. Like most countrywomen of her class, she was skilled enough to bind minor injuries, to treat common ailments, but she had no illusions about her capabilities in the face of life-threatening infection. Bysshe needed a physician, a good one, and he needed him at once. If anything happened to the boy, she would never be able to face his father again.

She looked up at Mrs. Harrison, and her countenance hardened with determination. "Find me a pen and paper," she said, "and recruit someone to serve as outrider. I need to send a message to Lord Chadwick."

Richard Glover, Lord Chadwick, peeled off his grey chamois gloves and passed them to the drowsy butler, who already held his hat and rain-spattered cape. With a terse nod the marquess dismissed the man and strode impatiently into his study, where he quickly located the brandy decanter and sloshed some of that vivifying liquid into a glass, heedless of the excess trickling down to stain the marquetry of the Chippendale table. He had longed for that drink all evening. He gulped down the brandy and regarded the empty glass ruefully as he flopped into the chair behind his desk. If he wasn't careful, he was going to become a hopeless tosspot before he was forty, a drunken degenerate without any of the mitigating charms of youth, like some of the highborn louts he had observed tonight at Little Harry's. As was his practice these days, he had remained aloof from the proceedings, but while he watched the diplomat he had escorted there—bald, belching, his overblown body constricted by tight stays—he had wondered with carefully masked distaste if the same sort of future awaited him; if he would ever find himself sprawled in some garish parlor, his fat sweaty hands groping moistly over the flimsily clad body of some young Paphian whose heavy face paint only partly concealed her disgust at what circumstances forced her to do. No doubt once the ambassador would have denied that he could sink to such depths, just as that girl's parents would have strangled her in her cradle rather than allow her to become a whore before she was even as old as Ginevra.

With a shudder of rage at himself and the world, Chadwick flung the empty brandy snifter into the low fire in the fireplace. For just a second the dregs of his whiskey flared and sizzled in the flames, and the bright new gaslight in the room made the shattered glass on the hearth sparkle mockingly at him.

Nowadays he preferred his dissipations to be . . . private, but he had only himself to blame for the continuing forays onto the town. Aeons before, when he was young, just after he was invalided from the Navy, he had been flattered when he was approached by members of the War Ministry, with their request that he help them ferret out the foreign agents hidden among the hordes of genuine *emigrés* resident in London. He had the perfect cover: he was a rich and aristocratic rakehell with no known connection to diplomatic circles, a man who could drink and wench and still remain alert for any furtive signal or unwary word. He had been seduced by the opportunity to serve his country now that his accession to the title made it impossible to return to the military, and he had thought privately that the assignment might help him in his quest to spirit his mother out of France. Besides, the job had sounded amusing, without the responsibilities of an official position. Over the years he had performed his duties with reasonable success, cynically aware that most likely he would have lived much the same way even had not the war given him an excuse to do so. He circulated as easily through the cockpits of Charing Cross as he did through White's or Almack's, and he listened with affected insouciance to all around him, watching with deceptively lazy blue eyes that missed nothing. Sometimes he had been required to distract suspects by taking them along with him as he moved not only among the Carlton House set but also into the haunts of the less savory denizens of the city. He had accepted such tasks as part of his duty to his sovereign, but now that the wars were at long last over and the Pax Britannica had dawned, when the foreign minister requested that he continue to escort visiting dignitaries on those dubious tours, Chadwick felt less like a loyal subject and more like a highborn pimp.

He was going to have to put an end to it. He was going to have to tell Castlereagh that henceforth he would serve his liege in the accepted fashion by occasionally assuming his seat in the House of Lords; that he intended to settle down to a life of pompous mediocrity as a country squire, devoting his attention to the growing of crops and the welfare of his tenants, living in unremarkable domesticity with his young wife.

Chadwick leaned back in his chair, booted feet resting on the edge of the desk, and he rubbed the bridge of his long nose and thought of Ginevra. A week had passed since he left her crying on her bed, a week during which he had cursed first her and then himself, for not turning back at the door to comfort her. How much less there would be to regret if only he had not left her! He was haunted by the memory of her wide gold eyes as she asked him timorously whether he would be seeing his mistress, and he despised himself for the ease with which he had wounded her with his taunting reply. She was not a worthy opponent. She was a confused and frightened child, trying desperately to cope with the situation she had been flung into, and he had been less than a man to take pleasure in hurting her.

He could not understand his reactions. He had never deliberately harmed a woman before, not even Maria, who had certainly given him justification; he had never cared enough about any woman to want to strike out at her, no matter what she did to him. Whenever a relationship had soured, he terminated it and dismissed the woman from his mind.

But Ginevra . . . This beautiful woman-child he had taken to wife affected him in ways he did not recognize, stirred him with her very vulnerability. She made him question the validity of the pride that had served him so well and so long, a bulwark against the slings and arrows life had thrown at him. She made him wonder whether he might not find more strength in humility—

A rap at the door interrupted his agitated thoughts. "Come in," he barked.

The butler appeared at the door in his robe, skinny

shanks visible beneath the hem of his long nightshirt. In his hands he carried a small silver tray with an envelope on it, and his demeanor was as dignified as if he were dressed in livery and powdered wig. "Milord," he said, "a rider just arrived with a message from her ladyship."

Chadwick frowned. "From my mother?"

"No, milord. From her young ladyship. From Dowerwood."

Chadwick's scowl deepened. "Dowerwood!" he exclaimed impatiently as his long fingers ripped open the envelope. "There's some mistake." When he unfolded the single sheet of paper, he saw with trepidation that Ginevra must have written the note hurriedly, under the compulsion of fierce emotion. Her usually painstaking copperplate hand was ragged and blotched, and the letters faded out repeatedly, as if she resented the time necessary to redip her quill into the inkwell. His blue eyes scanned the missive with growing apprehension. He winced when he came to that last frantic plea: "I beg you, my lord, send someone at once! I remain, your dutiful wife, Ginevra." His dutiful wife. Yes, she was certainly that—while in a matter of days he had proved the most lax and unworthy of husbands. He should have been there. God alone knew what phantasm from childhood had drawn Ginevra to the mouldering ruins of Dowerwood, or why Bysshe should be there, laid low with a fever, instead of safely ensconced at Harrow, where he had left him. The boy must be ill indeed, the marquess realized with dismay, if Ginevra admitted she could not treat him. She should not *have* to treat him, nor should she be forced to deal with a "drunken charlatan," as she mentioned. Chadwick should have been there to handle the situation, instead of leaving those two children to cope on their own.

But they were not really children, and he caught his breath as in his mind the pairing of his wife and his heir suddenly took on ominous dimensions.

The marquess jumped up, startling the stolid butler, who awaited instructions. "The rider," Chadwick demanded, "did he have any further message?"

"No, milord, the letter was all. The man could scarce

talk, he was so exhausted. He said he had been in the saddle since midday, the last two hours in rain."

Chadwick nodded, his movements jerky. His voice was harsh as he rapped out orders. "Of course. See that he has food and a place to sleep. Then rouse Hobbs and instruct him to start packing. While you're at it, you'd better get someone who can deliver messages for me, one to Dr. Perrin in Harley Street, another to Whitehall." Yes, he thought grimly, tell Castlereagh that he will have to find someone else to do his dirty work for a while. Aloud he snapped at the dazed butler, "Be quick about it, man! I'm going home!"

"Miss Ginevra, you must rest."

"No, Emma, I'll be all right." She rubbed her weary eyes and gazed at the boy who drowsed fitfully in his drugged stupor. The waning light disclosed a stiff fuzz of reddish-gold whiskers on his chin; she wondered if she ought to ask one of the footmen to shave him. Not yet, she decided. Now that his fever was at last cooling slightly, his skin was beginning to peel away in those areas where the rash had been most severe, exposing pinkly new flesh beneath. A razor might irritate it.

Emma said, "My lady, you've scarce stirred from that chair for days. The servants you summoned from Queenshaven have prepared a room for you. There's a bed aired and waiting, and a tub ready to be filled at a moment's notice. Let me watch while you bathe and take a nap. You can't go on this way, you'll make yourself ill. Give a thought to your own needs for once."

Ginevra shook her head doggedly. "No, Emma. When the laudanum wears off he'll be in pain again, and he'll want me. I intend to be here." She looked up at Emma, and her companion was horrified by the dark shadows bruising her gold eyes, the hollows punched into her cheeks by fatigue. Ginevra said, "I would dearly love a cup of tea, though, Emma."

"Of course. May I get you something to eat as well?"

"No, thank you. I don't care for any breakfast."

Emma chided gently, "My lady, it's dinnertime now."

Ginevra raised her head to meet her friend's speaking glance. She smiled ironically. "Don't look at me that way. Mrs. Harrison's disapproval is quite enough. Truly I could not eat a thing now. I promise you I'll go to bed as soon as the physician arrives from London."

"But we don't know when that will be, or even if—"

"Emma," Ginevra reproved sharply, "there is no doubt in my mind that his lordship will dispatch someone directly he receives my note. I am appalled that you could think otherwise."

"Yes, my lady," Emma murmured.

"And when the doctor comes," Ginevra continued, as if speaking to a child, "I shall be waiting to tell him all he must needs know about . . . about my stepson's illness." And when he reports back to the marquess, she added silently, my husband shall know that in this respect at least I am capable of acting a proper wife.

Emma regarded her young mistress as she leaned back in her chair, eyelids drooping, aching with exhaustion. In her stained blue silk dress, which she had not changed since reaching Dowerwood, the girl looked wraithlike, almost intangible. Emma had seen her work herself to the point of collapse before, always a devoted nurse, but this time she sensed that Ginevra was driven by some compulsion far beyond her compassion for the sick boy. It must have something to do with the absent Lord Chadwick, Emma thought resentfully, and she cursed the man again for deserting his bride. Aloud she said, "I'll go fetch you that tea now."

Ginevra was hardly conscious of her leaving. Her attention was directed to the recumbent figure on the wide bed. He twitched as if the opium were losing its hold on him, and one bloodless hand began to flail weakly, batting at his ear. Ginevra caught his lanky wrist and held it immobile at his side. She knew that Bysshe was going to suffer greatly as soon as the laudanum wore off, and she would have her work laid out for her, to prevent him from hurting himself in his frenzy. Once, after an epidemic of measles, she had seen a toddler at Bryant House almost claw off his ear in an effort to escape the pain. After the agonizing infection finally subsided, the child was left stone-deaf, and the tenants said it was God's mercy when he died two months later, overlaid in the bed he shared with his parents.

Bysshe stirred, and his brown eyes opened slowly. He stared up at Ginevra, his mind still clouded by the drug she had administered. "The doctor," he asked hoarsely, "has . . . has he gone?"

"Yes, Bysshe, yes, my dear," she crooned, brushing the boy's limp hair away from his face. "I sent him away long ago. I won't let him hurt you."

"That's good," he sighed, his agitation lessening. "I . . . I didn't like him." His lids drooped shut again, only to open almost at once.

Ginevra watched apprehensively. Bysshe was struggling to throw off the last soporific coils of the opium, and she did not know what she would do if help did not arrive soon. It had been a day and a night and most of another day since the messenger set out. Agony lay in wait for the boy, just this side of consciousness, yet she dared not give him more laudanum, not right away. His immature body had already had as much as it could tolerate. More would poison him.

As if in answer to her thoughts, Bysshe moaned. His long fleshless form twisted restlessly, and his fingers flew to his head again. Ginevra caught his wrists in her small hands, and this time she was shocked by the power that had returned to his thin arms. He pulled away from her easily, and his nails scratched at his ears, making the skin raw and sore.

"No, Bysshe, you mustn't!" she cried, trying futilely to stop him. Had his strength really come back with such force, or was she just weak from fatigue? "Stop it," she sobbed, biting her lip as he thrashed out of her reach.

Dazed, he whimpered in a little-boy voice, "It hurts . . ."

She glanced around frantically for someone to help her restrain him, but the room was empty. She called out, but there seemed to be some kind of commotion belowstairs, and no one heard her. Until Emma returned with her tea, Ginevra would have to cope with Bysshe on her own, pitting her waning energy against the vigor of his wiry body. After a moment's hesitation she kicked off her slippers and climbed onto the bed beside him. She flung herself across him, using all her few stones of weight to pinion his arms so that he could not touch his ears again. His head thrashed back and forth, tears escaping from beneath his tightly closed lids. "It *hurts*," he repeated pathetically.

"I know it hurts," she said in soothing tones, trembling with the effort to hold him down. Beneath her she could feel the heat of his tensed body radiating through his thin nightshirt, and she did not know how long she would be able to confine his movements if somehow she could not calm him. "Settle down, Bysshe," she pleaded. "Help is on the way, I promise you. I've sent for a doctor."

He jerked convulsively beneath her. "Not him!" he cried, his words blurred. "He looked . . . he looked like the gravedigger when . . . when Tom—"

"No," she said quickly to hide her anguish, "not him. I've sent for a fine London doctor, someone who'll know how to take away the pain. I asked your father to find one."

Bysshe's eyelids flew open yet again, only inches from hers, and he stared up wildly, his brown irises murky with delirium. He blinked hard, and momentarily his eyes cleared. "Don't let him touch you," he said.

Startled, Ginevra asked in confusion, "What? Why should the doctor want to—"

"Not the doctor!" Bysshe cried, shaking his head fiercely. "Him—the marquess! Don't let him touch you."

Ginevra gasped, stunned. When she could find her voice, she said breathlessly, "Bysshe, I don't understand." His expression troubled her. Suddenly she was aware of the hardness of his body beneath hers, the provocative intimacy of that sexless embrace. With great care she released his arms and eased her weight off him.

Before she could slide from the bed, his fingers captured her wrists, preventing her escape. She tried to tug her hands out of his grasp, but he would not let her go. He was sweating with pain, but he held her gaze as he begged, "Ginnie, listen to me! Stay away from him. You and I—we'll run away together."

"Oh, Bysshe, no!" she protested.

He said, "Yes, Ginnie. Please. Don't you know? I love you. Ever since we were children. I've always loved you!"

Ginevra paled. "Don't say that," she rasped. "You're sick. You're delirious. You . . . you mustn't say things like that."

"I quite agree," a deep voice interjected harshly, and Ginevra jerked her head around in the direction of the door, where her eyes met the burning blue gaze of her husband.

❧⟨ 6 ⟩❧

"My lord!" she cried, her voice shaking with astonishment and relief. Bysshe's bruising grip loosened, and she jerked her wrists out of his fingers and flung herself across the room at the marquess. "Thank God you've come!" she sobbed, throwing her arms around his waist and clinging to him so hard that the chased brass buttons of his long waistcoat left their imprint on her smooth cheek. She could hear his heart thudding under her ear, and she waited for the reassuring pressure of his arms to wrap about her thin shoulders. He did not move. His hands remained resolutely at his sides, and with a sickening sense of rejection Ginevra released him and backed away, her face crimson with embarrassment. How could she have so forgotten herself? He had come because his son needed him, not her. "F-forgive me," she stammered lamely, not hazarding to look at him. "It's . . . it's just that I dared not hope . . . did not expect you to accompany the physician. You . . . you *did* bring a doctor?"

"Yes, of course. He is belowstairs supervising the unloading of the supplies he brought with him. He'll be here forthwith." Ginevra schooled herself to lift her gold lashes, and she saw that her husband was gazing not at her but at the youth who stared back ashen-visaged from the bed. With two long strides the marquess crossed the room to Bysshe's side, and the boy shrank against the pillows, brown eyes wide and defiant in his colorless face, as if he expected the man to strike him. Chadwick picked up his limp hand and felt for the pulse; it was weak and rapid. He said smoothly, "Well, my boy, I was right

102

amazed to learn that you were here, rather than at Harrow, where I expected you to be."

Bysshe gaped at him, disconcerted by the mildness of his attack. He made a grimace of resentment and muttered sullenly, "I didn't want to be quarantined there all summer."

"Of course not. School is seldom the most salubrious of environments; during a quarantine I expect it would be well-nigh unbearable. Naturally, however, I should have preferred you to obey my wishes, but if you felt you could not endure staying there, you ought to have gone home, rather than troubling the Dowerwood caretaker and putting her family at risk."

Bysshe's glance shot furtively toward Ginevra; then he met the marquess's gaze squarely. "I had no wish to intrude upon your honeymoon, sir," he said, and he turned his head away. The instant his sore ear touched the linen pillow cover, he groaned, and at once Ginevra flew to him. She forgot her husband's presence while she tried to soothe the boy's pain as she had done for days now. Lord Chadwick leaned against the bedpost and watched enigmatically, arms crossed over his chest to prevent them from reaching out to her. He noted the intense, set expression in her amber eyes, their glimmer the only color in a bloodless face bruised with fatigue. She blinked hard several times, shaking her head as if to clear it, and when she reached for the napkin that lay in the basin on the table, he could see that her slim fingers trembled. She moved like an automaton. She was on the point of collapse, her inadequate reserves of energy long since spent—yet he knew if he tried to stay her hand before she delivered Bysshe's care over to the physician, she would lash out at him with all the unsubstantial fury of a spitting kitten.

When at last the doctor appeared at the doorway, accompanied by Emma, Ginevra lifted her head, her eyes alight with hope for the first time in days. As soon as she met the man's kindly and intelligent gaze, her apprehension began to abate. She set down the damp napkin and rose from the stool, extending her hand in welcome. "I am most grateful you've come, Dr. . . . Dr. . . ."

As she hesitated over his name, the man approached her, and she noticed that he limped slightly. Yet when he caught her thin fingers in his own, he bent his head over them with all the grace of a practiced courtier. "Jules Perrin, *à votre service, madame,*" he murmured.

Ginevra's startled eyes flew to her husband's face, and he smiled ironically. "The doctor is one of my mother's French cronies," he explained in an undertone. "He was kind enough to accompany her when she returned from the Continent two years ago."

Ginevra looked again at the man. He appeared to be about the same age as the marquess, of no more than medium height, with one of those handsome-ugly faces so difficult to describe. Despite his elegance of manner, he was dressed soberly and modestly, as befitted one of his profession, and he seemed an unlikely companion for the formidable dowager. Ginevra nodded uncertainly. "As a . . . a friend of my husband's mother, then you are doubly welcome, sir. I hope you will be comfortable here. All that we have is at your disposal."

"Merci, madame," he replied smoothly. When he switched to English his accent was almost unnoticeable. He said, "My first duty, my lady, is to ensure that that young man there is made comfortable." He inclined his head toward Bysshe, who had drifted into a delirium where he seemed unaware of what was going on around him. His hands were at his ear again, and Ginevra saw with dismay the red weals forming on his livid flesh. She wanted to reach for him, but the doctor said, "I shall attend him, madame." He looked at Ginevra critically. "In the meantime," he continued in a voice that brooked no opposition, "I would suggest that you retire to your own room and get some rest."

Ginevra shook her head fiercely. "No," she insisted. "You will require someone to assist you, to explain what treatment has already—"

"Madame, you are in no condition to assist anyone," he interrupted bluntly. "Your devotion does you credit, but I have only to look at you to know that if you do not cater to your own needs at once, you will fall ill yourself." He glanced sharply at Emma, who waited in silence at the door, her face its usual impenetrable mask. "This young woman will help me, will you not, mademoiselle?" he said. Something flickered in Emma's green eyes, but after a moment she nodded impassively. The doctor addressed Ginevra again, punctuating his words with a Gallic shrug. "You see, my lady, everything marches. Now, please retire, you are no longer needed here."

The girl, who had been functioning by sheer force of will for days, was stunned and bewildered to find control wrested from her small hands so easily. She appealed frantically to her husband. "My lord, I beg you—"

He caught her by her thin shoulders. "Ginevra," he said sternly, "even a marchioness must bow to the dictates of her physician. You heard Perrin. You must rest."

Ginevra swayed slightly, and suddenly from the doorway Emma snapped, with a bitterness she made no effort to disguise, "It's been too much for her, she never should have been left alone. She has neither eaten nor slept in days!" Ginevra cried out at this betrayal, but as she uttered Emma's name, the word faded to an incoherent moan. Her knees gave way, and she slipped out of Chadwick's hands and crumpled to the floor.

Chadwick swooped down and caught her before her head could strike the oak planking. When he swung her into his arms and held her high against his chest, he could feel her pathetically light body twitch with exhaustion. Her head lolled weakly against his shoulder, and her bright hair tumbled down the front of his coat like military braid. His blue gaze took in Emma, whose resentment and defiance for once showed clearly on her face. His eyes swept to the doctor standing beside Bysshe, who stirred restlessly on his bed, and he addressed his friend in deep, hard tones. "Perrin, I leave the boy in your capable hands. Emma will assist you however you may wish. In the meantime I shall attend my wife." And he carried Ginevra from the room.

Richard Glover tugged the collar stud loose from his shirt and dropped it onto the untidy heap of coat, waist-coat, and cravat already piled on the chair next to him. He was glad he had decided to send Hobbs on to Queens-haven with the rest of his luggage, while he himself jour-neyed to Dowerwood with no more than a change of linen in his valise. Although it was true that he would probably have to summon his long-suffering valet in a day or two—by all indications the stay at Dowerwood would be lengthy—for the moment he was grateful not to have the man shadowing him, casting silent, reproachful glances his way each time he mussed the starched perfection of his neckcloth or creased the tail of one of his elegantly cut coats. "No man is a hero to his valet," the Duc de Condé observed once, and Chadwick's hard mouth quirked in a wry smile as he admired once again that rare French apti-tude for the epigram. To Hobbs he was certainly no hero, nor hardly a man; he was still the bewildered, resentful little boy who would hide in the cupboard in the butler's pantry after being flogged for disobeying one of his fa-ther's more arbitrary edicts, sniffling in the musty darkness until the then second footman would bribe him out with a piece of marchpane or a ginger comfit.

Chadwick rarely thought of his father nowadays. He had put his memories of the stern and erratic eleventh marquess somewhere far behind him, somewhere where they could not hurt—the same place he had stowed his memories of his first wife. The two were forever inter-mingled in his mind. Since the age of sixteen he could not call to mind his father's harsh admonition, "You *will* marry the Beecham chit, her old man'll pay through the nose to make the little doxy a viscountess!" without also hearing his bride's coarse, scornful laughter when, on their wedding night, before his trembling fingers could even pull her gown up over her parted thighs, his eager and untried member had spurted its seed into the virgin folds of his own nightshirt.

He clenched his fist in exasperation. God! what had ever possessed him to remember that? And to what pur-pose? Rare indeed was the man who, if truth were told—

as it seldom was—had not begun his own novitiate in the temple of Lord Priapus in equally inept fashion. Why should he think of it now? Why should he remember Maria?

He knew why. The answer had been scorched into his brain ever since that instant when he flung open the door to the sickroom and found Maria's son supine and half naked on the bed with his arms around the struggling Ginevra.

Chadwick stood up and moved quietly to the bedside, taking care not to disturb his wife's repose. She lay fully clothed on the bed, her slight figure unnaturally still, drugged by her exhaustion as if by opium. Thinking she would rest more comfortably if she took some nourishment first, before she dozed off completely, he had tried to feed her, but she had resisted him, and he succeeded only in spilling her soup. After that he left her alone; there would be plenty of time for her to eat when she wakened.

When she wakened. . . . Chadwick stared down at her, his blue eyes hotly intent as he surveyed her body outlined by the limp, soiled sarsenet of her dress. She had twisted restlessly before sinking into that profound slumber, and her dress was wrapped about her like a swaddling garment, delineating her burgeoning breasts, the sleek line of her thighs. Gently he reached down to tug her skirts out from under her, loosening the silk where it cut into her soft flesh. He brushed her burnished hair from her eyes. He had known her since she was a little girl, watched her blossom from a merely pretty child to a young woman of remarkable beauty. He had intended her for his son, would have welcomed her with all honor and respect as his daughter-in-law, but circumstance had decreed it otherwise. She was his wife now, a woman of courage and dedication and devotion, a woman in all ways but one. Like the princess of the fairy tale, she was still asleep to the promise of her own body. When he found her on the bed with Bysshe, it had been abundantly clear that she was only marginally aware of the effect she was having on the boy, that she had been stunned and dismayed by his declaration of love. She had run to the marquess as to a refuge, and even immobilized with shock he had in that moment been piqued to think that she considered him "safe," somehow less of a threat than Bysshe. A fine blow to his pride, he thought with wry humor; a misapprehension he must clarify ere long. Chadwick's fingers curled into the mouldering fabric of the bed curtain as he contemplated her inert form, his body already stiffening like his resolve at the thought of the moment when he would claim his young bride. Very, very soon he was going to awaken the sleeping princess.

He heard a gentle knock at the door, and he turned just as Emma glided silently into the room. Her face had donned its imperturbable mask again. At his terse nod she curtsied and said, "My lord, I came to ask whether her ladyship needed anything."

Chadwick regarded her enigmatically. "I thought I instructed you to assist the doctor."

"Yes, my lord, and so I did. Your son is resting comfortably now, and Dr. Perrin is taking supper downstairs while a footman keeps watch over the boy. I thought you might wish to consult with the physician, and I could . . ."

Chadwick noticed the way Emma's green eyes flickered repeatedly toward the still figure on the bed. "Yes, yes, I understand," he said abruptly, softening his tone with a smile of such charm that Emma quickly lowered her lashes. "You want to ensure that your chick has not suffered in the brutal clutches of the ravening wolf—am I not correct?" Emma would not look at him. He continued lightly, "You don't like me very much, do you, Emma?"

He could see the astonishment in her eyes. She lifted her chin and met his gaze squarely. "No, my lord," she said.

He shrugged. "I thought not, and truly I do regret your ill opinion of me. You appear to be a capable and sensible woman, and I think I would value your regard."

"I'm flattered, my lord."

He shook his dark head. "No, don't be. I speak but the truth." He paused before adding, "Think not that you must pretend to change your opinion of me. I do not require that you like me, only that you continue to serve your lady with all the care and affection your have bestowed on her in the past. Will you do that?"

Emma looked again at the sleeping girl. "Of course, my lord, for as long as she needs me. I am surprised that you ask. I have loved Miss Ginevra since she was a child."

His fingers tightened on the folds of the draperies. Slubs of faded wool broke off in his hand. He concentrated on those shredded threads as he murmured, "Yes, haven't we all?" After a pause he gestured to the half-eaten supper tray on the table. "I was able to make her swallow a few spoonfuls of Mrs. Harrison's sustaining broth, but in the process her dress was irrevocably stained. I would have changed her garments myself, but I could not find a nightgown for her. The dressing room appears to be in disuse."

Emma nodded uneasily. "The staff her ladyship summoned from Queenshaven were only able to make a start at restoring the house to some semblance of order, and Miss Ginevra told them not to worry with the dressing room now. However, behind that screen there you will find a linen press, if you . . ." She hesitated for the first time.

Chadwick suggested gently, "Why don't you attend to her needs, Emma? I am not the most adequate of ladies' maids, and I am sure you could make her comfortable far more efficiently than I. While you do that, I shall consult with Dr. Perrin about Bysshe's condition."

"Yes, my lord." She kept her eyes respectfully downcast as he donned his waistcoat and pulled his jacket over his broad shoulders. He picked up the flaccid cravat and let it drop to the chair again. He made as if to stride from the room, but Emma halted him. "My lord, if I may trouble you about one last detail?"

"Yes, what is it?"

She said, "Because of the limited time, only two bedrooms have yet been made habitable abovestairs: this one, and the once across the hall where Lord Bysshe is. That Frenchman—that is, the physician you brought—has already requested that the maids prepare for him the room adjoining his lordship's, so that he will always be within easy call, should his patient require him." Her mouth hardened, and Chadwick gathered that she considered the doctor's request presumptuous. She continued, "However, that room is the master bedroom, the one used by Sir Charles Bryant whenever he was here at Dowerwood, and by rights it should go now to you. I must know, sir, may we give that room to Dr. Perrin as he wishes, or will you be wanting it for yourself? If you do not want it, then which room should we prepare for you?"

Chadwick looked down at her. The time had come to make his position clear, not only to his wife and Bysshe but also to the remainder of the household. Slowly his mouth widened into a lazy and disturbing smile. "By all means, give Perrin the master suite," he said. "I want him to have everything he needs. As for me, trouble yourself no further. I shall be sleeping here."

The maid was just bearing away the tablecloth, leaving the doctor to his port, a dish of cracked walnuts before him, when the marquess strode into the dingy dining room. He pulled back a chair from the table and flung himself into it. "Well, Perrin?" he demanded harshly.

Perrin bowed his head in mock deference. "Well, my lord?" he echoed.

Chadwick pulled up short at the undertone in the man's voice, and he grinned with self-deprecating humor as he realized how he had sounded. "Forgive me, my friend," he said contritely. "I did not mean to sound bumptious. Tell me, do you have everything you require for your comfort? How was your meal?"

"Everything is acceptable," the doctor said.

The marquess nodded as he plucked a walnut from the bowl. "How discreet you are! Acceptable . . . but not really good. I'm sorry, but you must appreciate that the facilities here at Dowerwood are limited at present."

Perrin let his eyes roam over the peeling, mildewed wallpaper, the sun-faded draperies that looked as if they would fall apart at a breath. Even the flattering glow of soft candlelight could not disguise the decay eating away at the house. He observed, "Indeed the house is unique."

Chadwick reached for the decanter and splashed some sweet wine into a glass. " 'Unique' is hardly the word," he said acidly. "The place is a mouldering ruin. It has been neglected for years, and I am not sure that it can be restored now. I suspect it is riddled with everything from dry rot to water rats. Of course I dare not tell Ginevra that, not yet at any rate. She loves this old house, even in its present state. I intend to have an architect look over the premises with an eye to their restoration, and woe betide him if he informs her that the building should be razed."

Perrin pursed his lips sententiously. "I can sympathize with that," he said. "Did you not tell me your wife lived here as a child? One becomes unreasonably attached to the setting of one's earliest memories. It is a common weakness. I know I returned to Beauclair more than once, even though once the mob had finished, there was nothing left of it but the chimneys and the foundation." He paused, and his grey eyes darkened. "I went back one last time, just before I agreed to accompany your dear mother, Madame la Comtesse, on her journey to London. I discovered even the chimneys gone. An *haut bourgeois* silk merchant had built a very large, very vulgar new house over the old foundations. When I saw that, I knew at last that there was nothing left in France for me."

After a moment Chadwick asked, "How fares young Bysshe? Will we soon be able to remove him to Queenshaven?"

Perrin spread his fingers wide in a gesture of indecision. "Only time will tell. For the moment I think it would be advisable to leave him where he is. He is reasonably comfortable, even if the rest of the household is not. He recovers rapidly from the fever. As for his hearing . . ."

"Yes, the ear infection. What about it? Ginevra was very worried. Do you think there is a possibility of permanent damage?"

"There is always a possibility," Perrin said darkly. "Such complications are common after *la scarlatine,* but equally commonly they clear up with no lasting effect. The lad is of a strong constitution, and your wife has tended him with great care. I have lanced the eardrum to relieve pressure and reduce his pain, and if it heals without further suppuration, then probably all will be well."

"Thank God!" Chadwick swirled his port, noting the fruity bouquet and the way the syrupy liquid clung to the sides of the glass. After a moment he murmured, "I should have been here. I never should have left her to cope with all this."

The doctor popped a walnut meat into his mouth and chewed thoughtfully. "I believe others are of the same opinion," he said mildly. "The pretty but forbidding lady's maid, *par exemple*. Mademoiselle . . . Jarvis—that is her surname, *n'est-ce pas?*"

Chadwick's brows came together, as if the question puzzled him. "Her name? I really don't know. Ginevra always calls her Emma, and I never thought to inquire further." He glanced at the other man. "You're interested in her?"

Perrin shrugged meaningfully. "*Peut-être.* You must admit, she is *très jolie, très . . . plantureuse.*"

"Buxom? I suppose she is," Chadwick said, looking surprised. "I hadn't noticed."

"Why should you notice the maid? You have just acquired a beautiful new bride to keep your eyes occupied."

"Why indeed?" A fleeting vision of Amalie passed through the marquess's mind, and he rigorously repressed it. He regarded his friend seriously. "Perrin, if you are serving notice that you wish to pursue the wench, you certainly needn't ask my permission. However, I would advise you that Emma is very important to Ginevra, and I should not care to see her hurt in any way."

The doctor nodded. "*Je vous écoute, mon ami.*" He smiled sardonically. "You need not worry. I do not think the lady likes me very much."

"I don't think Emma has a very high opinion of any man," Chadwick retorted dryly.

"*Quel gaspillage!* What a waste!" Perrin sighed as he reached once again for the decanter. For a few moments he concentrated on his wine and the nuts; then he piled the shells into a little mound on his napkin. Looking up, he glanced around the decrepit room and observed airily, "You are ever an original, Chadwick. Dowerwood is certainly a most remarkable spot in which to spend a honeymoon. *Formidable!*"

The marquess stared at him. "By God, man, I didn't bring Ginevra here. I took her to Queenshaven, of course, which may be grim, but at least it isn't falling down about our ears. She made her own way to this aging relic after I . . . after I . . ." He hesitated, uncharacteristically embarrassed by his own behavior. Considered under the wise and watchful eye of his friend, that headlong flight to London suddenly struck him as incredibly puerile.

The doctor reproved sternly, "Glover, *la petite marquise* is very young."

"Yes, dammit, I know!" Chadwick gulped down his port, then grimaced at the cloying sweetness. He preferred claret after meals. He pushed the empty glass to one side and wound his long fingers together. When he spoke, he bit off his words savagely. "Don't you think I am acutely aware that I am nearly twice Ginevra's age? Don't you think I realize I ought to have paired her off, not with me but with that boy she nursed so tenderly?"

"Then why didn't you?" Perrin asked reasonably. "For that matter, why don't you now? I believe I am not incorrect in my assessment that it is not yet too late for an annulment. With your wealth and position, the matter could be handled discreetly, I am sure. . . ."

Chadwick's blue eyes narrowed fiercely, and he brought his fist down on the scarred tabletop so hard that the glass stopper rattled in the decanter. "Never!" he shouted.

The physician regarded him enigmatically. "You needn't rage at me, *mon gars*, I merely made a suggestion. But I admit I am curious why, if you are so sensitive to the difference in your ages, you did not marry her to your son."

Lines of strain appeared around Chadwick's hard mouth as he said tightly, "Bysshe is far too young, barely sixteen. Hardly an age to take a wife, as I well know."

"The boy might dispute that. While I was treating him, he called her name repeatedly." Perrin rubbed his big nose thoughtfully as he studied the man sitting opposite him. "I think, Glover," he ventured, "that you have a very . . . delicate situation here. 'Tis said my late king delayed some seven years before consummating his marriage to Marie Antoinette, which sorry fact no doubt contributed to that good lady's peccadilloes. Louis's problem was physical—a slight defect that would never have troubled him had he been Jewish—and a surgeon's knife ultimately corrected it. I trust you suffer from no such handicap?" Chadwick's dark brows lifted. Perrin continued, "Then, *mon ami*, it might be prudent of you to—as they say—stake your claim at the earliest opportunity."

"I . . . intend to."

The doctor frowned. "I denote a certain hesitation in your voice. May I inquire its cause?"

The marquess felt himself blushing, something he was sure he had not done since childhood. After a moment he rasped, "Damnation, Perrin, the girl is terrified of me! I . . . I frightened her on our wedding night."

The silence in the room was emphasized by the erratic whirring of the pendulum clock someone had tried to restart. Rust had corroded the teeth of one of the gears, and the hands moved fitfully or not at all. Perversely the chimes struck seven at the quarter and half hour, and were mute on the hour. At last the doctor said, "You frightened the little one? I am surprised. You are not usually so clumsy."

Chadwick snapped, "I am not usually dealing with a virgin!" He laughed humorlessly. "In fact, after reviewing the procession of women in my misspent life, it occurs to me that I have never yet deflowered a maiden."

Perrin smiled wryly. "It is a highly overrated experience, I assure you."

The marquess did not seem to hear him. He snorted, "Oh, there were one or two who would have had me think I was the first, but I am an old campaigner and not easily gulled."

"I see," Perrin said. He rested his chin on his thumbs.

"Then am I to understand that you are asking my advice as a physician?"

Chadwick's blue eyes met his grey ones. "I suppose I am."

"*Bien entendu.*" The Frenchman leaned back in his chair, absently rubbing the knotted muscles of his injured leg. "Well, then," he began in the dry voice of a lecturer giving a tutorial, "you must remember that this is the one time when your first concern is not to give your partner pleasure, but to lessen her pain. . . ." He continued in precise, clinical terms for some minutes, at last concluding, "Above all, be patient and reassuring, and help her to look forward to a more satisfying future."

One of Chadwick's brows had arched sharply upward. "A tall order, my friend," he drawled.

The doctor eyed him squarely. "Oh, I expect you will rise to the occasion."

Chadwick gave a yelp of laughter. "You may be right," he declared as he pushed his chair back from the table. He stood up and clapped the other man on the shoulder. "Forgive me for deserting you, but I think I will bid you a good night now."

"So soon?" the doctor mocked dryly. "Ah well, it has indeed been a long day. *Bonne nuit,* Glover. *Dormez bien.*" Perrin watched the marquess leave. It occurred to him that he should have inquired about the location of Emma's quarters. After a moment he shrugged, and with a windy sigh he reached for the port once more.

Chadwick gazed down at his sleeping wife. She lay snuggled under the downy coverlet like a cygnet beneath the sheltering wing of its mother. Her left hand rested pale and defenseless on the pillow next to her smooth cheek, the jeweled rings only just visible under the flounced cuff of her white linen nightdress. Emma had brushed her long hair and braided it loosely into a thick plait that streamed over the top of the quilt, gleaming as brightly as her rings in the wavering light of the lone candle. Her repose seemed more normal now, more restful and regenerative than that near-cataleptic stupor he had noticed before, and she stirred slightly, as if she were dreaming. He wondered if he dared rouse her.

He perched on the edge of the bed and with mothlike delicacy trailed the tip of one finger across her cheekbone, ruffling her gold lashes, outlining her soft mouth. Her nose twitched. He traced the line of her jaw back up to her ear; then his hand stroked lightly over her hair. Under his sensitive fingers it felt like satin, and he began to un-braid the fine strands. Soon her tresses spread over the pillow, over her shoulders, like a mantle of silk, with a sheen whose richness made him catch his breath. He swivelled away from her, and with uncharacteristically jerky movements he began to remove his boots.

When he slid his lean, naked body between the cool, lavender-scented sheets, he was already tumescent, and he regarded his swollen organ impatiently. Cool down, he ordered himself. You're not sixteen anymore, and if you go off half-cocked this time, it'll put paid to the night's work!

He looked at Ginevra again, at the heartbreaking purity of her young face, and he sobered at once. He did not want to think of her in such terms, to defile her innocence even in his mind by describing their union with the same offhand and salacious phrases he had bandied with the doctor, language he might have used for coupling with a tavern maid. Ginevra was his wife, his marchioness. He ached to make her his in every possible way, yet he knew he wanted to do more than merely possess her. He wanted to cherish her, to . . . to reverence her, as it said in the marriage service. God help him, he wanted to love her.

The Marquess of Chadwick stared upward into the shadows of the threadbare tester, and he thought with bitter irony that hell must reverberate with the laughter of whatever demon had arranged this little prank of fate: that he who had sworn as a youth never to touch another woman with anything but his body, had at the ripe age of thirty-five given his heart to a green girl who cared nothing for his wealth or title, who feared his temper and despised him for a libertine. Who might just be in love with the boy he called son.

He turned to her and gently but insistently drew her sleeping figure into his arms. She stirred, and he held his breath as he waited to see if she would waken completely. She stilled again, nuzzling her face into the coarse black hair on his chest. He could feel the warmth of her slender body radiating seductively through the flimsy ruffled fabric of her long gown, and his hands trembled as they moved slowly across her back. He bent his head and brushed his lips across her ear, her cheek, her brow, teasing her fair flesh until almost instinctively in her sleep she turned her petal-soft mouth to his. The instant their lips met he was possessed of a fierce desire to abandon his gentleness, to force open her mouth and delve its sweetness in a relentless search for the center of her being, for her unique essence that must surely at last satisfy his sickening hunger. Her gold lashes fluttered uneasily against her cheek, and he felt her mouth retreat from the pressure of his. Sweat broke out on his forehead as, with ruthless self-control, he restrained himself.

Ginevra dreamed. The dream seemed familiar, yet she knew it could never before have been so vivid, so achingly real. She stood on a promontory overlooking the ocean. She did not know what had brought her to this place; it made her wary. Far below her the rocks rose sharp and cruel, with cold grey foam licking at their bases, but here at the top of the cliff for the moment she was warm and safe. The sun beat down from a bright blue sky, and dew-rich grass sprang thick and inviting under her fingertips when she bent to touch it. A temperate breeze blew from the west, ruffling her hair, billowing her long skirts behind her. She grew languid yet curiously alive as it stroked her face, her body. She could feel her small breasts lifting, firming, under its gentle caress. When, as always in her dream, the breeze from the water stopped abruptly, she was left bereft, and she wanted to sob with disappointment.

He pushed back the coverlet. In the candlelight her white nightgown gleamed in virginal contrast to the darkly tanned contours of his lean body. His breath quickened as one by one he fumbled with the long row of pearl buttons. His hand paused at her waist, and the soft fabric fell away, revealing her high, well-shaped breasts, the rosebud nipples erect even in her sleep. He began to shake. His lips moved greedily over her skin, savoring her salty nectar. For one heart-stopping moment he felt her arch her back, as if to give his questing tongue better purchase. He tugged at the remainder of her buttons. He was drugged with her delicate perfume, and he closed his eyes to stop his dizzy spinning. He did not open them again until his seeking fingers stroked over her rounded belly to encounter the soft mound with its triangle of silky golden hair. Then all control snapped.

The ocean breeze grew stronger, breaching with hot insistence the unsubstantial protection of Ginevra's garments. She ripped off her clothes and the wind tore them from her hands and sent them flapping away like some large ungainly bird. Ginevra presented her naked body wantonly to the caress of that fiery, urgent gale. She knew now why she stood at the rim of the precipice: she was Psyche, and the wind must surely be Zephyrus, come to bear her away to her lover. If only she would submit to its invisible embrace she could at last find the nameless bliss she had sought all her life. But even as realization came to her the gusts increased, began to scorch, and frightened by their sudden torrid ferocity, she cried out in terror. The wind swirled up around her, murmuring her name while it propelled her over the edge. She was falling, falling, her tawny tresses streaming behind her like the tail of a comet. In the back of her mind she thought with momentary clarity: *But it's only a dream.* She struggled to escape the coils of that dream, the long hair that wrapped tightly about her slender body like tentacles, like a man's hard arms. As she plummeted into the abyss, the velocity of the passing air became a weight crushing her breath from her lungs, and something wet and darting forced her startled wail back into her mouth. She could only moan helplessly under the glaring blue skies—blue eyes—as the rocks rose up to impale her.

"Ginnie . . . oh, God, Ginnie!" He shuddered with the force of his release, groaning against her bruised lips as he plunged relentlessly into her slight body and spewed his seed deep inside her. He was beyond thought, almost beyond sensation; the only reality was Ginevra's novice flesh enclosing his—possessing the possessor. He buried his flushed face in her bright hair to muffle the rasping sobs that ripped through him with each spasm of his not-quite-spent member, and only gradually did he become aware of her unnatural rigidity. He lifted his dark head to look at her. Her eyes filled his universe, as he knew his own must fill hers, but he was stunned by the shocked vacancy of her stare. Beneath her trembling lashes he saw glassy emptiness, as if the vibrant girl he loved had suddenly retreated somewhere very far away, leaving behind only a beautiful husk.

Still holding her tightly, he eased his weight off her. He tried to catch his breath so that he could speak to her, reassure her. He knew he had hurt her, and—sweet Jesu!—he had never intended that. Despite Jules Perrin's cautionary advice, he had wanted to do more than merely avoid pain, he had hoped to pleasure her. He had thought that if he used her fatigue as an opiate to soothe her fears, once the initial discomfort had been overcome he could draw on his considerable experience to gentle her toward fulfillment, so that she would literally awake to glorious womanhood. Instead his own throbbing desire had driven him mad, throwing off all restraint as he shattered her innocence. Forgotten was the suggested pillow to go under her hips, the careful lubrication—forgotten was everything but the urgent need at last to slake his own wild hunger. Now he was abjectly aware that in doing so he had dragged her from her chaste dreams to what must have seemed a nightmare of ruthless violation, even rape.

"Ginevra," he murmured, his deep voice hoarse and unsteady. She turned her gaze to him, but he was not sure that those wide unblinking eyes saw him. "Ginevra," he repeated, "listen to me. I promise it will not always be this way. I know this is strange to you now, but there will come a time—very soon, I hope—when you will find great pleasure in my arms." Still she did not respond. His hands began to move intently over her body, stroking, caressing, as he tried desperately to give her some inkling of what he meant.

She lay impassive and immobile in his searching embrace until he sought to part her clenched thighs. She flinched. "Please," she said hollowly. Her voice seemed to come from a great distance. "Please, I need to . . . I must . . . I beg you, excuse me for a few minutes." Reluctantly he released her, and she sat up in the bed. For the first time she became aware of her nakedness, and even in the dim candlelight he could see bright flags of color form in her wan cheeks. She slid from beneath the coverlet and retrieved her nightgown from the floor. Quickly and silently she pulled it on, her unsteady fingers groping with the buttons. When she was dressed, she picked up the candlestick and stumbled to the screen on the opposite side of the room.

As he watched her he decided that she must have no idea her every motion was silhouetted on the yellowed chinoiserie silk screen. The guttering candlelight caused her image to waver somewhat, but he could see her outline clearly, her stilted movements. She squatted over the chamber pot, then returned the vessel to its discreet hiding place in the bottom of the washstand. She smoothed her long hair with her fingers and shook it so that it streamed unconfined down her back. She poured water into the basin and bathed her face and hands. After a long pause she took the washcloth, and bunching the skirt of her gown with her other hand, bent over to clean her private parts.

Because the shadows cast by the candle oscillated with each flicker of the small flame, Chadwick watched for some time before he realized that Ginevra's hand had stilled, that she seemed frozen in that awkward hunched position. "Ginevra?" he called uncertainly. She did not answer. He swung his long legs over the edge of the bed and stalked across the room to her. He yanked back the screen. She did not look up. She was staring transfixed at the cloth she held, its rough cotton stained with a sticky mixture of semen and blood. With a quiver of some fierce emotion—guilt? rage? he wasn't sure what—he pulled the cloth from her unresisting fingers and flung it savagely to the floor. Then he jerked her into his arms. Only when he felt the buttons of her nightgown press into his bare skin did he remember his own nakedness, and he glanced down to find her eyelids tightly and resolutely shut against the sight of him. He shook his head with wry impatience, and his hold on her changed, softened. He cradled her against him, running his hands over her back, rocking her tenderly and crooning in his gravelly baritone. At last she seemed to relax.

He murmured, "It will be better, little Ginnie, you will see. But whatever happens now, you belong to me. No matter where you go or what you do, nothing can ever change that. You understand me, don't you?"

When he felt her body tense again, he swore silently at his clumsy tactlessness. He caught her chin in his fingertips and tilted her head so that her shimmering gold eyes stared upward into his, round with mute reproach. Her expression stabbed at his heart. His grip tightened brutally. "Don't look at me like that!" he grated. "Say something. Do something. *Cry!* But for God's sake, don't look at me like that."

She blinked, and moisture beaded on her lashes. "I won't, m-my lord," she stammered, biting her lip. Then with a sob she buried her face in the comforting, scratchy warmth of the hair on his chest, and at last the tears came.

7

London alarmed Ginevra. After her near-cloistered life in the country, she was frightened by the vast size of the city, the hordes of people, the noise. The filth appalled her, as well as the sea-coal smoke that hung thick in the streets, and the stench that rose from the polluted waters of the Thames. When she remembered Wordsworth's paean to the glories of the city—"All bright and glittering in the smokeless air"—she decided that the poet must have been in his altitudes the morning he stumbled across Westminster Bridge.

But here in Mayfair, in Chadwick's elegant town house of warm red Georgian brick, she would have been indeed hard to satisfy if she did not admit that life was very pleasant. From the moment the marquess had introduced his bride to the household, she had been cosseted and pampered, treated with an indulgent deference so utterly divorced from her former life that she hardly knew how to react. She had always been respected by her servants, but their regard had derived in part from their knowledge that she worked as hard as any of them. Now she discovered she could lie abed until noon, turn her hand at nothing more strenuous than a bit of fancy needlework or the choosing of a wine for their evening meal, and she found all this leisure gratifying, if a little boring.

Ginevra picked up the silver hairbrush from her dressing table and began to brush her hair with long, practiced strokes. On the wall within easy reach hung a bell rope: one tug was all it would take to summon Emma or any of the maids to tend her hair for her, as if she were incapable of performing even that not-very-oner-

ous task for herself. She was wryly aware that she lacked
the courage to question the staff's behavior toward her,
for they patterned their attitude after that of the marquess, and since that first traumatic night at Dowerwood
he had treated her with extreme consideration, a rare
gentleness and concern that made her feel almost as if she
were convalescent following a long illness. When, the day
after her husband's return, Ginevra had tried to resume
the tasks she had given herself, he told her that she
needed to rest; with dispatch he summoned a sizable
party from Queenshaven, who set about putting the old
house to rights, under the supervision of Chadwick himself. He turned Bysshe's care over to the doctor and for-
bade Ginevra entry into the sickroom, saying that the
boy's slow recovery would only distress her. Dr. Perrin
did request that Emma assist him, and Ginevra was able
to monitor Bysshe's progress through her friend. Several
days later the marquess allowed Ginevra a brief courtesy
call on the patient, but for some reason the visit had
proved stiff and unrewarding; Bysshe seemed unwilling
even to look at her.

As her honeymoon passed quietly, with a serenity almost unreal after the stress of the first days, Ginevra
slowly realized that her husband had deliberately relieved
her of all responsibility so that she need worry about
nothing but coming to terms with her marriage. He was
trying to alleviate the fear he saw in her wide gold eyes
each time he approached her. After the way he had ridden roughshod over her emotions in the past, his consideration frankly bewildered her, but she knew she was
learning to accept if not enjoy her situation. At times only
the benign and knowing glances of the servants reminded
her that this holiday was different from those she had
spent at Dowerwood as a child. She rested, ate Mrs. Harrison's savory gingerbread, and strolled about the grounds
with little Jamie, who had been crowded out of the
kitchen now that his grandmother had maids to order
about once more. Sometimes, at Emma's suggestion,
Ginevra spent the afternoon teaching the little boy his letters; other days they watched as the workmen began to

restore the house to some semblance of order. She laughed along with the child when someone cut loose the thick runners of ivy that clogged the rain gutters, and the whole viny mass fell to earth in an avalanche of green leaves. When she saw her husband throw off his coat and scale a ladder, hard muscles rippling across his back as he helped a carpenter reattach a heavy piece of iron fretwork that had come loose from the eave, she grew silent, blushing as she recalled the strangely pleasant feel of those muscles under her sensitive fingertips when she clung to him in the night.

The evenings at Dowerwood had been spent in the parlor, where, Ginevra remembered vividly, Tom had proposed marriage to her. Looking at the marquess as he conversed quietly with the doctor, she wondered sometimes if he ever thought of that fateful day so long before. If he did, he gave no sign. Whenever his blue eyes surveyed the room, clean now but in dire need of redecoration, they seemed to note nothing but the disintegration of the furnishings. The cherrywood chairs were reasonably sound, but the upholstery was moth-eaten. Moisture had collected behind the glass of the framed engravings, leaving them streaked and mottled. Assuming he would want to discard the lot, Ginevra was surprised when, after she hesitantly mentioned the rusty duelling swords crossed over the mantelpiece, Chadwick said with a smile, "I thought I might have the pair polished and honed, and then we could send them to your father as a gift, if you like. I believe he told me once that the rapiers were a memento of his salad days." As Ginevra looked up at him from across the card table—they had been playing whist, with Emma as a fourth—she was suddenly captivated by her husband's grin. Something deep inside her stirred in a most peculiar fashion, and she was hardly aware of the doctor's wise chuckle when she rose and made her excuses shortly thereafter.

Ginevra glanced at her reflection in the swivel mirror on her dressing table: her image was framed like a Tudor headdress by the canopy of the pleated and draped fourposter behind her, and her cheeks colored as she thought of the nights she had spent there in her husband's arms. She knew his body as well as her own now, his lean, hard muscles, the deep scar on his hip from his old war wound. She had not slept alone since he returned to Dowerwood for her, and even now that they had come at last to London, each morning she had wakened to find herself snuggled against him in the granite cradle of his embrace. Sometimes he simply held her; more often he touched her with a disarming tenderness that made it increasingly difficult for her to recall the driving passion he had shown her that first night. His caresses were always butterfly soft, controlled even when he was moaning his own pleasure into her bright hair; he treated her as though she were a piece of rare porcelain, and it was hard for her to believe that this was the same man whose body had breached hers so ruthlessly while in the throes of some urgent need she still could not begin to comprehend.

She found herself longing for his touch. Her childhood had been singularly devoid of affection, and she responded hungrily to the cuddling, the gentle stroking—but his passion confused her.

She wished she understood him, she wished she knew what it was he was seeking from her. Despite his kindness, their union seemed at best tenuous, held together only by the desire he felt for her, and she feared that soon even that frail bond would break. Already she was aware of a gulf between them. She had thought at first that he had taken her merely to brand her as his wife, his possession, but now whenever she lay passive under his touch she was aware that he watched her intently for something else, some reaction other than acquiescence—and when he did not find that unknown response, he would fling himself away from her while he still shuddered with his own satisfaction, his muffled groan tinged with disappointment. Ginevra would watch him helplessly. She longed to beg him to explain what he wanted, but she remained silent, unable to frame the words.

She was failing him, as she had always known she must. He had had his pick of seductive, experienced women since before she was born, and there was no way she could hope to match their skill. Soon the novelty of their relationship would fade, and the marquess would abandon her entirely while he returned to those other women, perhaps even to that Madame de Villeneuve. She was sick with dread that soon his tenderness would change to impatience, then disdain, then indifference, and he would resume his old ways, leaving Ginevra, lonelier than ever, to cope with only the shell of a society marriage, a hollow life that would have to be carried out among strangers, in a city she disliked intensely.

One of her long curls snarled in the stiff bristles of the brush, and Ginevra yanked at it until the pain brought tears to her eyes. Since their arrival in London the signs of their impending breakup had become more distinct. That very morning she had awakened in his arms as usual, and she had nestled closer without opening her eyes, luxuriating in the feel of his hair-roughened skin rubbing intimately against hers. When she slowly lifted her lashes, she had found him staring closely at her with a dark intensity that made her nervous. She murmured, "Good morning, my lord," and his blue gaze had narrowed into a scowl as he snapped, "For God's sake, Ginevra, don't call me 'my lord'! My name is Richard, and I want you to use it. When you call me by my title, you sound like a servant. I almost expect you to leave my bed and creep furtively back to your quarters in the attic." Ginevra, still half-asleep and stunned by the suddenness of his attack, could only gape at him, her face pale with shock. He took a deep, rasping breath and continued irritably, "And contrary to what you are probably thinking, I do not make a habit of seducing the housemaids. It has always seemed to me less than a noble act to take advantage of one's dependents in that fashion. Every woman I have ever been with has had the right to say no."

Sickened by the images of all those other pliant female bodies that had curled invitingly around his, Ginevra retorted before she could stop herself, "Every woman but me!"

His glare became glacial, and his hard mouth turned up

in a smile that had no hint of humor in it. Suddenly apprehensive, Ginevra tried to move away from him, but his arms were a vise trapping her, and his long fingers caught in her burnished hair and pulled it so taut that her eyelids stretched. "As you say, madam wife," he mocked mildly, too mildly, "every woman but you." Slowly his face had lowered to hers, and with grinding, irresistible force his lips ravaged hers until she could taste her own blood, salty and metallic. She whimpered with pain. When he lifted his dark head to stare at her, she could see red flecks on his mouth. With a muttered curse he flung her away from him. He slid from beneath the blankets and stalked naked across the room to the communicating door of his own chamber, slamming it behind him so hard that the canopy on Ginevra's bed swayed.

She set down her hairbrush and regarded her reflection in the mirror. Her lower lip was still slightly swollen, giving her face a sensual cast she had never seen there before. She looked older. She looked . . . kissed. She reached for one of the tiny cut-glass pots that adorned the dressing table, and she delicately rubbed a salve of refined and perfumed oil into her aching lip. After she closed the lid she returned the vial neatly to its place on the table, her fingers tracing the graceful G engraved on the silver cap. The marquess had given her the luxurious dresser set the night before they left Surrey for London, handing the fitted case to Ginevra with the dry, offhand comment, "By the way, don't forget to tell Emma to pack this." When Ginevra squealed her delight, he had shrugged as if the gift were only a casual one, of little import, yet she knew he must have ordered it for her weeks before, perhaps even prior to the wedding. Ginevra shook her head in bewilderment. How did one reconcile such a thoughtful and tender gesture with the anger that had driven him to hurt her deliberately that morning?

With a sigh she tugged on the bell rope to summon Emma to help her dress. Today the marquess was going to present her to his mother at last, and she wanted to look especially well. She had no time to waste questioning why her husband was moody and unpredictable. Such fluctuations of temper seemed part of the male condition. Certainly Sir Charles had been equally capricious, and young Bysshe showed the signs as well. Ginevra's eyes narrowed. There was nothing she could do about her husband or father except learn to cope—but it was high time she confronted the boy.

Bysshe's grumbled "Come in" was barely audible. Ginevra opened the door to his sitting room and found him by the window, hands shoved deep in his pockets as he stared sullenly down at the street. He was fully dressed, except for his coat, and his clothes bore the unmistakable stamp of his father's tailor. Ginevra was struck again by how tall he had grown. His lanky body retained its adolescent thinness, but he was very nearly a man; only his face, still youthfully round, reminded her of her childhood playmate. She noticed that he had shaved his few whiskers, and someone, perhaps the invaluable Hobbs, had carefully trimmed his straight sandy hair. The one remaining sign of his recent illness was the sickly pallor lingering around the ear that had been bandaged.

Ginevra said lightly, "Good morning, Bysshe—or perhaps I should say good afternoon. I'm not yet accustomed to city hours, I fear. I thought I'd see how you are faring. I'm delighted you're looking so well."

The boy turned away from the window, and his brown eyes surveyed her comprehensively. When his glance reached her mouth, his expression hardened. He nodded coldly. Ginevra bristled and said, "I think it's time you and I had a talk."

With a sweeping gesture he motioned her to a seat. "As you wish, my lady."

She sank into the chair, more hurt by his rudeness than she cared to admit. "That's exactly the sort of thing we need to discuss," she noted, making a pretense of adjusting her skirt. "I want you to explain why you are being so . . . so stiff with me. At first I thought it was your illness, but you've recovered now, and still you treat me like a leper. You wouldn't even ride in the carriage with your father and me when we journeyed from the country."

Bysshe shrugged. "The doctor wanted me to stay with him, in case I became overtired."

Ginevra looked steadily at him. "I don't think that's it at all. The pair of you could have ridden very comfortably with us, yet you chose not to. You have been deliberately avoiding me, and I don't understand why. What have I done?"

He scowled down at her, his young face troubled. "You truly don't understand, do you? You have no idea at all what it does to me to think of you as my . . . my stepmother."

Ginevra shook her head impatiently. "Don't be silly, Bysshe. No one is asking you to think of me as your stepmother. I'm Ginnie, your old friend, just as I've always been."

He glared at her, and his color heightened. Suddenly he exploded, "Yes, but now you're also *his wife!*"

Ginevra shrank back against the soft cushions, shocked by the force of his outburst. She thought she could hear the glass shade vibrate on the gas fixture. "For God's sake, lower your voice before someone hears you."

She could see the effort it took for him to restrain himself. His flush ebbed, and his hollow chest rose jerkily with each harsh breath. He sank to his knees before her chair, catching her arm in a bruising grip as he demanded, "How could you, Ginnie? How could you give yourself to him? How could you let him . . . ?"

Ginevra patted his linen sleeve in the same sort of gesture she might have used to comfort a toddler. "It doesn't matter now," she said gently, "it's done. My father . . . your father . . . Dowerwood: you know they've always wanted the properties joined, and after Tom died, it was the only way."

"The hell it was!" Bysshe gritted. "You could have married *me!*" His hands slid up to her shoulders, and he shook her as he begged for understanding. "Why didn't you tell them you wanted to marry me, Ginnie? I'd be a good husband. Don't you know I love you? I told you."

"You were out of your head when you said that."

"I'm perfectly sane now, and I want you to listen to

me. I've always loved you. I used to be jealous of Tom, because you were destined for him. You were as beautiful as an angel, and even when we were little I used to dream about you. I used to imagine that I was the viscount, and you were going to be mine." His fingers tightened on her thin shoulders, and his face moved closer to hers. "At Dowerwood when the pain finally stopped and my mind was working clearly again, I thought at first that I had imagined everything, that this crazy nightmare of you marrying him was just something that had come to me while I was delirious. When I found out it was true, I got sick all over again. Late at night I'd lie there in bed, and when he would look in on me, I'd pretend to be asleep. Then in the dark I'd watch the light from his candle shining in a big crooked rectangle on my wall after he left the room. I could see it clearly as he crossed the corridor to your room, and when it finally narrowed and disappeared, I would know that he had shut the door, that he was alone in there with you." Ginevra stared at him, mesmerized by the feverish glow in his brown eyes. He was so close that she could feel his warm, moist breath stroking her face as he whispered, "Sometimes it seemed to me that I could hear the bed creak . . ."

He regarded her hungrily. "Oh Ginnie," he murmured. His arms slid roughly around her and he lowered his mouth to hers in an awkward kiss. Stunned, Ginevra remained immobile as his trembling lips moved wetly over hers. He took her passivity for encouragement, and one hand groped for her breast.

Tentative, shaking fingers, so different from her husband's gentle but firm caress, pulled at the low neckline of her dress, and Ginevra shuddered with revulsion. She pushed her palms against Busshe's chest and shoved as hard as she could. Caught off-balance, he tumbled backward, sprawling in an undignified heap at her feet. She leaped up from the chair, her face livid with anger as she readjusted her bodice. "How dare you!" she raged, stamping her small foot, glaring at him indignantly as he picked himself up from the floor. "How dare you treat me that way! Whether you like it or not, Bysshe Glover, I am a married woman, and you dishonor me when you speak as if I were some . . . some Cyprian!"

Bysshe recoiled, his head jerking back as if she'd slapped him. "Ginnie!" he gasped. "How can you even think I'd ever insult you? I love you. I thought you . . . I wanted you to . . . I had to tell you . . . Dear God, Ginnie, it's *his* touch that dishonors you. The man's twice your age and he has a French mistress!"

Ginevra spun away from him and flung herself out of the room, sickness welling up in her throat. She fled along the carpeted hallway, brushing past a startled footman, not halting until she was out of sight of Bysshe's door. She stumbled to a standstill in front of a flower-laden console table at the head of the staircase, and she leaned heavily against it, shaking, uncertain her legs would support her. She peered closely at her unnatural pallor, her face so bleached that by contrast her gold lashes seemed almost dark against her white cheeks. She could feel her heart pounding erratically, and she crossed her arms over her chest as if to protect herself from the outrageous knowledge that she had heretofore avoided: Bysshe loved her. This was not some fantasy brought on by his fever; her husband's son was in love with her. The boy whom she still regarded as a childhood friend had grown to a man who wanted from her something much more profound than mere affection. Oh, Lord, the idea was disgusting . . . deplorable . . . *incestuous*—and she did not know how to cope with it.

It wasn't fair, she thought with resentful irony, remembering how she had opposed this marriage because of her previous engagement to Tom. She had just been coming to terms with the situation, no matter how bleak those terms seemed, and now this! Someone ought to have known what would happen. Her father and Lord Chadwick were both men of the world: even in their haste to arrange the match they ought to have had enough insight to foresee that Bysshe could not be so casually dismissed as they pretended. But they had ignored him, and now it was left to Ginevra to find a way out of this labyrinth of jealousy and desire. God help everyone if the marquess ever suspected . . .

"Ginevra?"

She spun around, her eyes stretched and startled, just in time to see Chadwick mount the stairs by twos. When he reached the top, he caught her in his arms and demanded, "My dear, what's wrong? Are you unwell?"

Not daring to look up, she shook her head fiercely. She wondered if Bysshe's kiss had somehow branded her, as that of her husband had done earlier, and she could feel guilty color painting her cheeks. She stared resolutely at the mirror polish of his boots and murmured huskily, "No, my . . . no, Richard, I'm quite fit, I assure you."

One long finger curled under her chin and tilted her head upright while his blue eyes studied her hectic features. She lowered her silky lashes in an effort to hide her expression from his discerning gaze. He frowned. "You seem feverish."

She shook her head. "I'm not ill. I'm just a . . . a little apprehensive about the prospect of meeting your mother, that's all."

The hard line of his mouth softened. "Of course you are. Meeting one's in-laws for the first time is enough to make anyone nervous. But believe me, you have nothing to fear. My mother can be formidable, but I know she will love you." A teasing light danced in his eyes. "She has always had an affinity for small, helpless creatures."

"Richard!" Ginevra squawked indignantly. "You make me sound like a puppy."

He smiled indulgently and pulled her closer, his hands moving over her soft hair. "No, not a puppy—a kitten. A tawny Persian kitten with tiger eyes, one that purrs sometimes when I stroke it, and other times hisses and lashes out at me with its sharp little claws." He paused. "I'm sorry I was rough with you this morning," he said. "God knows I don't mean to fly up in the boughs that way, but you have no conception of how it makes me feel when you . . . when you . . ." His deep voice faded as his arms tightened about her.

"It doesn't matter," she said quietly. She relaxed

against him, closing her eyes as she nuzzled her face into the intricate folds of his cravat. The fresh smell of crisply starched linen filled her nostrils, not quite masking the deeper, more elusive scent of tobacco, imperial water, and warm brown skin that Ginevra identified with her husband. She sighed, her earlier alarm abating. In the safety of his arms she had the tantalizing feeling that she was on the verge of some momentous discovery, some grand revelation that could change her life. She clung to him, waiting.

Just as Chadwick's mouth lowered to Ginevra's, he suddenly noticed Bysshe standing frozen in the corridor, staring at them. His fingers clamped down convulsively, digging into Ginevra's delicate skin. He nodded curtly and said, "Good morning, my boy. You're looking well."

Bysshe's reply was equally laconic, his gaze never wavering. "Thank you, sir. I understand we are to call on *Grandmère* today."

Chadwick nodded absently and returned his attention to his enrapt wife. Gently he eased her away from him. He surveyed her at arm's length, his eyes stroking warmly over her slender figure. She blinked, her small face bemused and faintly disappointed. He patted her cheek and urged, "Go, my dear, fetch your hat and we'll be on our way. My mother will be anxious to meet you."

"Yes, Richard," she murmured, and she turned in the direction of her room. When she brushed past Bysshe, she glanced furtively at him, and something about his expression made her uneasy.

In the open phaeton Ginevra sat sandwiched between her husband and his son. A freshening breeze had cleared the air, and the sun beat down on her jaunty straw bonnet, but she was most acutely aware of hard-muscled thighs pressing against her from either side. On her way out the door the butler had handed her the post, and to divert her attention from the disturbing nearness of the two men, she busied herself thumbing through the envelopes. After a moment she looked up in confusion. "These seem to be mostly invitations, but none of the names are familiar to me."

Chadwick took the cards and scanned them quickly. "No, you would not know these people, but I assure you they are anxious to meet you." He grinned. "On our wedding day I warned you how it would be." He riffled through the invitations a second time. "You should be flattered at the number of hostesses who have contrived to put together some form of entertainment for your benefit. Usually this late in the year everyone has retired to country homes or else Brighton or one of the other watering places."

"Then I collect we are reversing the normal process?"

He shrugged. "To some extent. As it happens, I do have duties that require my presence in town now. I tried to get out of it, but the foreign minister insisted."

"You ought to be flattered that you are so indispensable," Ginevra said.

Chadwick snorted, "I think I would be more flattered if I were *not* needed. Ah, well, perhaps I should regard it as penance." He selected one of the notes and handed it to her. "Here, why don't you reply in the affirmative to this one? It will be all the way out in Greenwich, but Lady Thorndike's card party should be innocuous enough. It will give you an opportunity to meet people without all the fal-lal of a formal debut."

"Thank you. I should prefer that."

"I thought you might. Just don't let Jane Thorndike talk you into joining one of her everlasting committees. She can be very convincing. If you're not careful she'll have you teaching factory children to read or collecting clothing for the poor."

Over Ginevra's head Bysshe glanced at the marquess. He muttered waspishly, "Maybe she could get *you* to join the Committee for the Suppression of Vice."

Ginevra gasped. At the sight of Chadwick's clenched jaw, she interjected hastily, "I'll look forward to meeting Lady Thorndike. I think her charitable work sounds most commendable."

"Oh, it is," her husband agreed slowly, relaxing. "It's just that I don't want you taking on any duties right now. You're here to rest and enjoy yourself."

Ginevra frowned. "Richard," she ventured uncertainly, "truly I think I might enjoy myself more if I had something to do. All this . . . this relaxation is becoming rather monotonous. It seems to me—"

"It seems to me that this is something we should discuss later," Chadwick said, noting the familiar gate just ahead. "We have nearly arrived at my mother's house." As he helped Ginevra stuff the letters into her reticule he said to Bysshe, who was scowling sulkily, "The invitation includes you, and I shall expect you to accompany us to the party. The Thorndikes have children about your age, and it's high time you mixed with young people again. You've stayed secluded too long." Before Bysshe could reply, the carriage pulled to a halt.

Ginevra was uncertain just what she had expected of her husband's mother: someone tall and stately, perhaps, with a long nose and an imperious expression—but certainly not this petite and fragile woman lounging on a divan floridly carved in the Egyptian style. Her apparent indolence was belied only by the sharp intelligence of her bright blue eyes. Bysshe stooped so that she could brush her lips across both his cheeks after the French manner, and the sweet smile he exchanged with his grandmother struck Ginevra as the first genuine look of happiness she had ever seen on his young face. Chadwick bent over his mother's hand with courtly grace; then he caught Ginevra by the arm and nudged her forward. "Mother," he said, his deep voice throbbing with a note his wife had never heard before, "this is Ginevra. Ginevra, I'd like you to meet my mother, Lady Helena Glover, Dowager Marchioness of Chadwick and Comtesse d'Alembert."

Lady Helena's dark brows rose sharply. "Honestly, Richard," she drawled, tipping her head so that her grizzled curls bounced, "if you insist on announcing me in the grand manner, you really should tap your staff on the floor and signal a flourish of trumpets. This is not a royal presentation, you know. You're liable to terrify the child." She held out a beckoning hand. "Come, my dear, let me take a look at you. Despite what that wretched boy of mine has told you, I don't bite."

Ginevra slipped her hand into the frail grasp and gazed
down at the woman, noting the piercing eyes so like
Chadwick's and the silvered hair that must have once
been as black as his was now. Her husband's mother.
They were dissimilar in stature, but yes, she would have
known, even had no one told her. Slowly she sank to her
knees beside the divan. At close range she could see the
translucent quality of Lady Helena's skin, blue veins
clearly visible, and her mind harkened with remembered
pain to the last summer of her own mother's life, when
she had languished on the sofa at Dowerwood. As
Ginevra leaned over to kiss Lady Helena's cheek, her
gold eyes flicked up to meet her husband's intent stare,
and in his grave expression she found the answer to her
unspoken question.

Tea was served, and the visit progressed without un-
toward incident. Bysshe seemed on his best behavior in
his grandmother's presence, and Chadwick watched indulgently as Lady Helena regaled Ginevra with her memories
of the building of Dowerwood, at about the same time as
Lady Helena's arrival at the Glover estate as a bride.
"The Gothic style was just coming into fashion," she said,
"and I always admired that house greatly. By contrast
Queenshaven seemed a mouldering behemoth. I'm delighted that the properties have been joined now. I hope
you spend many happy years there." She spoke of sum-
mertime in Surrey, Christmas in London, the giddy whirl-
wind that had marked her debut and presentation. She
spoke so eloquently that it was some time before Ginevra
realized that not once did Lady Helena mention her husband, Chadwick's father.

She was beginning her account of a trip she had made
once to Scotland with her late sister, a tedious and
uncomfortable journey made even more unpleasant by
their constant fear that at any moment highwaymen
would swoop down upon them, when her butler announced the arrival of another guest, Jules Perrin. The
doctor greeted them with surprise and pleasure, kissing
both Lady Helena's and Ginevra's hands with an elegance
of grace only emphasized by his slight limp. When

Ginevra noticed him looking about surreptitiously, as if searching for another visitor, she murmured in an amused undertone, "Emma did not accompany me this time, monsieur. I thought she deserved an afternoon's holiday."

Perrin frowned. "I trust Mademoiselle Jarvis is not un-well?"

"Oh, no, of course not. Emma enjoys the best of health, but she has been very busy of late, and it seemed only fitting that she have some time to herself for a change. She made some mention of visiting the book-stores."

Perrin's grey eyes showed their approval. "She is a very capable and diligent woman. I was most impressed by the assistance she gave me at your country home. Please—extend to her my regards." Ginevra promised to do so, and the doctor turned to Chadwick and Bysshe. "With your permission, I plan to call upon you tomorrow, if that is convenient. I think I ought to have one last look at that ear."

"I shall be busy," Chadwick said; then he glanced at the boy, who was unconsciously rubbing the side of his head, as if to stave off remembered pain. "Bysshe, do you have any objection to—?"

With a wave of her hand Lady Helena interjected, "Why don't the three of you go upstairs and attend to that now?"

"Ma chère Hélène," the doctor protested, "I did not mean to spoil—"

"Oh run along, all of you. It will save your making a call tomorrow, and besides, Jules, I know you will refuse to relax and enjoy our company as long as you have medical matters on your mind."

Rather to Ginevra's surprise, the men left the room without further demur. She sipped her tea and noted conversationally, "I like Dr. Perrin. I had almost given up hope for Bysshe before Richard brought him to Dower-wood."

Lady Helena agreed. "Jules is a very dedicated physician, and his qualifications are excellent. I doubt that I should have survived the journey back to England had he not agreed to accompány me." She sighed. "I had hoped that he would find here some of the happiness that was so lacking for him in his homeland, but as yet I do not think he has. Despite Richard's patronage, his practice is very small, and he is, I believe, rather lonely."

Ginevra ventured uncertainly, "It must be difficult for him to live among strangers, foreigners."

The dowager's blue eyes darkened, and she scowled. "I expect Jules feels less alien in England than he did in the company of his own kind—the people who murdered his family."

Ginevra gasped, and her mother-in-law sighed heavily. "An old story, and not an uncommon one in France these days. Jules is of noble birth. By rights he should now be Chevalier de Beauclair, but during the Terror his parents and sister were killed by a mob that then proceeded to raze his ancestral home. Jules was only a child, and he was spirited away by servants loyal to the family. In the flight his leg was broken, and because they had escaped with nothing beyond the clothes on their backs, the only doctor they could find who would treat the boy was an incompetent quack who set the leg improperly, leaving Jules permanently lamed. I have always thought that Jules's bitterness over his injury was one reason he studied medicine himself. He has a burning determination to provide the best care available to anyone who requires it, no matter how poor."

Ginevra was horrified by the tale, but she could not help observing dryly, "Madam, the Chadwick family can hardly be called poor."

Lady Helena laughed and poured herself a second cup of tea. As she stirred sugar into the steaming liquid with a vermeil teaspoon, she said, "No, my dear, but we can provide the support he requires if he is to benefit those who are truly needy. My late husband—Henri, my second husband—was Jules's patron prior to his death, and I have tried to carry on in his place. It has not always been easy: Jules is a very proud man, and he still carries within him the scars from his childhood."

After a pensive silence Lady Helena continued with

seeming nonchalance, "Tell me, how do you get along with that son of mine?"

"We . . . contrive, my lady," Ginevra said carefully.

Lady Helena responded impatiently, "Don't call me 'my lady,' I dislike such formality among family members. If you feel you cannot call me 'Mother' as Richard does, then 'Lady Helena' or perhaps 'belle-mère' will suffice."

Ginevra blushed, touching her fingertips to her still-tender lips. Indeed, there were great similarities between her husband and his mother.

The older woman watched her with speculation. She added gently, "Bysshe called me grandmère, and because of your age you might feel most comfortable with that. Unfortunately, I suspect Richard would not like it at all." She paused, studying the girl closely. "You are so very young," she said.

Ginevra grimaced. "My youth is one deficiency that time will remedy soon enough—belle-mère." She stumbled over the word. "I'm sorry, did I pronounce that correctly? I don't speak French."

Lady Helena's brows arched. "Not at all? I'm surprised your parents did not require your governess to teach you."

Color rose in Ginevra's pale cheeks. "I didn't have a governess," she mumbled in embarrassment. "I was running my father's household, and there wasn't enough . . . time for formal studies. I made use of his library as much as I could, but there was none at hand who could tutor me in the usual niceties of a young woman's education, such as French or drawing or playing the pianoforte." Her hand began to tremble, and she set her cup and saucer on the low table before her, lest she humiliate herself further by spilling something.

Lady Helena watched compassionately. "Forgive me, my dear," she said sincerely, "I spoke without thinking. Richard has told me of the way you assumed your mother's responsibilities after she died. He has spoken with great admiration of your devotion to your father and his tenants, abandoning your own childhood. I think now he would like to help you recapture some of the carefree days you missed before. He wants to spoil you a little."

Ginevra's tawny eyes darkened. "Is that what he is doing? Indeed, I thought he was merely being arbitrary,"

"I don't doubt that it seemed that way to you," Lady Helena said. "Glover men are notoriously peremptory, even when their intentions are the most laudable. Richard is no different, although he is much more amenable than, say, his father was." She peered thoughtfully at Ginevra. "Just how much," she asked slowly, "do you know about Richard's father?"

"Nothing at all, except that he died many years ago."

Lady Helena nodded. "Geoffrey succumbed to apoplexy when Richard was not much above the age you are now. I think his death was a blessed release."

"You mean he suffered some painful and lingering illness?"

The dowager smiled ironically. "No, dear. Geoffrey was always a strong man, robust, still in his prime. I meant his death was a relief to everyone else." She watched the color drain from Ginevra's face. "You think that a hard thing for me to say, don't you?"

Ginevra floundered, "Well, I suppose if a person were truly of an evil and irredeemable disposition . . ."

Lady Helena said, "I would hesitate to call Geoffrey *evil*; that is not the correct word. He was not depraved, his dissipations were quite normal—but he was proud, cold, inflexible, and utterly impossible to live with."

"I'm sorry."

"Don't be," the older woman said, "it has nothing to do with you. And I managed to make a new life for myself after Geoffrey's death." She smiled gently, wistfully. "The happiness I found with Henri compensated for so much. . . . No, it is Richard who still suffers from his father's foibles." She fell silent, and her blue eyes clouded again with memories, unpleasant ones this time. "Geoffrey never asked, he demanded. He expected instant, unquestioning obedience to his every edict, no matter how unreasonable. Richard was his son and heir, his link to eternity, and as such he bore the brunt of his father's strictures.

Geoffrey tried to fashion the boy into a miniature of himself, and this was hard on Richard, for from a very early age he showed an intelligence and sensitivity lacking in his father, a compassion for the needs of others. I'll never forget how once, when Geoffrey was having trouble with poachers, he ordered his gamekeeper to shoot any on sight. Richard, who was only nine or ten, ran ahead to warn off one of the tenants he had seen trespassing in the woods, a man with a great brood of hungry children. The man escaped, but Geoffrey and the keeper caught Richard beside a sprung trap, which was smeared with fresh blood. Geoffrey was in a rage, of course. When he ordered Richard to identify the poacher, the gamekeeper whispered for the boy to say that the man had fled before he got there. Instead he faced his father and declared, "I am not a liar. I know who did this, but I won't tell," and nothing, not even the beating his father gave him, could make him change his mind." Lady Helena glanced sidelong at Ginevra. "Tell me, does he still carry those scars on his back?"

Sickened, Ginevra muttered, "Not that I've noticed."

"Thank God. I've always been afraid that . . ." Lady Helena paused, shaking her head sadly. "Men are so irrational. Geoffrey wanted a son just like himself, and when he got one, the two of them, both proud and obstinate men, made life hell for each other."

Ginevra watched the emotions that creased the woman's face, aging her. She said gently, "It must have been very difficult for you, caught as you were in the middle."

"But I wasn't in the middle. I wouldn't fight. I retired from the battlefield very early—and for that I shall always feel guilty. Instead of helping my son, I nursed my own hurts—had I been of the Roman persuasion, I think I might have secluded myself in a convent—and I left Richard to face his father alone. I ought to have helped him. I could never have withstood Geoffrey on my own, but I should have given Richard some support, especially in the matter of Maria." She reached for the teapot, scowling when she touched the cool surface. She rang a small crystal bell, and at its crisp tinkling sound a young maid appeared, who addressed her mistress in French. After the girl had borne away the silver salver to the kitchen, Lady Helena leaned back on the divan, wincing as she twitched an arthritic shoulder.

Ginevra quickly crossed the narrow space separating her from her mother-in-law. She leaned over the low couch' and with great care plumped up the cushions and adjusted Lady Helena's shawl. The woman reached up and patted her cheek with a frail, bloodless hand, while her blue eyes searched Ginevra's face anxiously. "You are a sweet child," she murmured. "I wish my son had found someone like you when he was young. I think his whole life might have been different if he had not married Maria."

Ginevra was full of guilty curiosity about her husband's first wife. "Then . . . then you felt the marriage was not . . . suitable?" she asked hesitantly, despising herself for prying.

Lady Helena made a face. "Oh, it was suitable enough, on the surface. Maria was of fairly good family, her father was rich and more than willing to sell his daughter for a title. She was not unattractive—she was tall, and her coloring was much like Bysshe's—and I thought it surprising that she had reached the age of twenty-one without snaring a husband, but no one asked my opinion. I also thought sixteen was far too young for Richard to marry, and when Geoffrey and Maria's father arranged the match between them, at first Richard was reluctant too. But Maria set out to dazzle him, and by the time of their wedding, the boy was wildly in love. I have no idea how long it took him to discover that Maria's dash and sophistication had been acquired through intimate contact with half the men of the *ton*, but I do know that when she promptly became pregnant, an entry was placed in the betting book at White's regarding the paternity of the child. Thank God even as an infant poor Tom was the image of Richard!"

Ginevra recoiled, and her mind reeled at the thought of the unspeakable humiliation her very proud husband must have suffered, a sensitive boy publicly cuckolded. Her voice quivered with outrage as she asked, "When Richard's father arranged the marriage, did he know what Maria was?"

"I don't know," Lady Helena said bleakly, and her face twisted with anguish. "He might have. It could have been his way of revenging himself. You see, he was so very jealous of Richard. He knew the boy was going to be twice the man he ever was . . ." She sighed, and after a pause she continued, "Tom's birth made a divorce out of the question, even had Geoffrey consented to Richard's seeking one, which I am sure he would never have done. No Glover would ever disgrace the family name by airing his marital problems in public."

The maid returned with fresh tea, and Lady Helena was silent until the girl had curtsied and left the room. "Will you pour, my dear?" she asked Ginevra. "My shoulder, I'm afraid . . ." While Ginevra hefted the massive silver teapot, she marvelled that the frail woman had been able to lift it at all earlier. She busied herself replenishing the cups while her mother-in-law said, "Richard and Geoffrey had one last violent row, and Richard said that he was going to join the Navy whether his father liked it or not. Ironically, Maria's dowry gave him the funds he needed to buy his commission. Geoffrey was livid—and a little afraid too, I think, because war was imminent—but Richard said he had provided for the succession with Tom, and it made no difference if he was killed."

Ginevra stared at the woman with shimmering eyes. "Dear Lord, and you had to hear all that?" Before Lady Helena could reply, they heard sounds of the men returning from abovestairs. Ginevra felt almost guilty. Somehow she knew her husband would not thank his mother for her revelations.

As the men's booted heels clattered on the staircase, Lady Helena murmured quickly, her voice low but insistent, "When Richard came back from the war, everything was different. Maria and Geoffrey were both dead, and Richard had changed. He was hard, wild. I have seen no

gentleness in him since then, until now—with you." She
held out a supplicating hand to the girl. "I beg you, be
kind to my son."

Ginevra was clutching Lady Helena's hand when the
men reached the parlor. With dismay she felt thin, brittle
bones under crepy skin, signs of a weakness far more ad-
vanced than the woman's age warranted, and she knew
the dowager had not long to live. She glanced sidelong at
Lady Helena, and she saw that her sharp blue eyes had
softened with longing as she gazed at the marquess. Was
this the reason she had made the wearisome and risky
journey back from France? Ginevra wondered. She
claimed she had been happy on the Continent. Had she
been driven home by the desire to make peace with the
tall, handsome son she felt she had deserted?

Gently Ginevra squeezed the fragile fingers and declared with forced brightness to the men, "Well, you all
seem excessively pleased with yourselves. Are we to assume then that the examination went well?"

Dr. Perrin nodded. "I believe I can safely say that Lord
Glover is now completely recovered from his illness, with
no side effects, *grâce au bon Dieu!*"

"Yes, thank God," Lady Helena echoed, and she
waved them to their chairs. "Make yourselves comfortable,
all of you. This sweet child and I have been having a
pleasant enough coze while you were busy, but now that
you are finished, you must acquaint us with all the latest
on-dits. Since I no longer get about, you know I depend
on you to bring me my daily ration of scandal. . . .
Ginevra, my dear, will you be so kind as to pour for
them?"

As they drove back toward the marquess's house in
Mayfair later that evening, Ginevra could not stop staring
at her husband. She knew he must think her regard odd,
to say the least, but as she looked at his strong, stern
profile, she kept remembering the boy who had been hurt
so cruelly. No wonder he seemed implacable sometimes;
after being abused by his harsh and forbidding father,
then failed by an ineffectual mother and a promiscuous

wife, he must have decided long ago that he would never allow himself to be vulnerable to anyone again.

Bysshe, who had resumed his usual sulky pose the instant they departed from his grandmother's house, had climbed up onto the high perch beside the coachman, and Ginevra, with a little more room to move around, turned slightly on the leather seat so that she could watch Chadwick without craning her neck. She studied the granite planes of his face, the deeply engraved lines that were only emphasized by the softness of the raven curls that ruffled in the breeze beneath his flat-crowned beaver hat. She tried to picture a time when his features would have been rounder and less rigidly defined, as Bysshe's still were, a time when those deep blue eyes had sparkled with innocence. She could not conjure up the image. His mother claimed he appeared to have softened toward her, and yes, Ginevra knew now that her husband could treat her gently, with care and consideration, but even in his tenderest moments his face still showed the marks of past bitterness, carved there long ago by callous hands, and she knew that nothing she did could every truly erase them.

Ginevra blinked. Chadwick was staring back at her. His face was intent and oddly pale as he tried to decipher her expression. "Ginnie?" he murmured uncertainly, his voice strangely husky.

A jerky movement on the perch diverted her attention. Ginevra looked up to find Bysshe, flushed and grim, biting his lip and peering at something off to their right. Ginevra glanced around. The phaeton was moving at a steady pace through Hyde Park, its progress unimpeded by the usual afternoon crush of traffic now that most of fashionable society had departed the city. Only a handful of carriages and riders made the leisurely circuit through the park, and it was toward one small cluster that Bysshe directed his gaze. Ginevra looked in that direction and saw a couple on horseback. The man was dressed in the rainbow hues popular among the more dashing of young gallants, but it was the woman who captured Ginevra's attention. She noted with surprise that she in turn was also being scrutinized thoroughly, although she could not imagine why, for she knew she paled to insipidity beside that statuesque and fiery beauty. The two riders did not come closer, but even at a distance Ginevra could see that the woman's skin was a warm gold, as if she hailed from some tropical clime, and the eyes staring back at her seemed dark and magnetic. But it was her hair that caught and held Ginevra's enrapt attention. From beneath a diminutive feminine shako, in defiance of all rules of fashion, her long curls flowed like liquid flame over her shoulders, and against the hunter green of her very stylish riding habit they seemed almost alight.

Ginevra tore her eyes away and turned to her husband. "What . . . what an astonishingly lovely woman," she stammered, unaccountably shaken. "I don't think I've ever seen anyone like her. Do you know who she is?"

Chadwick's face was absolutely expressionless, and he said nothing. "Richard," she repeated, "do you know . . . ?" Her voice died away as she became aware of her husband's unnatural stillness, and under her gaze his rigid cheek twitched spasmodically.

As she watched him, his silence began to beat against her ears, louder than the clatter of the horses' hooves on the packed earth of the drive or the normal muted roar of the city. She could feel her pulse become erratic as blood seemed to drain from her body, seeping with inexorable slowness into the great hollow cavity forming at the base of her stomach. She sank back against the seat and drooped her head limply so that the brim of her straw hat hid the bleak expression in her eyes. She knew who that stunning beauty was. One look at the marquess, and she didn't need the confirmation of Bysshe's low, spiteful voice raining down on her like shards of shattered glass: "I'll tell you who she is, Ginnie. That's your husband's mistress!"

She wished she were older. She wished she had the sophistication to greet Bysshe's sneering announcement with
a shrug and a casual smile, as if it bothered her not one
whit to come face to face with the woman who competed
for her husband's attentions. Instead, all Ginevra could do
was bow her head and gnaw her lip painfully in a frantic
effort to hold back the sickness that threatened to spill out
of her as she visualized Chadwick making love to the
Frenchwoman, his naked skin rubbing erotically against
hers, bronze on gold. As if the images were seared into
her brain by the heat of their desire, Ginevra could see
the two of them wound together intimately, that glorious
hair pouring over his strong throat like lava, and she
knew there was no way she could hope to compete with
that sultry and exotic beauty.

She kept her eyes resolutely downcast as she tried to
compose herself. She did not want Bysshe to see the effect
his words had had on her. Instinctively she knew that he
had been striking at her as much as at his father when he
threw that poisoned barb, for he still resented the way she
had rejected him that morning. When he muttered her
name again, she did not respond. At her side her husband
growled in a harsh, icy undertone, "You've said quite
enough, Bysshe," and the boy fell silent. The marquess
must have signalled the coachman to quicken his pace, for
the phaeton accelerated as it left the park, its iron-rimmed
wheels clattering over the cobbled streets. The carriage
rocked slightly, and Ginevra swayed against her husband.
He steadied her and caught her lace-mittened hand in his.
She tried to pull away. His grip tightened painfully over

her thin fingers, and he did not release her until they reached the house in Mayfair.

When he assisted her down from the carriage, Ginevra thanked him and murmured, "If you will excuse me, I'd like to go to my room."

"I'll join you in a few minutes."

Her voice sounded strained and unnaturally high even to herself as she protested, "I'd really rather you didn't. I'm tired and I'd like to rest."

"I see. Will you be down later for dinner?"

She managed a semblance of a shrug. "I don't know. Perhaps not."

Chadwick sighed. "Very well. Enjoy your nap, my dear." He watched her pensively as she made her way up the long staircase, her slender shoulders drooping as if pressed down by some great weight, while her stylish bonnet dangled limply from her fingers. When she had disappeared into the upper hallway, he turned and caught sight of Bysshe slipping stealthily into the billiard room. He barked the boy's name, and Bysshe jerked around, his face alternately pale then flushed under his unruly straight hair as he met the marquess's glare. Chadwick said, "In my study. Now." Without waiting for a reply he turned on his heel and stalked away.

In the study Chadwick did not mince words. "Your conduct toward your stepmother is unconscionable," he declared, facing the boy across the desk.

Bysshe stared down at the carpet. "I don't think of Ginnie as my stepmother," he mumbled sulkily.

Chadwick inclined his dark head. "No, of course not. In the circumstances it would be ridiculous for you to do so. However, the very fact that Ginevra is an old friend of yours makes your actions even less excusable."

Bysshe regarded him balefully. "I just thought she ought to know."

The marquess snorted, "You mean you thought you could spite me. Well, my lad, I hope you enjoyed your little moment of triumph, because in the process you have managed to hurt and humiliate someone who has a deep affection for you. After the way she cared for you when you were ill—"

Color built up in Bysshe's face; then suddenly he exploded, "If anyone has humiliated her, it's you! You're the one with the fancy ladyfriend! You're not worthy to be Ginnie's—"

"Quiet!" Chadwick roared, and the boy fell silent. Slowly the marquess rose to his full height, powerful and overwhelming. Bysshe retreated. With rigid control Chadwick stated flatly, "You forget yourself, boy. Ginevra is my wife, and neither your relationship to me nor your long-standing friendship with her gives you any right whatsoever to question the quality of our marriage. Do I make myself clear?"

"As glass."

Chadwick continued, "I have tried to be lenient with you of late, overlook your increasingly surly behavior because I attributed it to the lingering effects of your illness, but now I can no longer do so. I think perhaps it would be advisable for you to return to Queenshaven and remain there until September when the new school term begins."

"I won't be packed off to the country," Bysshe shouted, "and I'm not going back to school, either!"

"Indeed? This is news to me. I had assumed you would continue at Harrow until you were eighteen and could enter Oxford, as your brother did."

"Why?" Bysshe demanded. "Are you hoping I'll get thrown by a horse too?" Chadwick's jaw clenched, and after a moment Bysshe muttered, "I'm sorry. That was uncalled-for." His voice rose. "But . . . but I think even a broken neck would be better than going back to school. 'Chief nursery of our statesmen,' they call it. Hell! I'll wager sailors pressed onto warships don't have it much worse than boys in school. In wintertime you rise at six; the sun's not up yet, and the washwater is frozen in the basins. There's never enough food, and what there is is foul. The smaller boys go hungry because some bully has stolen theirs, and when you're not standing at attention while some tutor drones on and on in Greek or Latin, you work in the birch room making rods for the proctors to beat you with."

"You needn't convince me," the marquess said quietly. "I went there too, you know, and somehow I survived."

"Yes, but you quit when you were sixteen!"

Chadwick stared at Bysshe. Then, nodding, he agreed with an ironic sigh, "So I did." After a pause he continued matter-of-factly, "It occurs to me that you may be suffering from a malady much more common than scarlet fever, and one that responds more readily to treatment. I should have realized sooner, but it is difficult to acknowledge that the children one knows do make a habit of growing up. Your sixteenth birthday fast approaches, does it not?"

Bysshe said warily, "In three weeks."

"Very good. I'll tell you what I propose. If you will give me your word that henceforth you will conduct yourself as behooves a gentleman and a Glover and will cause your stepmother no further distress, I shall ask Harriette Wilson to arrange a very private, very intimate . . . celebration for you."

At the mention of the most notorious courtesan in London, Bysshe's eyes widened and he choked, "You mean you . . . you want me to consort with a . . . a . . ."

"I mean," the marquess amplified impatiently, "that there is—or should be—as much etiquette employed in the bedroom as in the ballroom, and it's high time you learned it. Little Harry is intelligent and discreet, and she will know which of her associates would be most suitable to instruct you."

"Damn you!" Bysshe shouted, almost sputtering with embarrassment and fury. "I might have known a rake like you would think of something like that! You think by playing pander you can make me forget I'm in love with—" As if suddenly realizing whom he was talking to, Bysshe cut off his words abruptly.

Chadwick smiled grimly. "That is one sentence you would be wise never to finish," he said in a harsh undertone. "Once the words are spoken, they will have to be dealt with, and it would be far better for everyone if that sorry turn of events does not take place." He paused. "I collect you do not care for my birthday suggestion?"

"No. I will never defile my feelings in such a shameful manner."

"Oh, Lord," the marquess groaned, shaking his head. "I forgot that no one is so self-righteous as the very young." He shrugged and stood up, weary of the conversation. "As you will. Certainly you have the right to choose your own method of initiation. I will tell you bluntly, however, that when you do make that choice, I shall demand certain standards of conduct from you as Viscount Glover. You will offer insult to no lady, nor will you impose upon any of our dependents. Beyond that you must suit yourself, although I sincerely hope that you will have enough presence of mind to avoid acquiring either French pox or English bastards."

"Yes, sir," Bysshe murmured. His brown eyes were still rebellious as they watched the marquess exit the study.

When Chadwick knocked on the connecting door between his and Ginevra's suites, there was no answer. Quietly he pushed open the door and stepped into her room. She lay fully clothed on the bed, motionless except for her eyes which followed the progress of a coin of sunlight across the wall. Only when her husband loomed over her did she glance up at him.

Frowning, he asked, "Are you feeling unwell?"

"No, only tired. It's been a . . . a trying day." Her voice was flat and expressionless.

"Yes," the marquess agreed. When she did not speak again, he noted, "You should have removed your dress. You'll wrinkle it."

"It doesn't matter. Emma has not returned yet, and I couldn't be bothered."

"Shall I help you undress?"

"No, thank you." With an air of languid indifference she looked away.

He sat down beside her on the edge of the bed and caught her chin in his long fingers. Only when he tried to turn her face back toward him did he discover that her studied lassitude was false, that she lay rigid and unyielding. Muttering an oath, he hooked his fingertips under her jaw and jerked her around with irresistible force. Bright blotches of red sprang up in the soft skin just under the bone, and he knew that by morning she would have four parallel bruises there. With an air of contrition he said, "Ginevra, we must talk."

She rubbed her tender skin and glared at him through half-lowered lashes. "You mean you want to explain about that woman?"

His mouth hardened. "No. I owe you no explanations about my past life."

Ginevra tried to shrug, an awkward movement in her reclining posture. She said, "I don't think explanations are necessary, in any case. She is very beautiful. You . . . you have good taste."

He smiled sardonically. "Thank you, I expect Amalie would appreciate your approval." He regarded her enigmatically before saying brusquely, "I'm sorry Bysshe acted like such an ass. His behavior was most definitely not that of a gentleman, a fact that reflects unfavorably on his upbringing. I'd make him apologize himself, but somehow I think that would only create more ill will. So I must ask you to be generous enough to forgive him without an apology." His voice softened, became cajoling. "Perhaps it will help you feel more charitable if I tell you that his statement was incorrect: Madame de Villeneuve is no longer under my protection."

Ginevra bit her lip to keep from crying out in surprise. She stammered, "You mean . . . you mean you gave her up before we were married?" Her shimmering gold eyes widened momentarily with hope, a hope that subsided as she waited for his answer that was not forthcoming. She repeated hesitantly, "Richard, you . . . you haven't seen her since the wedding, have you?"

At length, wtih a sigh he replied, "My dear, that's not . . . precisely what I said."

Ginevra winced. "I see."

She rolled away from him to the center of the bed, where she lay huddled, eyes screwed shut, arms clenched tightly across her chest, her knees drawing upward against the pain gnawing at her vitals. When he leaned over her and stroked her trembling shoulders as he murmured against her ear, "Ginnie, please listen . . ." she shook him off fiercely.

"Don't ever touch me!" she gritted, her eyes still closed. "Don't ever touch me again!"

For just a second his fingers bit ruthlessly into her flesh; then she felt the mattress shift as he eased his weight off the bed. His voice was stiff and clipped as he inquired, "Am I to assume then that you would prefer I did not come to you tonight?"

For the space of a heartbeat she almost relented, remembering the comforting warmth of his hard, lean body, the security of his arms about her in the night—but then she thought of those same arms wrapped about the pliant body of Amalie de Villeneuve, and her resolve firmed. "I think it might be better if you stayed away."

"Indeed." His tone softened, became almost conversational. "In that case I shall not trespass here again until you ask me." He turned and strode across the room without looking back at her, but at the door he paused, and she heard him groan, "Damnation, I am sick to death of fractious children!"

The days passed slowly after that. Each morning Ginevra would wake behind the draperies of the great four-poster and her hand would reach out instinctively for her husband, only to remember that he no longer slept beside her. The sun that had roused him, blue-black curls shining with iridescent delight on the white pillow, now reflected only the gleam of bleached linen, pristine and somehow accusing. Chadwick made no attempt to cross the threshold into her bedroom, greeting her instead with a chaste kiss at the breakfast table before he embarked each day on that mysterious male enterprise known as "business." Often she did not see him again at all unless he returned briefly to change into evening dress before leaving the house again.

Bysshe also kept very much to himself, a fact for which Ginevra was now grateful, although she worried that the boy seemed so isolated and brooding. Her concern lessened somewhat when the marquess presented his son with an early birthday present, a magnificent young stallion that even Ginevra's untutored eyes could see would someday be the equal of Giaour, Lord Chadwick's great roan. For just a second as Bysshe stroked the animal's gleaming grey coat he smiled gratefully at the marquess, and Ginevra thought it was the first time she had seen the boy regard his father with anything but antagonism. But the atmosphere of tense hostility quickly returned when Chadwick asked Bysshe what he would name the horse. "His sire is called Aeneas," the man noted, "so something classical might be appropriate."

Bysshe looked thoughtfully at Chadwick and Ginevra standing side by side, and he suggested slyly, "What do you think of Hippolytus?"

Chadwick's expression did not waver, but Ginevra observed with surprise the line of white that appeared around his thin mouth. When he spoke, his deep voice sounded steady but strained. "Well, lad, I'm delighted to know that you have retained some small portion of what you were taught at that school you hated so much, but perhaps you have forgotten that Hippolytus came to a bad end. I think something less . . . provocative might be more suitable."

"Of course, sir," Bysshe said, his brown eyes veiled. "Anything you say, sir."

Ginevra followed this exchange with some confusion, aware of undercurrents she could not explain, and it was not until much later that she recalled from her diverse reading at Bryant House that Hippolytus had been the son of the mythical hero Theseus, and his affair with his father's wife Phaedra had led ultimately to the destruction of all three of them.

Bysshe's birthday present reminded Ginevra of Houri, the little chestnut mare the marquess had given her, and she began riding lessons under the supervision of one of the grooms, venturing out in the early morning when traffic was still light and the only pedestrians were bucket-laden housewives hurrying to the public standpipes to draw their daily water before the crowds built up. But even this pleasurable new activity could not lessen the fatigue and depression that had settled over her.

Her mood was not eased by the letter she received from her father, his first communication with her since her wedding day. In it he expressed conventional wishes for her continued health and happiness; then he announced without further preamble that he was closing up Bryant House and travelling to Italy. He had always had a desire to see the Continent, he said, and now that the wars were over and he no longer had a daughter to contend with, he could journey where he wished. Ginevra read his crabbed handwriting with resentment. Her anger and hurt came not from her father's curt dismissal of her from his life—she had always known that to him she was no more than a pale and annoying replica of his dead wife—but rather from the cavalier fashion in which he abandoned his tenants to the dubious supervision of a steward, a stranger. When Ginevra remembered the shameless way in which Sir Charles had used the welfare of his staff as a lever with which to force her into marriage with the marquess, she screwed the letter into a knot and flung it furiously into the empty fireplace.

Ginevra was still staring blindly at the wadded paper when she heard a knock on her sitting-room door. She glanced up just as Emma glided silently into the room, her pretty face unusually solemn. Ginevra asked worriedly, "Emma, is something wrong?"

The older woman smiled gravely. "No, not . . . not really, my lady. I wondered if I might have a word with you, that's all."

Something about her quiet voice sent a tremor of apprehension through Ginevra's slim body. She gestured to the chair opposite her. "Perhaps you'd better sit down."

"No, thank you, my lady."

Ginevra snapped impatiently, "Confound it, Emma, I've told you before, I don't like you to be so formal with me! Why do you persist?"

Emma's green eyes lit up now with genuine amusement. She said dryly, "I do it because I enjoy it. It pleases me to know that the little girl I raised has grown to be a great, noble lady."

Matching Emma's tone, Ginevra said, "Well, in that case, this great, noble lady is ordering you to sit down." She watched her friend curtsy with exaggerated deference before sinking into the proffered chair. When she was settled, Ginevra asked frankly, "Well, now, Emma, what's troubling you?"

After a moment's hesitation Emma said slowly, "Miss Ginevra, I would like permission to leave your service."

Ginevra gaped, speechless. At last she choked, "My God, what are you saying?"

"I want to leave your service," Emma repeated.

"But why?" Ginevra cried. "Have I offended you in some way? Oh, Emma, I'm sorry. You know I wouldn't—"

"No," Emma silenced her, "it's nothing you've done! You've been the kindest, most considerate mistress anyone could wish, as dear to me as my own child."

"Come, now, you're not that much older than I am," Ginevra chided.

"Near enough. I was nineteen when I came into your household, somewhat older than is usual for girls entering service, but then I . . ." Her voice faltered. "I had had different plans for my future."

"You were betrothed," Ginevra prompted.

Emma nodded. "Days before the wedding my Harry made a delivery of leather goods to the port at Bristol, and while he was there he was grabbed by the press gangs. When word came back to the tanner, his master, who was a good man, the two of us rushed to town, his master to see if he could buy Harry back out of the Navy, I to plead with the captain at least to let us be wed before they set sail. But by the time we reached the port, the fleet was gone, already on its way to Spain." She winced, her face bleak, and it occurred to Ginevra that for the first time she was seeing through the impassive mask that Emma had always worn. Emma's voice sounded low and desolate as she said, "I was glad Harry was in Nelson's fleet; they say no one on the admiral's ships was ever logged. I comforted myself with that thought after Harry died at Trafalgar." She paused. "The victory celebrations were just beginning—I could hear the fireworks—the night I lost the babe I had been carrying."

Ginevra stared down at her hands and wove her fingers together. How, she wondered, had she lived alongside Emma for eleven years, considered her her closest friend, and yet had remained ignorant of the anguish, the pain the woman kept bottled inside her? She said simply, "I'm sorry. I had no idea."

Emma shrugged. "It was a long time ago." She regarded Ginevra with tender affection. "After I recovered from my . . . my illness, the wife of Harry's master heard that your mother was looking for a new nursery maid, and she sent me to her. Since then most of the joy in my life has come from watching you grow."

Ginevra said slowly, "And now you want to leave me. Why?"

Emma met her gaze frankly. "You don't need me anymore. You're a grown woman, a lady of exalted rank. You require people who can serve you properly in your new position, who can advise you on fashion and etiquette. I am too much of the country, and I am no longer adequate for you."

"But you know I don't think of you as a maid. You're my companion, my . . . my friend."

"Yes, I know that," Emma cried, "but I also know it is impossible for me to remain in London!"

Ginevra's eyes widened at the outburst. "Emma," she asked thoughtfully, "is something bothering you? Some person, perhaps—some man? Has some man insulted you or . . . or threatened you in any way?" She remembered the errands Emma ran daily for her, venturing out into the streets where no lone woman was ever entirely safe. "Dear God," she choked, "has someone . . . ?"

Emma shook her head fiercely. "No, I am unharmed." She flashed a quick, wry smile. "There's precious little these Town dandies could try that a country girl hasn't learned to cope with very early from farmhands and stableboys." Her expression darkened. "You are right,

however, there is a man. Lately every time I go out I
seem to encounter that physician, the one who cared for
Lord Bysshe. At shops, at bookstores—it happens too often to be other than by design."

"Jules Perrin?" Ginevra exclaimed. "How marvellous! I
knew he liked you."

Emma looked at her with horror. "It's nothing to be
pleased about."

"But why not? I admire Dr. Perrin. He is a very kind
and dedicated man. Any woman should be flattered by his
attention." She faltered. "His advances have been honorable, have they not?"

"Oh, yes," Emma snapped sarcastically, "he has been
everything that is proper and correct."

"Then whatever is the problem?"

Emma's green eyes flared. "He's French!"

Ginevra stared, speechless, trying to interpret that cryp-
tic remark. At last she shook her head and said, "I still
don't understand."

"Maybe you would," Emma declared with unconcealed
bitterness, "if you had lost someone you loved in the
war."

Ginevra blushed. She thought of the doctor, a good
man who carried profound scars from his own past. He
and Emma had worked well together at Dowerwood. It
all seemed so pointless, somehow. She suggested gently,
"Emma, the war is over."

Slowly her friend shook her head. "Not for me, it
isn't."

Ginevra took a deep breath, and the ache in her throat
made her realize how tensely she had been holding herself. She murmured, "I see. Then there's nothing more to
be said, is there?" She unbraided her fingers painfully and
watched the blood seep back into the whitened knuckles.
She said much more lightly than she felt, "In that case,
what do you wish to do? You're a freeborn English-
woman, you do not need my permission to leave me or
London, but obviously I am not going to dismiss you out
of hand. What plans have you made? If you wish to remain in service, I can give you excellent references. If you

prefer some independent enterprise, your options are somewhat limited, but I shall—"

"I want to start a school," Emma said. When Ginevra looked puzzled, Emma continued fervently, "I want to go back to Surrey and provide a place where children like Mrs. Harrison's Jamie can learn to read and write and cipher. Town children who really desire it always have access to some form of education—even those who work in the factories can go to the new Sunday schools—but there is little available for the boys and girls in outlying districts. Times are hard for everyone now, and without at least the rudiments of learning, these children can hope for nothing better than a marginal existence on the farms or sixteen hours a day minding looms in the woolen mills."

Ginevra considered. She thought about little Jamie, who had been so inquisitive and eager to learn. Now that the party had left Dowerwood, she wondered if he would retain any of what she had taught him. His grandmother was barely literate. Her mind turned to Queenshaven, to the tenants and their families whom she had visited. Without education, what future awaited them in a world where one minister had declared of the agrarian poor: "They don't live; they just don't die."

"You would accept girls as well as boys?" Ginevra asked with concern. "Not all schools do, even nowadays."

"Of course," Emma agreed, smiling as she watched Ginevra's enthusiasm grow. "Otherwise how will they hope to achieve the ideal of 'the educated mother in equal union with the educated male'?"

Ginevra blinked. "I didn't know you had read Mary Wollstonecraft."

Emma's mouth quirked. "How else do you surmise a copy of her book came to be in the Bryant House library?"

When Ginevra tendered the suggestion to Lord Chadwick at one of their infrequent meetings at the breakfast table, he expressed surprise at Emma's departure but accepted Ginevra's casual explanation that her friend was unhappy in London. When she asked about setting up a

small school for the tenant children, her enthusiasm
bubbled up, and he favored her with one of his rare
smiles. He said the idea sounded sensible and she was free
to handle the matter as she wished. Ginevra might have
enjoyed his approval more had she not suspected he was
simply humoring her whims.

After that events proceeded apace, and almost before
Ginevra realized, she was waving good-bye to Emma,
who was journeying by coach to Dowerwood, there to
make her home in the caretaker's cottage with Mrs. Harrison while she set about her project. When the vehicle
disappeared into the London traffic, Ginevra returned to
the house and made her way up the long staircase, her
steps as leaden as her heart. First my father, now Emma,
she thought.

When she reached the top of the steps, she gazed at her
reflection in the mirror over the console table. She saw an
attractive young woman in an elegantly fashionable day
dress, her hair styled *à la* Psyche with amber combs. The
tawny eyes that stared back at her had a maturity and sophistication that had not been there a dozen weeks before.
She frowned judiciously. Emma was right: she didn't need
her anymore. She was growing up, and while she would
always love her friend dearly, the time had come to put
nursery maids aside.

Resolutely she walked back to her room. She needed to
discuss with her new maid just what she ought to wear to
Lady Thorndike's card party.

Susan, the new maid, was meticulous but slow, and her
slowness, plus the unusual amount of traffic on the long
drive between Mayfair and Greenwich, conspired to delay
Ginevra and Chadwick's arrival at Thorndike Place almost an hour beyond what they had intended. Their
hostess greeted them warmly. She laughed at Chadwick
with the ease of long acquaintance, expressed her sorrow
that Bysshe had been unable to come, and took Ginevra's
hand the instant she had been relieved of her pale blue
silk evening cloak. "Come, my dear," Jane Thorndike
gushed, "I know you must need some refreshment after

that ridiculous drive. Everyone says we were mad to build so far out of town, but my husband is an avid astronomer, and he insisted that we live near the observatory. Personally, I sometimes suspect he wanted to discourage the charity cases I sponsor from imposing further on us." She directed Ginevra toward the dining room, where, she could see through the archway, tables laden with all sorts of summer delicacies waited upon the guests' pleasure. Lady Thorndike exclaimed with self-deprecating humor, "Enough food to feed a needy family for months. My little card party seems to have grown beyond all recognition! So many people anxious to meet you, my dear . . ." As if to give proof to her words, guests began to crowd around, and in the welter of introductions that followed, Ginevra lost track of her husband.

An hour later she sought refuge in a curtained alcove just off the salon where the Thorndikes' teenage children and their friends were romping through a series of country dances, accompanied by a string trio. Before she pulled the drapery shut, she watched them wistfully. In years she was very close to those lighthearted youngsters who frolicked, giddy as butterflies. She sank onto the love seat that filled the cubbyhole. Sometimes she thought she had never been young.

She had hidden behind the curtains to rest and to escape momentarily the avid curiosity of the other guests—the men whose polite formality scarcely masked their intrigued appraisal, the women whose bland smiles only just covered frustration and envy. Most of them already had husbands of their own, but clearly they had coveted the marquess for themselves, and they resented the fact that a rank outsider had connived, so they thought, to snatch the most eligible man in London.

As she prepared to depart her hiding place, her attention was captured and held by the voices of two men slowly sauntering past the alcove. When they paused, she was trapped.

"The wench is a beauty," the first judged, "but not, I should have thought, Glover's usual style. He likes them buxom and vivacious, usually, and she's just a bit of a thing. Hardly said a word."

The second voice drawled, "The filly is still very young, probably skittish. But obviously prime blood, the kind that takes careful handling when you break her to the saddle." He laughed ribaldly. "Anyway, they say she is a fabulous heiress from the Midlands, and of course there was never any chance that he would marry the arresting Madame de Villeneuve."

"It should be intriguing tonight, watching her come face to face with the girl."

The other voice exclaimed, "Never say Amalie has dared to put in an appearance here!"

"Yes, just a few moments ago, didn't you see? She arrived with young Carstairs, who's been sniffing around her every time his mama's back is turned. Our hostess turned the color of an unripe cheese when she saw her, but she couldn't get her husband's attention quick enough to have him turn the jade away before she was announced. You know old Thorndike: if he doesn't see something through his telescope, he doesn't see it at all."

The men were quiet, and Ginevra began to think they had finally moved on. But just as she rose weakly from the sofa, the first voice asked, "Would you care to lay a small wager on which of them will take the prize?"

The other snorted, "I'd have to be as green as that girl to take a bet like that! The little chit versus a vampire like Amalie? That's no contest, no contest at all."

When the two men at last wandered on, Ginevra huddled on the short couch, surprised that her glowing cheeks did not illuminate the walls of the dim alcove. She shook with humiliation, rage, and disgust, mostly directed at herself for failing to make her presence known. If she had stepped forward, she could have quelled that boorish pair with a speaking glance, and they would have prostrated themselves in their effort to make amends for speaking disrespectfully of a lady. Instead she had lurked guiltily behind the curtains and listened to every scornful word—and if those words hurt her, she had only herself to blame.

Oddly, the words that hurt most were those that charged that she was too immature for the marquess, for that was the accusation that was so patently true. If he had returned to Amalie, it was only because despite her grand claims that she was grown up now, that she had never been young, where her husband was concerned Ginevra continued to act childishly. She sulked, she spurned his overtures, she shrank from him because retreat was easier than facing what he demanded of her as a woman.

She wondered why she was such a coward. Chadwick had a temper, of course, but he kept it rigidly under control around her, except when she provoked him past all endurance. Even then his treatment of her was often remarkably gentle. No, it was not his anger she feared, nor even the enormous social demands on her as his wife. When she was twelve years old and had been thrust without warning into the position of mistress of Bryant House, she had faced that without flinching, and in many ways now her duties were much easier. No, the antagonism between Ginevra and Lord Chadwick had much deeper roots in something she began to think must date back even to childhood. Very early in life she had learned rejection, and after that she had permitted herself to care about people only in a superficial way. She was kind because it was her nature, diligent because she had a strong sense of duty, but even those persons closest to her, such as Emma, had in a real sense remained strangers. To them she seemed mature, when in fact she was merely aloof. Only with her husband . . .

Ginevra winced, shaking her head as if she thought she might faint. She had always been afraid of the Marquess of Chadwick because he alone had the power to touch her heart.

Love, she thought; my God, I'm in love with him!

The pain she had felt when those two men gossiped about her husband had nothing to do with embarrassment or offended vanity, it was the anguished acknowledgment that she loved Richard Glover and through her own stupidity had driven him into another woman's arms. He had been tolerant and tender with her, but at last his patience had come to an end; even now it might be too late to salvage anything of their marriage. By his own admission he had been with Amalie de Villeneuve since the wedding, and certainly the woman must feel confident of her position if she dared confront him publicly. If Ginevra tried to establish her rights, she risked the humiliation of an equally public rebuff.

Suddenly a scrap of conversation repeated in Ginevra's mind, two short sentences spoken in a voice weighed down by a lifetime of regret: "I wouldn't fight. I retired from the battlefield early on." Lady Helena's entire adult life had been colored by the remorse she felt for the spiritual cowardice she had displayed during the conflicts between Chadwick and his father, and now Ginevra faced the same prospect if she did not garner the courage to fight for her husband's affection. Her enemy's weapons were formidable—sophistication, audacity, and the security of a long-established relationship—but Ginevra was Chadwick's legal wife, and, as he had told her in another context, nothing could ever change that. She had to try.

She was just smoothing the white silk of her dress, adjusting the blue velvet ribbons that adorned the low, square-cut neckline, when the curtain across the alcove was flung back and Lady Thorndike exclaimed, "My dear, whatever are you doing in here? I've looked everywhere for you."

Ginevra held out a cajoling hand. "Forgive me for being so rude, but I was so overwhelmed by your hospitality that I needed to relax for a few minutes."

Her hostess said with concern, "Child, if you're tired, you have only to say the word. My bedrooms are all at your disposal, should you wish to lie down."

Ginevra shook her head. "Oh, no, I'm quite refreshed now, thank you." She smiled winningly. "Tell me, please, what has become of that wretch of a husband of mine? I've not laid eyes on him since we first arrived."

Lady Thorndike looked uncomfortable. She said reluctantly, "I believe I saw him last in the parlor on the far

side of the music room. He was talking to . . . to someone."

Ginevra did not need to ask who that someone was.
She thanked the other woman graciously and wended her
way through the salon where she had seen the young
people dancing earlier. Some of the older guests were beginning to join the lighthearted fun, and Ginevra only just
avoided being pulled into a circle for the schottische.

The parlor was full of people laughing and joking in
small groups as a liveried butler passed among them with
a tray of brimming champagne glasses, but Ginevra had
no difficulty spotting her husband and the woman he
talked to. They made a striking couple, both tall and
well-built, handsome of feature, with vibrant coloring.
Ginevra accepted a glass of wine and sipped it as she lingered by the archway, studying her enemy. She noted
with a certain malicious pleasure that the Frenchwoman's
bright red hair clashed uncompromisingly with the bur-
gundy-colored tailcoat the marquess wore now that he
had put off his somber mourning entirely. Madame de
Villeneuve's remarkable tresses were arranged in artful
disarray with a number of silver combs, and her dress of
silver-grey tissue might have looked drab against her
golden skin were it not embroidered thickly with ruby-
colored silk. From her ears dangled sparkling clusters of
gems, and around one slim wrist was a heavy ruby
bracelet with the largest stones Ginevra had ever seen. As
she watched, that wrist was laid lightly across the velvet
front of the marquess's coat, and long gloved fingers began to toy with the intricate folds of his cravat.

Ginevra observed that deliberately intimate gesture
with narrowed eyes, and she thought fiercely: Take your
hands off him, you slut—he's mine!

She looked intently at her husband, at the lithe and
powerful body she knew so well yet not at all. Yes, he
was hers; he belonged to her. Whenever she wished, she
could caress that broad chest, those heavily muscled
shoulders . . . She alone had the right to touch him, and
to her amazement she realized now that she had never
done so. She had accepted his lovemaking passively,

afraid to respond. The incipient awareness she had felt when they married had been quickly overpowered by the trauma of their first connection, and only now, when it might be too late, did she understand just what she had given up.

"I will never give him up," she murmured hardly, and an amused chuckle, quickly stifled, made her uncomfortably aware that she had spoken aloud, that her enrapt stare was attracting the attention of people standing nearby. She glanced about casually. Some of the guests were making an elaborate pretense of ignoring her; others looked back at her with candid, knowing smiles. She wondered if any of those smiles belonged to the men she had overheard earlier. She returned their gazes blandly and gulped down the remainder of her champagne. She squared her thin shoulders. So they thought there was no contest! When she marched across the room, a strand of her golden hair fluttered and gleamed like the plume on a helmet.

The marquess did not see her until she slipped her small hand possessively through the crook of his arm. Beneath the wine-red velvet she could feel his hard muscles tense with surprise at the first deliberate overture she had ever made toward him, but the blue eyes that smiled down at her were welcoming, if a little wary. "Ginevra, my dear," he murmured, "where on earth have you been? I was beginning to think you had been spirited away by Gypsies."

She laughed. "I was just meeting your friends, listening to them tell me the most outrageous stories about your misspent youth."

"Methinks I need a new set of friends," Chadwick said wryly.

"Perhaps you do," Ginevra rejoined, grinning. "I'll see to it right away." Their eyes met and locked, and his free hand closed warmly over hers.

The woman standing with them muttered in an acid undertone, "*Sois prudent, mon brave, ou la petite te mènera par le bout du nez.*" Chadwick's mouth hardened. He was already irritated by Amalie's presumptuous appearance at the party, and now he began to wonder if she had been drinking. Her persistence might have been pitiable had it not been so damned embarrassing.

Ginevra looked inquiringly at her husband, and after a moment's hesitation he interpreted, "Madame de Villeneuve is afraid you will try to turn me into a henpecked husband."

Ginevra caught her breath, aware that every eye in the room was trained on them with acute interest. So—the woman was wasting no time with preliminaries, belittling her with her very first words, and now their audience listened avidly for her response. In a voice that carried across the hushed room, Ginevra said sweetly, "I think, Richard, that if Madame de Villeneuve knew you better she would realize that no woman could ever control you. Only a fool would try."

Bravo! the marquess thought with admiration. A hit, a very palpable hit. His mouth quirked as he looked down at his wife. "And you're not a fool, are you, little Ginnie?"

"Not anymore," she said. In the ensuing silence they could hear the strains of a waltz coming from the salon. Ginevra asked coyly, "Richard, could I be so bold as to ask you to dance with me? We've never done so, you know."

"Of course, my dear. At once. What a delightful idea." He turned to lead Ginevra into the other room, and she shifted her glance back to the flame-haired beauty, who was looking stunned. The simpering miss over whom Amalie had expected an easy victory had been a camouflage; to her amazement she discovered that beneath that soft girlish exterior was a woman who would fight ruthlessly to keep her man.

Ginevra said with cool formality, "Forgive us for deserting you, madame. It was a pleasure to meet you. I meant to compliment you on your lovely gown."

Still reeling, Amalie tried to lash back. She extended her arm clumsily, shaking her wrist so that the ruby bracelet flashed hotly against her pearl-grey kid gloves. "And what do you think of my bracelet?" she demanded desperately, her black eyes glittering. "This *joli bijou* was a recent—a *very* recent—gift from an . . . an admirer!"

The arm around Ginevra's waist tightened painfully, but her expression did not falter. She could feel her husband waiting anxiously for her reply, as if he were afraid he would have to rush to her defense. The knowledge of his support gave her added courage, and she answered in cold, clipped tones that indicated she had absorbed more of the marquess's personality than either had heretofore suspected. "How interesting, madame," she said, her tawny eyes hard above a pasted-on smile. "You are fortunate indeed to be of such large stature that you can wear masses of jewelry without being overwhelmed. I, on the other hand, find I must make do with my wedding rings." She turned and exited proudly, and the faint laughter that rippled through the room was not directed at her.

When she passed the music room, the marquess pulled to a halt in the corridor and declared, "I thought you wanted to dance."

Victory bubbled in her veins like champagne. "I do—but not now," she said breathlessly.

He gazed down at her, at her small, glowing face. Her cheeks were rosy, and her eyes were alight with triumph. He thought she had never looked more beautiful. Her chest heaved rapidly, as if from exertion, under the clinging white silk of her gown, and he had to force himself not to yank down the low, blue-laced neckline and bury his dark head between her milky breasts. When she did not speak, instead staring up at him as if she had never seen him before, he asked huskily, "What is it, Ginevra? Why do you seem so different?" Still she was silent. He said, "Forgive me for allowing you to be put in such an awkward position, but you handled it magnificently. I could hardly believe the change in you."

She blinked and licked her lips. "I . . . perhaps I just grew tired of people pushing me around."

Another waltz came to its tuneful conclusion, followed by scattered applause. "The dancing," Chadwick murmured, but Ginevra shook her head.

"I want to go home," she said. "Please, Richard, I want to be alone with you."

His blue eyes bored into her. "Ginnie . . ." he said, his deep voice unsteady.

"You told me you wouldn't come to me again until I invited you," she continued impetuously, troubled by his incomprehension. She cried, "Oh, Richard, what more must I say?"

He let out his breath with a hiss. Heedless of anyone who might be watching, he pulled her hard against him, her gentle perfume rising like incense to drug him. Into the brightness of her hair he rasped, "You needn't say a word, Ginnie. Dear God, not another word. . . ."

In the dimness of the closed carriage she faced him across the space between the two seats, as aware of his deeply engraved features as if, catlike, she could see them in the dark. The coach rattled over the rough pavement, its superior springs softening the long, rutted road between Greenwich and Mayfair to a smooth swaying action that would have seemed almost soothing were not the two passengers so impatient to reach their destination. Their mutual tension was almost tangible, filling the shadowy interior of the vehicle. Ginevra stared at the obscure figure of her husband, smelled his musky scent, and ached to touch him. An hour at least before they reached home—how could she bear to delay another hour?

"Waiting be damned!" the marquess growled, and he hauled her across the space into his arms.

She squealed, "Richard, heed the coachman!"

He stretched over her and pulled the leather curtain securely across the small communicating window behind the driver's box. "There," he chuckled grimly, "now he's blind to our activities, and unless he wants to be banished to my hunting box in northern Scotland, he'll be deaf as well." He wound his arms tightly, almost painfully about her. "Now, my girl," he muttered thickly, "be quiet and kiss me."

Like a reluctant student suddenly inspired by a brilliant teacher, she followed his tuition eagerly, absorbing in one late but breathtaking moment the import of the lessons he had tried so fruitlessly to teach her in the months since their marriage. She was dazed by her newfound knowledge, drunk with the sensations that flowed through her under the demanding pressure of his seeking hands and mouth, and her body tensed as he brought her closer to the final, devastating revelation.

"This is madness," he groaned, lifting his head from the breasts that gleamed naked and inviting even in the dim light. "I can't take you in a carriage like some light-skirt . . ."

"Please," she wailed, uncertain of what she begged for. She was out of control now, all inhibition lulled by the heady, erotic atmosphere inside the dark cab. The air was moist with their rapid breathing, perfumed and heavy with the mingled odors of their bodies. The gentle sway made her languid even as the ever-present throb of the horses' hooves picked up the beat of her own pulse. "Please," she said again, more softly, and she laced her fingers through his black curls and pulled his face down to hers.

She tugged at his cravat, her lips seeking the delicious warmth of his bare skin. She felt the pounding of his heart under her fingertips as if it were a new and momentous discovery.

She was not aware of the disarray he had made of her own clothing until he braced his long legs against the seat opposite and pulled her astride his lap, cupping her buttocks beneath her bunched skirt as he guided her quivering flesh down over his. She gasped at the ease and depth of their union, jerking in surprise, and he murmured, "Softly, softly," as his hot mouth closed on hers.

She did not know when she began to sob, when the dizzy pressure welling inside her forced her breath from her in low, hoarse gasps that she tried futilely to stifle against his strong throat as she clung to him. She could feel him shaking with joyous triumph. He urged, "Don't fight it, Ginnie, I want to hear you."

Her voice was a high, thin thread of sound. "But I think I'm dying . . ."

"No, Ginnie," he soothed, his lips moving hungrily over

her flushed face, "no, my darling. You're just now coming alive." His arms crushed her against him convulsively as they finished their dance of life together.

She lay against his chest weakly, helpless and bemused, conscious only of the steady throb of his heart beneath her ear, and comforting hands that sleeked back her tumbled hair. When he pulled her gown up onto her shoulders and smoothed the skirt down over her thighs, she looked at him in confusion. He said quietly, "We're almost home."

"Oh, no," she choked. "My clothes . . . the servants . . ."

"Don't worry," he chuckled, kissing her lightly on the nose, "they're all deaf and blind, remember?" Quickly he repaired his own dishabille, and he reached for her blue silk evening cloak. As he draped it modestly about her, he smiled infectiously so that she too began to laugh. When he carried her still giggling into the house, swaddled in the protective folds of her cape, the only sign that anyone noticed them was the bedroom door that closed with deliberate slowness just down the corridor from their own.

❧❧ 9 ❧❧

"You are certainly in a gay mood, my lady. The party last night must have been a good one."

Ginevra glanced up, bemused, to stare at her companion, who sat facing her in the open phaeton. "I beg your pardon, Susan?"

The maid repeated, "I said, you must have enjoyed the party, my lady. You've been humming a bit of waltz music ever since we left the house."

Ginevra blinked. "No, we didn't dance," she said. After a moment she shook her head hard and declared, "Oh, Susan, you must think me quite bird-witted today. Forgive me, I suppose I'm still a little tired. Yes, thank you, I did enjoy the party very much."

"That's good, my lady." Susan smiled benignly. As soon as she had entered her mistress's bedroom that morning she had noticed the rumpled pillow beside Ginevra's own, the sensuous shadows beneath her sleepy gold eyes, and Susan had felt a great rush of relief that, whatever the argument that had estranged the master and his young bride these last weeks, it had apparently been settled to their mutual satisfaction. She asked, "Will you be going out tonight, my lady?"

"No," Ginevra said, "I shall stay home. His lordship will be abroad, however. Some kind of political meeting."

"I have to go," he had sighed that morning, reluctantly unwinding her arms from around his neck, "but I promise this will be the last time. From now on I shall devote myself entirely to you."

"You mean you truly *are* becoming a henpecked hus-

172

band?" she had teased lightly, and his punishment for her audacity had been swift and highly pleasurable. . . .

Ginevra still tingled with the memory when she instructed the coachman to wait while she and Susan made their way into the covered promenade of the Burlington Arcade. Sunlight streamed through the high arched sky-lights, striping the narrow storefronts with their bow windows full of attractively arranged merchandise. When they entered Madame Annette's exclusive establishment, they were quickly escorted into the private room reserved for Madame's better customers, where they could await the couturiere in comfort. Just as the burly female clerk closed the door behind them, Ginevra was seized by a wave of dizziness so intense she almost collapsed.

"My lady!" Susan cried, catching her arm and half-dragging her to the velvet settee. Ginevra sank weakly onto the scratchy upholstery, her hands pressed against her white face. "Dear Lord," she gasped in astonishment, trying to catch her breath, "what could have brought that on?"

Susan hovered about solicitously. "Has the megrim passed, my lady? Shall I fetch you a glass of water? Do you have your vinaigrette?"

"I don't carry smelling salts," Ginevra said, shaking her head to clear it. "I've never needed them." She blinked hard and massaged her throbbing temples. "Lord," she said again, "I haven't felt like that since . . . no, I'm not sure I remember ever feeling quite like that."

"Perhaps you're hungry," Susan suggested. "Did you eat much breakfast?"

"No. Only coffee, and little of that. Lately nothing seems to agree with me, and I . . ." Her voice trailed away at the knowing smile that began to spread across Susan's placid features. "Susan?" she asked uncertainly.

"Oh, my lady!" the girl exclaimed with amusement. "Don't you know?"

Ginevra stared at her. Slowly, slowly, one hand slid down from her bloodless cheek, along her throat, and over her soft breast, to spread gently and protectively across her belly. Her gold eyes clouded and became opaque as she turned her vision inward, bewildered and elated, frightened and . . . and exalted. Was it truly possible that she was increasing? Of course it was, and yet the idea had never occurred to her. She wondered why she had not considered the obvious consequences of submitting to her husband's potent strength. She thought back, calculating the signs: it must have happened very soon after the marquess returned to Dowerwood for her, perhaps even that first traumatic night, although she sincerely hoped not. She would have preferred their child to have been conceived in mutual joy such as they had shared the night before, not in pain and fear—but suddenly that didn't matter anymore. A baby. She was going to give her husband their baby.

She looked up at Susan and said firmly, "Of course I shall want the doctor to confirm it before I tell anyone, so I hope you will refrain from spreading the news to the rest of the servants until we are sure."

"As you wish, my lady," Susan said with a grin. "Not that there can be much doubt. There's but one reason I know of why a healthy young woman—"

Their conversation was interrupted by the arrival of Madame Annette, a rake-thin grey-haired woman with sharp eyes, whose thick French accent was superseded in moments of stress by the nasal twang of her native Ipswich. She gushed, "*Madame la marquise,* you honor my humble establishment. How may I serve you today?"

Still dazed by her discovery, Ginevra had to think hard to remember the purpose of her errand. "The orchid-colored lace gown you included in my trousseau," she said after a moment, indicating the long box that Susan held out. "The style and cut are exceptionally attractive, but my husband feels the color does not become me, and he has instructed me to ask if you would make a new dress, in another color, something softer." She recited her instructions by rote, realizing even as she did that soon the style and cut of the dress might be unsuitable as well.

The woman did not seem to notice her distraction. She held the gown to Ginevra's face and studied it critically. "*Oui, monsieur le marquis* is correct as usual. This fabric is far too matronly for you, the purple color makes Madame's beautiful complexion look dull and sallow. I shall go *toute de suite* and personally choose something that will complement that young skin *comme la pêche*."

Ginevra watched her go, and she wondered what the woman would say if she told her that a few months before, her wardrobe had consisted entirely of sturdy, graceless dresses she had fashioned herself. She suspected that few of Annette's customers would even know how to thread a needle.

When the door from the lobby opened, Ginevra paid no attention, instead musing dreamily about the strange and wonderful changes that had come into her life in the past several months, the even greater changes yet to come. She did not notice the tall woman who loomed over her, shredding a swatch of fabric with her long crimson fingernails, until she uttered harshly, "*Mon Dieu*, so he sends you here for your dresses as well! I did not realize that he was so partial to Annette's designs—or perhaps it is simply that he finds it easier to maintain one account for both his wife and his mistress!"

Ginevra looked up at the statuesque beauty and recoiled instinctively from the hatred radiating unmasked from her, now that they were alone. Beside Ginevra, Susan gasped, and the girl's patent fear revived Ginevra's waning courage. She held up one hand in silent warning to the maid, and she stared back at the striking red-haired woman who towered over her. She must never ever let the Frenchwoman know that she rattled her. She said coolly, "Madame de Villeneuve, when you try to cause a scene in this manner, you do nothing but play the fool."

Amalie was shaken and infuriated by Ginevra's unbreachable confidence. She was not used to being bested by other women, especially not half-fledged girls, and her frustration made her crude. "*Merde!*" she snorted. "You are the one being played for a fool. Do you fancy he is in love with you? Not two days after he married you he came back to my bed!"

"Yes, I know," Ginevra said quietly, her expression impassive, although inside she felt limp with relief. How ironic that Amalie's charge, intended to devastate her, had quite the opposite effect. Two days after the wedding he would yet have been reeling from Ginevra's rejection, and, thwarted and angry, he would have sought out the woman in order to reaffirm his manhood. Of course it hurt to think of him touching Amalie, but Ginevra could accept his action, knowing that the fault was partly her own. The pain would have been less bearable had he gone to his mistress after consummating his marriage to Ginevra. She said again, "Yes, I know he went to you. You serve a cold dish." She turned to her maid, who listened with an ashen face, gossip in the servants' quarters never having prepared her for a situation like this. Susan was speechless with admiration at the way her lady said evenly, with subtle emphasis, "Please go tell Madame Annette that I must insist on privacy for my fittings. If she feels she cannot provide it, I shall be forced to take my custom elsewhere."

"At once, my lady," the girl gulped, plunging toward the door the dressmaker had disappeared through. In seconds she returned with the woman, who was laden with two great bolts of fabric. "*Ma chère* Madame Chadwick," she trilled, "I have found just the thing for you. This pale pink *peau de soie* will look *très ravissante* made up in that style you like, and while I was looking I also found—" She choked off her words when she noticed Amalie's presence in the room. After a moment's frozen shock her shrewdly assessing eyes quickly flicked between the two women, the young wife who radiated serene self-assurance, the overblown mistress whose star seemed to be in eclipse.

With a rush Amalie began, "I want to see those new Chinese silks you—"

Ginevra interrupted sweetly but firmly, "I really must have privacy, or I shan't be able to make a selection." Annette was galvanized into action, her decision made. She dropped the rolls of fabric into Susan's arms and stalked over to Amalie, grabbing her roughly with bony, work-hardened fingers and propelling her toward the door.

Amalie, used to unctuous deference in her position as *chère amie* to a prominent man, demanded, "How dare you! Have you forgotten I'm one of your best customers?"

"Not when you make trouble in my shop, you ain't, dearie," Annette growled, all trace of Paris absent from her voice. "Now, be sensible and get out before I have to call my clerk to help me."

Still Amalie resisted. She twisted from the seamstress's grasp and ran back to Ginevra, who was delicately fingering the silky texture of a bolt of honey-colored wool. Amalie looked down at the gleaming golden curls on that bent head, and she shouted with loathing, "He'll abandon you too, you know! He always does. He despises women!"

Ginevra resolutely ignored her. She said to her maid, "Tell me, Susan, how do you think this would do for a riding habit for this autumn? Is the color too light to be serviceable?"

Susan laughed. "Oh, my lady, you'd better give up all thought of riding, at least until next spring."

"Yes, I expect you're right," Ginevra agreed, her hand straying self-consciously to her abdomen again.

When Amalie heard this exchange, she was so stunned that she went peaceably when Madame Annette and her clerk ejected her from the shop.

Pregnant! she thought with a mixture of grudging admiration and disgust as she guided her yellow-wheeled curricle through the midday traffic. The little bitch was *enceinte*. No wonder she felt confident of her power over Chadwick: she had pulled off the one trick Amalie had never dared try, fearing it might prove as bad a miscalculation as her marriage all those years before to a young subaltern she erroneously thought was a close relation of the admiral who killed Nelson. More than once Amalie had considered "forgetting" the piece of vinegar-soaked sponge she always placed carefully deep in her vagina before the marquess's calls, but no—there was no guarantee he would marry her, and she was not about to risk her figure or her health for a brat that would quickly have to be foisted off to the baby-farmers. And if Chadwick had somehow got the idea that the child was not his . . .

Amalie was strangely thoughtful as she drove toward Hyde Park. She knew now that she had lost the marquess forever. She had been far too confident, had overplayed her hand, and that whey-faced little chit had taken the trick. But Amalie was not a woman to accept defeat meekly; the deeper strains of her Creole blood demanded satisfaction, revenge. She guided her horses into the park and began to make the slow circuit. A handful of starers loitered behind the rails and gawked at her, awed by the dashing red-haired beauty who dared to drive her own curricle publicly. Their admiration was mild balm to her wounded vanity, but she wasted no time on them. She was depressed by the small number of vehicles in the park, evidence of the annual flight of fashionable society. She ought to have gone off to Brighton and charmed one of the royal dukes, instead of hanging around London like a lovesick girl, waiting for Chadwick to call on her. Perhaps she could get the Carstairs boy to take her to the seashore. He was reasonably attractive, rich, and ripe for the plucking, and only the futile hope that she could regain her hold on Chadwick had kept Amalie from seducing him. Now that the marquess was gone, she supposed she ought to use her wiles on the lad. Perhaps it would relax her; certainly it would require little effort. Boys were utterly gullible and so cocky about their attraction that they never questioned a woman's motives. They always seemed to think that they were the first man ever to have an erection. . . . Yes, it might be amusing to see the expression on that *guenon* Lady Carstairs' face when she found out her little "angel" had been——what would she call it?——debauched. But before Amalie could enjoy spiting the old hag, she first had to think of a way to pay back Chadwick for spurning her.

From across the circuit Amalie noticed with interest a lone rider gazing at her, and she tilted her head down so that she could study him unobserved from under the brim of her stylish bonnet. Extremely young, but tall and fair. Well-dressed, and that grey stallion was certainly a bit of prime blood. Her black eyes widened with surprise when she recognized him. *Ma foi*, the little boy was growing up! And from the way he stared at her, he found her as fascinating as his father had done, once upon a time.

Amalie clicked the reins to speed her carriage's progress around the ring, closing the gap between her and Bysshe. Her mouth hardened into a smug grin. All at once she knew how she was going to get her revenge.

Ginevra wrapped her dressing gown about her and asked, "Well, am I right?"

Jules Perrin wiped his hands on the towel Susan held out to him, and he said, "Of course, madame. You didn't need me to tell you you are with child."

She smiled. "No, I suppose not." Her gold eyes became thoughtful. "Do you think there will be any difficulty? Pray be frank. I helped deliver a baby once, so I do have some idea of what is involved."

He spread his hands in a very Gallic gesture and said, "There is no way to tell at this point. You are in good health and are probably stronger than your fragile appearance would lead one to believe. However, you are also *très petite*. Your husband is very tall, and the baby may be a large one. Beyond that, it is impossible to surmise."

"I see. In that case, monsieur, I shall leave my care in your capable hands and will not worry unless you tell me to."

"A most sensible attitude, madame." He began to pack his medical bag. "Does your husband know yet?"

"No. I shall tell Richard directly he comes in tonight."

"Bon," the doctor said. "I know he will be delighted. If you wish, I can suggest that he take you out of London soon. You will be more comfortable away from the heat and the bad air."

"Thank you. I'd like that." When he made as if to go, Ginevra exclaimed, "Oh, please don't leave yet. At least have some refreshment first." She signalled for Susan to fetch tea, and when the girl had curtsied and departed, Ginevra led the doctor into her sitting room.

As they made themselves comfortable, Perrin noted with eager eyes that belied his outward placidity, "I do not see Mademoiselle Jarvis about. Is she frequenting the bookstores once again?"

Ginevra stared at him. "Didn't you know?" she asked in dismay. "I thought someone, perhaps even Emma herself, would have told you. She has left my service to return to Surrey."

He did not move. "Surrey," he echoed thickly, his face grey. "Why?"

Ginevra watched him with compassion. His pain was almost tangible. She stammered, "Emma had to get away from . . . from London. She . . . hates the city."

"Who does not?" he muttered. Under his breath he swore violently in French; then he looked up at Ginevra with bleak eyes. "Tell me truthfully, I beg you, did she leave because of me—or do I delude myself by thinking I might have influence on her actions?" Ginevra hesitated, and he continued desperately, "When we worked together at Dowerwood, Emma and I, we contrived well, I sensed a certain sympathy in her, and I hoped . . . But as soon as the young *vicomte* recovered, she changed, became distant, and here in the city I have scarcely seen her at all." He leaned forward in his chair to plead, "*Chère* madame, you know her so well: did I offend her in some way?"

Ginevra bit her lip and shook her head. "No, monsieur," she said gently, "the fault is not with you personally, nor with any deed of yours. I will admit, however, that she is attentive to the difference in your . . . stations."

"Station?" Perrin repeated ironically. "I have no station. My title disappeared when the rabble shouting '*Liberté, égalité, fraternité!*' burned my home and slaughtered my family. There is no difference now between a physician and a lady's maid."

"Schoolteacher now," Ginevra corrected, and the doctor looked puzzled. While she explained the plans Emma had outlined to her, Susan returned with refreshments, and they drank their tea in pensive silence. The doctor rubbed the aching muscles of his crippled leg, an action that Ginevra was beginning to recognize as a sign of tension. He said, "I approve very much of what Emma wants to do. We would have made a very good team, she and I, she attending to the minds of the poor, I to their bodies."

Ginevra ventured awkwardly, "Forgive me for prying, but truly I don't understand how you can feel such mercy toward the people who robbed you of so much."

He sighed. "I have tried to put bitterness behind me. Besides, the people who sheltered and cared for me in those days were no less indigent than the ones in the mob. The hungry have no politics."

"Monsieur," Ginevra asked suddenly, "if Richard takes me back to the country for my confinement, will you come with me?"

"Of course, madame. You know I am always at your service."

"I thought . . ." She paused, framing her request. She continued more firmly, "I thought you might use the time to look around the countryside, with an eye to remaining there permanently. You know we are in desperate need of a new physician at Queenshaven, and you said you prefer rural life. I am sure Richard would be delighted to provide you with a house, in exchange for attending the tenants, and you would be available to . . . anyone else who might need you . . ."

"Such as a certain schoolmistress?" Perrin asked dryly.

Ginevra colored. "It was but a thought."

He nodded. "And a thought I like very much. I should be delighted to do as you request."

Afraid she had said too much, Ginevra added hastily, "Of course, there is no guarantee that Emma would—"

"*Je vous écoute,* madame," he agreed sagely. "There is not a guarantee. But in any case it would not be a hardship for me to leave London. *Au contraire!*" He smiled warmly. "As to the other, I will just have to be patient, won't I?"

Ginevra sat curled up in a massive armchair in the library, leafing through a volume of Byron's poetry without absorbing any of it. The room was silent except for the faint whisper of the gaslight and the pounding of her heart. She had dressed and come downstairs once more to await her husband's return, and now every footfall in the hallway made her leap up expectantly, only to subside with disappointment when the steps passed by without pausing. At last she heard the front door open, and the butler greeted someone in a low monotone. Hard booted heels strode across the marble entryway and turned down the long corridor, approaching the library. She glanced up eagerly, her golden eyes shining with anticipation at the tall man who loomed in the doorway.

It was Bysshe.

Her hopes blasted yet again, Ginevra forced her mouth into a smile and said politely, "Hello, Bysshe, how are you? I haven't seen you all day."

His young face was oddly pale and intent as he stared at her silently for a long moment. "Ginnie," he gulped hoarsely. After another pause he stammered uncertainly, "The . . . the butler told me that . . . that Dr. Perrin was here to see you. You aren't sick, are you?"

Ginevra's smile was genuine now, sweetened with the secret she was determined to relate first to her husband. "No, I am excellent well, thank you. I merely needed to consult with him about something."

Bysshe glanced around, brown eyes furtive. "*He* is not here, is he?" he asked, and Ginevra knew at once that he meant the marquess. He never referred to his father by name, she noticed curiously.

She said, "No, Richard is out for the evening." She gestured to a chair. "Won't you please sit down? You make me quite apprehensive, hovering like that."

He looked at her strangely. "You mustn't be afraid of me, Ginnie. You know I'd never hurt you."

Her brows lifted. "I never suggested that you would. Whatever can be the matter with you, to think such a thing?"

He brushed one hand across his eyes. "I don't know," he mumbled. "Perhaps . . . perhaps it is just the heat."

She watched him with concern. Indeed the boy did not look well; she had the impression that he had been living on his nerves for weeks. She rose and crossed the room to him. "You're sure your ear is not troubling you again?" She touched his forehead experimentally, to check for fever. His skin felt clammy.

He caught her fingers in his own and smiled weakly. "Little mother," he mused fondly, "how you've always taken care of me. . . ." He dropped her hand and brushed his lank hair from his eyes. "I could do with a bit of fresh air," he said brightly, "and I expect you could too. Will you come for a ride with me?"

"A ride?" Ginevra hesitated, remembering Susan's admonition earlier. "It's rather late to be taking out the horses, isn't it?"

He shook his head. "You still think in terms of country hours. Here the evening is just beginning. Besides, I did not mean for us to go on horseback. I have a curricle we could—"

"But we don't have a curricle," Ginevra persisted.

He said impatiently, "I borrowed it from . . . from someone. I thought I would see how I like driving a light vehicle, in case I have a mind to purchase one later." When she still looked uncertain, his tone softened, became cajoling. "Please, Ginnie, it would do you good to get out of the house, and I promise I shan't put us in a ditch."

"I should hope not," Ginevra declared with a smile, relenting. It had been so long since Bysshe had spoken to her in anything approaching a normal manner that she hated to spoil this new-sprung amity by rejecting his overture. Besides, the alternative was to spend what might prove to be several hours alone, becoming increasingly tense and agitated as she awaited her husband's return. "Very well," she agreed, "let me fetch a wrap."

Susan's disapproval was evident as she helped Ginevra into her lightweight pelisse. "You must be extra careful now, my lady," she cautioned. " 'Twould be a sorry thing indeed if aught were to happen now that—"

"Susan," Ginevra laughed, "we're not going racing, for heaven's sake! Lord Bysshe is simply taking me out for a brief drive, a chance to enjoy the cool of the evening. I expect we'll be back in less than an hour."

"Whatever you say, my lady," Susan grumbled, and Ginevra was still chuckling at her tacit rebuke when Bysshe handed her into the jaunty yellow-wheeled curricle pulled by a pair of high-spirited matched blacks.

"This is quite an elegant equipage," Ginevra observed as Bysshe settled beside her and took up the ribbons. "Who did you say lent it to you?"

"A . . . friend." Bysshe shrugged, snapping the reins. The horses responded instantly, and the carriage pulled away from the block with a jolt.

"Must be a good friend," Ginevra said nervously as she clutched at the armrest. "Are you certain you can handle this?"

Bysshe growled, "Yes, Ginnie, I promise nothing will happen to you."

His increasing recklessness alarmed her suddenly, the stress that seemed to radiate from him. When the curricle did not turn into Hyde Park as she had expected, but instead continued unabated westward along the Kensington Road, passing the moonlit depths of the Serpentine and leaving the city traffic behind to plunge deeper into the darkness of the rolling countryside, she cried, "Bysshe, for the love of God, where are you going?" His only answer was to urge his cattle to greater speed.

The road out of London was twisted and bumpy, and the thick, eerie shadows cast by the silvery moonlight reminded Ginevra of just how dark a country night could be. Only the jouncy yellow light cast by the two lanterns on the front of the curricle gave any hint of the road before them. Bysshe snapped his whip and the horses raced still faster. "Bysshe!" Ginevra cried again. She grabbed at his arm, and he swore violently and knocked her away with his elbow. The galloping horses swerved at the tug on the reins, raising the light rig on one wheel and almost oversetting it. They seemed to sense the novice hand driving them, and they began to panic. Bysshe struggled fiercely to regain control, straining on the leather ribbons with all the power of his adolescent muscles, and by the time he was able to pull the panting, lathered animals to a halt on the grassy verge alongside the road, his coat was drenched with sweat and his hands were blistered and bleeding. He turned on Ginevra, who huddled in the corner of the seat shaking and nauseous with fright, and he shrieked, "You stupid fool, you could have killed us both!"

Her body felt battered and jolted, and her heart seemed unable to accept that that mad race had ended, that the carriage was now at a standstill. She bowed her head and clutched at her thin arms, trying to fight off the dizzy sickness that threatened to overwhelm her. Whenever she tried to look up at him, fear rose like gall in her throat and choked her. At last she was able to gasp, "Have you . . . taken leave of . . . your senses? Why . . . why are you doing this?"

One of the lanterns had blown out in their wild flight, and the murky light from the remaining lamp cast wavering shadows that distorted and aged Bysshe's youthful features. He gazed down at her with eyes that seemed sunken and unfathomable, and he said slowly, "I have to save you, Ginnie."

She could only gape. When she did not speak, he amplified urgently, "I have to get you away from him. I can't let him . . . defile you."

She forced her heart to slow its pounding; she commanded her breath to smooth its ragged gait. When she felt she had the strength, with great care she eased herself upright on the seat and asked, "Bysshe Glover, what on earth are you talking about?"

"Him—the marquess," he said. "I have to get you away from him before he ruins you."

Ginevra's warm eyes turned cold. "You are talking about my husband," she said steadily.

"So what? He was my mother's husband, and he drove her away!" The boy's voice rose clamantly. "Ginnie, you don't know the kind of man he is. Even since you've been married he's been seen in bordellos of the lowest sort. He likes to . . . to debauch women, to turn them into whores. Why, that Frenchwoman was virtuous before he seduced her!"

Ginevra snorted, "Who told you that—*her?*"

The sulfurous light could not disguise the bright color that painted his cheeks as he mumbled, "I . . . I met her today, Ginnie. In the park. At first I could not believe that she would dare to approach me, but when she did, I found I could . . . could not turn away." His voice grew firmer, more steady, and Ginevra listened in amazement as he spoke. "Madame de Villeneuve is a very beautiful woman," he said seriously, "and a greatly wronged one. When she spoke to me, I . . . I thought at first that she was trying her wiles on me, yet it soon became clear that her sole concern was for you, Ginnie."

"Me?" she choked, uncertain whether to laugh or scream. The woman's audacity was incredible, surpassed only by the boy's gullibility.

"Yes, Ginnie, you! Madame de Villeneuve told me frankly that she knows it is too late to save her, but she is much concerned that you should not suffer the same fate. She says she knows how easy it is for a young girl to be bewitched by the man's charms, and something must be done to save you from him now, before you are irretrievably lost."

Ginevra shook her head impatiently. "Oh, Bysshe, you idiot, can't you see what she is doing? She has told you only what you wanted to hear. Women of her . . . her profession are very good at that. But I am surprised at you. How can you believe such lies?"

His soft mouth hardened into a sneer of distaste. "I might not have believed her—had I not seen you come home last night." Ginevra blanched. He said, "I could hear the pair of you even before he carried you up the stairs. You were giggling like some drunken bawd, your clothes were half off, and your hands were all over him, and you . . . you practically reeked with the smell of him!"

Ginevra felt violated. She bit her lip and screwed her eyes shut to still her trembling. Tears spilled from beneath her silky lashes. Suddenly her patience with the boy disappeared like mist burnt away by the scorching, blinding anger that ignited in her, and she gritted, "Damn you, Bysshe Glover, damn you to hell! How dare you spy on something that was private and personal and . . . and beautiful—"

"Beautiful?" he exclaimed in horror, and he grabbed her shoulders and shook her as if to convince her of his sincerity. "Oh, Ginnie, can't you see? If you are so lost to all decency that you can think—"

She jerked her left arm free of his grasp and slapped him hard across the mouth.

The sound of that blow seemed to echo over the quiet, moon-drenched fields surrounding them. The two horses stirred uneasily in their harness. Bysshe lifted his hand to his face and touched his mouth gingerly; his fingertips came away stained with blood from where the stones on her betrothal ring had sliced his lip. His brown eyes narrowed and he took a deep, rasping breath.

Ginevra said, "Take me home, Bysshe. Take me home now."

Slowly he shook his head. "No, Ginnie. I must get you away before it is too late, before his hold on you becomes unbreakable."

She was beginning to think she had stumbled into some nightmare, some drug-induced fantasy that stubbornly refused to dissolve in the face of reality. She pleaded desperately, "Bysshe, I beg you—you must understand. It is already too late: I love him and I carry his child."

All color drained from his face, leaving behind in the dim jaundiced light a parchment mimicry of his features, like a death mask—the death of Bysshe's youth. Helplessly Ginevra watched his bloodied lips gasp for air. She wondered if he would faint. Then as she gazed at him, mesmerized, suddenly the color returned, flowing under his skin in waves of yellow, pink, red, until his face blackened with rage. All at once she became aware of the hazard of her position, her vulnerability, and she tried to retreat, moving backward across the leather seat until she was brought up sharp against the low armrest. Defenselessly she watched as Bysshe exploded, *"You bitch!"*—and when he raised his hand to strike her down, there was no place she could flee.

The Marquess of Chadwick felt young, younger than he had in years. He alit from the carriage with a spring in his step that had been missing since . . . Sweet Jesus!—could it really have been since Maria? He dismissed the coachman and strode up the shadowed walkway toward his front door. No, he decided, he refused to believe that his life's mood could have been dictated for almost twenty years by that travesty of a first marriage. Rather, he judged, his discontent must have settled upon him at about the same time that he started his stint as uncredentialled diplomat. Cynicism was inevitable when a man saw the future of Europe decided frequently not on battlefields but in brothels, the deaths of a thousand brave men as nothing compared to the charms of a whore with suitably exotic talents.

But all that was behind him now, he thought with relief as he reached for the massive brazen handle that gleamed in the glow of the porch light. He had at last kept the vow he had made to himself and had tendered his resignation, had resisted the blandishments of those at the ministry who urged him to stay on, and now he was going to devote his energies to the growing of crops and the welfare of his tenants. Times were hard and he had neglected them shamefully. In the brief time he and Ginevra had been married she had shown more concern for the people of Queenshaven than he had in all his years since acceding to the title.

"M'lord!"

His hand froze and he jerked his head around to peer blindly in the direction of that furtive hiss. The voice seemed to arise from the penumbral depths of the shrubbery lining the walk.

"M'lord!" came the call again, and as he watched, a small shape wrapped in a plain dark cloak of a servant crept out of the shadows and approached him timidly, with the stiff labored gait of one who had been waiting for hours. When the hood of her cloak fell away to reveal the face of a young girl of no more than twelve or thirteen years, he recognized her vaguely as one of Amalie's maids, one of the anonymous figures that had moved about dimly in the background of that sultry erotic fantasy that had been his affair with the Frenchwoman. It occurred to Chadwick that he ought to know the child's name because he had probably been paying her wages.

The thought of Amalie annoyed him, and he demanded irritably, "What do you want?" The girl shrank back. After a moment she stepped forward again to offer him a pale green envelope that reeked of patchouli even at a distance. His mouth thinned, and he refused to take it. She held the note closer and implored, "Oh, please, m'lord! If I didn't deliver her note my mistress would . . ."

He looked down at her wide, frightened eyes, and he shook his head impatiently, sighing. "Very well. Far be it from me to bring down Amalie's wrath on someone smaller than she is." He accepted the envelope, grimacing at the smell, and he asked, "Is there supposed to be an answer?"

The girl said, "No, m'lord. My mistress was just on her way out of town when she gave it to me. We don't know when she'll be back."

Chadwick received this news with an inscrutable expression. "That's a relief," he murmured, and he produced a coin and handed it to the maid. "Here, child," he said with a commiserating smile, "you've done as you were bid. Now, hurry home, it's much too late for you to be abroad."

"Thank you, m'lord." The girl bobbed a quick curtsy and fled into the shadows.

When Chadwick stepped into the brightly illuminated entryway, he discovered Susan huddled in anxious conference with the butler. In his surprise he forgot the note. In Chadwick's experience household servants were as territorial as cats, and the maid's presence downstairs in what was chiefly the butler's domain was unusual enough to make him faintly disquieted. "Is something amiss?" he asked when the butler scurried over to retrieve his hat and gloves.

The man smiled imperturbably. "I expect Susan is exaggerating, as is the wont of young women," he said. "I'm sure there is nothing to be concerned about."

"Yes there is!" Susan interrupted, crowding roughly between the two men. Ignoring the butler's squawk of outrage, she clutched at the marquess's lapels with trembling fingers and pleaded, so agitated that she stuttered, "M-my lord, y-you must do something! Oh, please, I know something dreadful has happened!"

Chadwick caught her wrists gently and put her away from him, studying her grey face as he did so. Beneath her neat cap the girl was shaking with fright. He said in quiet, soothing tones, "Compose yourself, Susan. I shall help you in any way I can, but before I can do so, you must try to calm down." He watched her struggle to regain her self-control, and when she seemed to have herself in check, he asked, "Now, girl, what may I do for you?"

Susan cried desperately, "But, my lord, it's not me! It's her ladyship. She's gone!"

He stared at her blankly. "What do you mean, she's gone?"

"She went for a drive and she said she'd be back within the hour—"

The butler, offended that a maid had bypassed his authority, interposed, "My lord, I'm sure the wench has merely misinterpreted Lady Chadwick's instructions."

Susan turned on him furiously, spitting with indignation. "No I did not, you old fool! I warned her ladyship she must be careful now, and she promised she and his young lordship would only be gone a short while—"

The butler yelped, "Don't get high in the instep with me, missy! I was here long before—"

"Quiet!" the marquess bellowed, and the squabbling servants fell silent instantly, quailing before the cold light of command that blazed in his blue eyes. "That's enough, both of you!" He took a deep, shuddering breath and said in a strained voice, "All right, I wish to have this clear: you say my wife left the house this evening and has not returned?"

"Yes, my lord. She went for a ride with his young lordship."

"I see. Who drove them?"

Susan looked at the butler, and he shrugged. She ventured, "No one, my lord. Her ladyship said they were taking a curricle."

Chadwick scowled. "My stable does not include a curricle."

"No, my lord," Susan agreed, "but that is what she said."

Little sparks of alarm began to shoot off in the back of Chadwick's head. He asked carefully, "And at what hour did they go out for this drive?"

Again the two servants glanced at each other, and the butler said, "I am not sure of the exact time, my lord, but it was not long after the doctor departed."

Silence loomed up between them. At last the marquess groaned, "My God, I think I must be surrounded by half-wits! Why was the doctor here? Why was I not informed at once?"

After another awkward pause Susan said quietly, "It was her ladyship's wish, my lord. She wanted to be the one to give you the news herself."

Suddenly Chadwick felt as if his breath had been punched out of him. "The news?" he echoed hoarsely.

"Yes, my lord," Susan said reluctantly. "Her ladyship is . . . is increasing. Forgive me for going against her wishes by telling you. I would never have done so, except . . ."

Chadwick turned away, his harsh features pale under his tan. "I see," he rasped. "Thank you, Susan. You were quite right to let me know." He stared down at his hands, amazed to find them steady. How fair she was, Ginnie, his beautiful child-woman, now gravid with child herself.

Susan called, "My lord, ought not someone go search for them?"

He blinked and looked back at the girl, surprised to discover that his feet had carried him across the gleaming marble floor almost to the door of his study. After a moment's hesitation he said with forced casualness, "I think perhaps it is too early to send out runners. After all, if there had been an accident, I am sure someone from Bow Street would have informed us by now; it is not as if her ladyship and Lord Bysshe were strangers to the city. I expect what has happened is that they called on my mother and lost track of time." Even as he spoke Chadwick realized how lame that explanation sounded. To conceal his growing apprehension he said firmly, "Susan, go you to her ladyship's room and lay out her night things. She will undoubtedly be extremely weary when she comes home."

He saw the look that flashed in the girl's eyes, and he thought she was going to protest, but after the briefest of pauses she muttered, "Yes, my lord," and trudged toward the staircase, her steps weighted with disillusion. He felt a twinge of exasperation. Damn the chit, daring to condemn him for not rushing headlong into the streets like some latter-day knight-errant to rescue his ladylove. Just what did she expect him to do, where did she think he should go? At this point no one even knew for certain that a "rescue" was necessary. As he had suggested, Ginevra and Bysshe might very well be with his mother. Or at the last moment they might have decided to attend the theatre, or they might yet be driving, or . . . or . . .

Sternly he refused to consider alternatives. He was not some moon-minded adolescent to fall into a jealous panic whenever his lady was out of sight. At the door of his study he glanced at the butler, whose face was more stony than usual, as if to atone for that gross breach of etiquette that had allowed him to be discovered quarrelling with the maid. Chadwick snapped, "Inform me instantly my wife returns," and he slammed the door behind him.

He splashed brandy into a glass and sank into the chair behind his desk, only to rise again at once, far too agitated to relax. He leaned against the desk and mused. Ginvera was pregnant. Inside her slender body a child grew and developed, the fruit of his loins. He was startled by the intense wave of desire that pulsed through him, engorging him with its heat. God, why wasn't she here with him now so that he could hold her, caress her, reaffirm his potency . . . He chuckled wryly. If Ginnie didn't hurry home soon, he would be damned lucky if he could walk up the stairs.

He lifted the snifter to his lips and relished the rich bouquet of the brandy, his sensitive nose discerning the faint tang of the charred oak casks it had been aged in: good French stock, and not even contraband, although there were those who claimed the liquor had lost some of its savor when the blockade was lifted. As he sipped his drink, his nostrils twitched, and they picked up a discordant note, a whiff of some odor that seemed thin and acrid against the heady aroma of the brandy. Chadwick scowled and set the glass aside. After a moment he realized that what he smelled was the heavily perfumed note from Amalie.

He retrieved the green envelope from his pocket with a grimace of distaste, aware that it would require all of Hobbs's skill to remove that cloying scent from the fine fabric of his coat. Poor Hobbs! His much-imposed-upon valet had probably dared hope that at last such trying duties were behind him.

Chadwick's blue eyes narrowed as he broke the thick wax seal that was stamped with an elaborate and explicit representation of Venus Astarte. Amalie had never been one for subtlety, be it in the employment of her perfume or the gratification of her appetites in bed, and Chadwick was amazed now to think that their relationship had continued for as long as it had without his becoming jaded much sooner. But now at last—praise God!—Amalie seemed to have accepted the termination of their affair. The little maid had said that her mistress had left town, and no doubt this message was a long and lugubrious farewell.

Thus Chadwick was surprised to flip open the single folded sheet of paper and discover but three terse sen-

tences penned in Amalie's distinctive spiky, back-slanted
hand: "*Adieu, mon chèr* Richard, *le jeu est fait.* Your
son has eloped with your wife. I wish you joy on becoming a grandfather."

ᨒᨑ 10 ᨑᨒ

He stared at the note, revolted and fascinated. He felt
awed by the depth of his mistress's malice, strangely
humbled to realize that the life he had lived so heedlessly
could have inspired such hatred. Amalie's revenge. Dear
God, had he dared to think she was not subtle? Obviously
she knew him far better than he had ever known her!
With deadly cunning and accuracy she had searched out
his most vulnerable spot and had probed it mercilessly,
stimulating half-dead hurts and hostilities to new and
painful life. She knew his ambivalence toward the son of
his first marriage, and somehow she had managed to em-
ploy the boy as agent in destroying the second. Bysshe
would have been an easy gull, Chadwick saw now: he had
been building to this explosion for weeks, and Amalie had
made skillful use of his burgeoning anger. As a final
ironic twist, the marquess realized with grudging admiration, Amalie must have arranged for the elopement to be
carried out in the very curricle he had bought for her.

The one thing the Frenchwoman had underestimated
was his trust in Ginevra. He knew there were many differ-
ences yet to be resolved between him and his young bride,
he knew she was still uncertain of her feelings toward
him, but never would he believe that she might he un-
faithful to him—especially not after last night.

But where were Ginevra and Bysshe now? He rubbed
his aching temples and tried to think. God alone knew
what lies Amalie must have fed to those impetuous children to make them flee into the night, and now he had to
find them before something regrettable happened. But
where could they be? Obviously with only a light vehicle

195

they could not have followed the fashion for elopements and gone haring off to Scotland, so they must be somewhere close at hand, perhaps even still in London. His blue eyes blinked hard. Was it beyond the realm of possibility that they might truly have gone to his mother?

Lady Helena's butler staggered back, almost felled by the impact of the door Chadwick flung open. "Is my mother stirring?" he barked, and without waiting for an answer he bounded up the steps two at a time.

When he burst into his mother's bedroom, he found her propped against a great mound of pillows, reading, a pot of some fragrant tisane warming over a fairy lamp beside her bed. "Thank God you are awake!" he exclaimed.

She looked up and observed dryly, "Well, if I hadn't been, I certainly would be now! You make enough noise for a regiment of hussars!" She glanced at his face again and set aside her book, her faint smile fading. "What's wrong, Richard?" she asked quietly.

He knew the answer before he posed the question. "Are Ginnie and Bysshe here?"

Lady Helena's sharp eyes widened. "No. Why did you think they might be?"

He stared down at the shrunken figure huddled in her downy nest. Her face was lined with fatigue, and the thin silver braid that emerged from beneath her linen nightcap dangled limply over one shoulder. One of his earliest memories was of watching reverently as Lady Helena's maid brushed the blue-black tresses that flowed in a thick, iridescent swath down her back; he remembered that when he begged to be allowed to stroke her hair, it had felt springy, almost alive under his chubby fingertips.

"Richard, what has happened to upset you?" she asked again, and for answer he handed her the note from Amalie. One eyebrow arched delicately at the perfumed paper, but as she read the letter her face was carefully expressionless. At last she passed it back to him and asked bluntly, "Do you believe this?"

He shook his head. "No, of course not. I do know that something has happened to make them take flight, although I am uncertain whether Ginevra went willingly."

He hesitated before adding slowly, "Her maid tells me that, as the note implies, Ginnie is with child."

The years fell away from Lady Helena's face as she smiled tenderly. "I thought so."

Chadwick looked surprised. "You did? How could you tell?"

His mother shrugged. "Women can always tell. It's the eyes, I think. Besides"—she chuckled in a way that reminded him of all the years she had dwelt in France—"one could hardly expect your wife to be otherwise." Her amusement subsided, and the look of weary age returned. "You must find them quickly, Richard."

"I know—but how? Where could they have gone?"

She eyed the note he clutched in his long fingers and suggested, "I don't suppose it would accomplish anything to question the . . . friend . . . who dispatched that nasty piece of business?"

He crushed the green paper into a reeking wad and flung it away from him as if it were unclean. He said tightly, "I have it on good authority that Amalie has already left town."

Lady Helena nodded sardonically. "Very prudent," she judged. "Then what about Bysshe? Where would he be likely to go? You must have some idea."

Puzzling hard, Chadwick finally admitted with a groan, "No. I have no notion of how his mind works. We are strangers."

His mother winced with remembered pain and regarded him sadly. "That's a sorry admission."

"A true one, nonetheless," Chadwick sighed.

"*Plus ça change . . .*" she murmured. She thought again and said, "But surely there was someplace he used to go when he was unhappy or confused? Some place that meant security to him?"

"I cannot think of anywhere, unless it be . . ." His brows lifted. "Dowerwood?" His mother nodded sanguinely. He protested with an irritable wave of his hand, "But that makes no sense! A man decamping with another man's wife does not go—"

Lady Helena intervened hardly. "Bysshe is not a man,

Richard, pray you remember that. He is a little boy *trying to be* a man. That is a very nice, very significant distinction." She held out a placating hand. "Please, my son, try to understand."

Gently he caught her fragile fingers in his strong ones. He bent with courtly grace to brush his lips across them. "I understand, *ma chère*. And when I find our infant runaways I promise that I shall be—".

"No!" Lady Helena snapped, jerking her hand away from him. "You do not understand at all. You cannot deal with them in the same manner. Bysshe is still a child; Ginevra most definitely is not. She is young, yes, but she is a woman, a strong and courageous woman—or she would be if you would ever make up your mind whether you should treat her as your wife or as your daughter!"

For perhaps the first time in his adult life the Marquess of Chadwick was truly shocked. "For God's sake, Mother," he choked, flushing hotly, "how can you . . . ?" His voice faded, and he seemed to feel his blood draining from him. He stared down at Lady Helena, his blue eyes naked with pain in a face otherwise bleached of all color. With appalled insight he realized the truth of her blunt words. He thought of Ginevra's fortitude in coping with the vast and bewildering changes he had wrought, the gallantry with which she had accepted his entry into her life, her bed. He remembered his own impatience and temper that had erupted whenever she questioned one of his edicts. Had there been even one time when he had tried to explain to her what he wanted from them, when he had listened to her opinions? He had imposed his own demands ruthlessly, even to the getting of a child—he could have prevented that, but in the satisfaction of his lust it had never occurred to him to question whether a girl of eighteen years might not be ready yet for motherhood—and he had excused his willfulness by cosseting her when it was convenient and did not contradict some expressed desire of his own. Whenever she retreated from his inconsistency, he drew himself up like a stern father and called her immature. Just which of them was the childish one? he wondered.

He rasped, "Mother, I love her."

Lady Helena watched him with eyes as blue as his own, and she wished with wistful regret that she could draw his dark head down to her breast and comfort him again as if he were little. She sighed and knew it could not be. They had been apart too many years, she had failed him too many times, and now, when he needed her, she could offer no comfort, only advice.

In a voice oddly humble he repeated, "I do love Ginnie."

"Then find her," Lady Helena said softly. "Find her, my son, and tell her, now, before it is too late."

Cold water trickled over her cheek, and Ginevra shook her head violently, only to still again with an anguished moan. She screwed her eyes shut and clapped her hands over them to shield them from the intolerable brightness of the single candle. As she lay there she felt the water drip once more, seeping in little rivulets between her fingers and beading on her gold lashes. When she tried to flick the wetness away, her fingertips brushed her cheekbone, and she winced.

Above her, Bysshe's voice begged, "Oh, Ginnie, please be careful."

Slowly, reluctantly, she lifted her lashes, blinking away the moisture as her eyes adjusted to the light. Bare inches from her face she encountered Bysshe's brown eyes frowning at her anxiously. He repeated hoarsely, "You must be careful," and he dabbed delicately at her cheek with a sodden cloth.

She batted away his succoring hand and looked around cautiously. Her pelisse and shoes had been removed, and she was lying on something upholstered and lumpy, like a worn settee. Beyond the range of the candlelight the grey radiance of approaching dawn limned a room that seemed vaguely familiar. With great care she raised herself gingerly on one elbow, her head throbbing at every movement, and she glanced about her, taking in the cherry-wood armchairs and framed engravings, the crossed swords over the mantel, all looking rather eerie and omi-

nous in the dim light, yet all known to her. Confused, she
returned her gaze to Bysshe. His mouth, she noted, was
swollen and discolored where she had slapped him. "Why
have you brought me to Dowerwood?" she asked.

He muttered, "I didn't know where else to bring you."
He leaned forward, and she shrank away from him. At
her retreat he cried, "I'm sorry, Ginnie!" and blushed
furiously. "Please believe me, I'm so very sorry!"

She watched him warily. "Where are Emma and Mrs.
Harrison?"

He shrugged with unconvincing nonchalance. "They're
at . . . at the caretaker's cottage, I assume." He hesitated
before adding sheepishly, "No one seemed to be stirring
when we arrived, and I . . . drove in quietly so as not to
wake them. I parked the horses in the wood."

She pushed herself erect and swung her feet around in
front of her so that they dangled over the edge of the
sofa. She could feel the blood pounding in her temples
with sickening force, and she clutched at the arm of the
settee to steady herself. When the dizziness subsided
somewhat, she brushed her hair out of her eyes, and with
her fingertips she cautiously prodded her bruised cheek.
There seemed to be a swelling on her nape as well.

Bysshe dipped the cloth in a basin of tepid water,
Ginevra could not help recalling the time she had sponged
him in like manner. So much for gratitude. He said,
"When I . . . when you . . . fell, you struck the bracing
of the curricle, and . . . Oh, Ginnie, for a moment I
thought . . . I was so worried!"

His anguished remorse irritated her. She challenged bit-
terly, "So worried that rather than seeking help you carefully ensured that no one would know we were here?"

His color deepened. "I . . . I was afraid." He added
quickly, "But I'll take care of you, Ginnie. I promise I'll
get whatever you need. I won't hurt you."

She said coldly, "Forgive me if I find your word less
than reassuring." She twisted away, and suddenly an intense wave of nausea swept over her. Lunging for the
water basin, she only just managed to avoid disgracing
herself on the parlor rug.

Bysshe watched with a green face. When the sickness had passed, he moaned, "Oh, Ginnie, what's happening to you?" She lifted her head and regarded him balefully, too weak to speak. He looked at the basin with a grimace of disgust. "I guess I'd better do something about that," he grumbled, and he bore it away to the back of the house.

While he was gone, Ginevra leaned back against the cushions and garnered her strength. Morning sickness, she thought, and her lips curved up into a ridiculously dreamy smile. She frowned again, and after a fearful hesitation she probed her belly gently through the light fabric of her skirts, unsure of what she expected to find, yet needing to know for certain that Bysshe's outrageous escapade had not harmed the precious gift she carried for Richard. . . .

Richard! she thought with a start. Oh, God, he must be going mad with worry by now. Whatever could he have thought when he finally arrived home and found her gone? Assuming that he did arrive home, of course, that he had not spent the night with . . . No, she shook herself firmly, she would not allow her mind to fall prey to the farrago of nonsense that woman had fed Bysshe. Her husband had said he would come home, and he never lied to her.

But what if he believed that she had eloped with Bysshe?

Agony pulsed through her like electric current, and she wanted to scream as at last she comprehended the full extent of the Frenchwoman's revenge: this elaborate charade had not been intended to make Ginevra distrustful of her husband; rather it was meant to convince Richard that his second wife, like his first, had betrayed him, that Ginevra was another Maria. "No!" she sobbed, ignoring the pounding in her temples. "No, I won't let her hurt him like this!" She sprang to her feet and stumbled toward the door.

Suddenly in the archway Bysshe materialized. The light in the room was rising quickly, the pure unsullied light of a new day, and Ginevra could easily read his look of surprise. He carried a tumbler of water in one hand, and he caught her awkwardly with the other. "Ginnie," he chided, "you shouldn't excite yourself."

She pulled away from him without difficulty, and in a cool voice that belied her agitation she said, "Bysshe, it's time you take me home."

For response he proffered the glass to her with the abashed air of a child presenting a flower to its mother. "Here," he said, "I thought you'd want this."

The water was fresh-pumped and cold, and she gulped it greedily, grateful to wash the vile taste of her sickness from her mouth. When she had finished it she said breathlessly, "Thank you. Now, may we go home?"

He shook his head. His brown eyes were regretful but resolute. "No, Ginnie, I can't take you back."

She stared at him, blocking the doorway, and her own expression firmed. "Then in that case, stand aside and let me go find Mrs. Harrison and Emma. They will help me."

He shook his head again, harder. "No, Ginnie. I won't let you go back to him. You don't seem to understand. I'm very sorry I lost my temper—that was unforgivable of me—but nothing has changed. I still have to protect you—from yourself, if need be."

"But I don't want to be protected!" She glowered at him, but he remained obdurate, and she knew further argument was useless. Slowly she turned away and shuffled across the room, her steps weighted with despair. In the center of the worn rug she halted, and she stood gazing down at the faded design. With one silk-stockinged toe she began to trace the pattern. The room was so quiet she could hear birds beginning to sing outside in the virgin morning, and somewhere in the distance a horse whinnied. In a husky voice that he had to strain to hear, she asked, "Bysshe, what is it you want of me?"

There was another silence; then, "I want you to love me," he said simply.

She completed the outline of one arabesque and began another. "I do love you, Bysshe. You've always been my very dear friend, the brother I never had."

"But that's not what I want, Ginnie."

She looked up at him now and smiled faintly, ironically. "I know. You want me to be your whore."

Bysshe blanched. "Ginnie!" he gasped, outraged.

She shrugged and glanced away again. "Isn't that what you want? Forgive me for misunderstanding you, but I don't see what other alternative there might be. I am a married woman, Bysshe, and the only way I could . . . be with you as you wish is by becoming your mistress, your harlot."

"But there must be some—"

In exasperation she gritted, "No, there isn't! Have you forgotten that I am your *stepmother*, that within me I carry a child who will be your sister or brother, just as Tom was? How can you dare to hope that—"

From the doorway a deep voice drawled, "It's of no avail to argue, Ginevra. Haven't you learned yet that the rutting male simply will not be gainsaid?"

Golden curls aswirl, she jerked her head around. The marquess loomed behind Bysshe, his tall, massive frame overshadowing the youth, who shrank from him.

"Richard!" Ginevra cried, her face alight with joy and relief. Ignoring Bysshe, she flew across the room to her husband. Her stocking feet scarcely touched the floor, and he caught and enfolded her to him in powerful arms that crushed her with sweet savagery. "Oh, Richard," she sighed against his chest as she clung to him. She nuzzled her face in his lapels, and her nostrils were full of the masculine scents of leather and horses and sweat. Beneath his coat his shirt was drenched, and she realized with wonder that he must have galloped through the night to find her. She marvelled, "I was so afraid you wouldn't . . . you wouldn't . . ."

He trembled as he brushed his lips across her gleaming hair, shaking with fatigue and something she could not yet identify. "Did you think I would not discover you, little Ginnie? Don't you know that I love you so much that there is no place you can hide from me?"

She looked up at him with shining eyes, unable to believe what she had heard. "Love?" she questioned, and he nodded wryly.

"Quite madly, my dear. I'm afraid you'll never escape me now."

"But I don't want to escape," she declared, and he caught his breath sharply. Her thin arms slid under his coat and tightened about him fiercely, so that her breasts were crushed against his chest and her hands stroked the powerful muscles of his back. Leaning against him, she could hear the heavy thud of his heart under her ear; then his strong fingers caught her chin and tilted her head so that his mouth could close hungrily over hers.

For endless moments they stood entwined in the silent room, heedless of the youth who watched them. Then gently, reluctantly, Chadwick eased her away from him. He stared down at her with tender concern, but when he saw the deep bruise on her cheekbone, his expression hardened ruthlessly. He rasped, "Tell me what happened, Ginevra."

Her gold eyes flicked charily between her husband and Bysshe, whose swollen lip glared against his livid countenance. The tension that had ebbed during those mindless seconds in Chadwick's arms now flooded back into the room. Ginevra stammered unconvincingly, "N-nothing happened. I . . . I fell."

"Ginevra . . ." Chadwick warned.

"Please, Richard, it's not important now." She reached up to stroke the stern line of his mouth, still wet with her kisses. "I am unharmed. Let us put an end to this."

He caught her wrists and drew them away from his face. "No," he said, "it's not that easy." He squeezed her fingers for emphasis, and she grimaced at his strength.

"Stop hurting her!" Bysshe shrieked. "Keep your hands off her!"

The marquess looked at the boy in surprise, as if he had forgotten his existence. "I am not hurting her," he said coldly, "and I will thank you not to interfere in my marriage. You have already intruded more than is . . . healthy."

"Damn you!" Bysshe swore, sputtering in his fury. "You think all you ever have to do is give orders . . . See what you make of this!" As Ginevra gaped, paralyzed with shock, he ripped Sir Charles's old duelling foils down from the wall over the mantel and flung one hilt-first at Chadwick.

Quickly Ginevra's husband shoved her aside, and she stumbled against one of the armchairs, sinking feebly into it as she watched. Chadwick caught the thrown sword easily, the thin, deadly steel flexing and flashing in the morning light. With an agile flick of his wrist he bowed the blade to test it, and when Bysshe moved toward him, Chadwick fell with lethal grace into the guard position, the well-balanced crouch that gave him freedom of movement and yet presented the smallest possible target to his opponent. His graven features were expressionless as he studied Bysshe with hooded eyes. "I wondered when it would come to this," he murmured.

Ginevra stared numbly at her husband and the youth who faced him. Bysshe was already sweating with tension, his lank hair plastered to his forehead, and it required no knowledge of swordplay to realize that Chadwick could swiftly overpower him. She supposed the boy must have taken fencing lessons in school, but to the marquess were all the advantages of stamina and agility and experience. Bsyshe had only recklessness and the wild, seething anger that drove him.

"En garde," the boy choked, raising the tip of his foil in salute. The point described little circles as his fingers trembled.

"En garde," Chadwick echoed, and when he slowly lifted his sword, his hand was rock-steady.

Ginevra had once seen two of her father's friends mix with swords on the lawn behind Bryant House. It had been a game, an impromptu exhibition of skill, no more, yet it had sickened her. While the other members of the house party shouted raucous encouragement, she had watched the darting blades, heard the jarring clang of steel and the labored grunts of the combatants, smelled the feral odor of their heaving bodies, and she had wanted to scream. Now the prospect of such violence unleashed seemed even more terrible, almost blasphemous, in the sedate confines of the Dowerwood parlor.

She leaped from the chair and shouted, "For the love of God, Richard, don't do this!"

His blue eyes never wavered as he waited for his opponent to make the opening thrust. Through lips that barely moved, he noted almost conversationally, "The challenge was his, Ginevra. Would you have me delope?"

"But, Richard . . ." she pleaded, her voice trailing off when she saw that his features were adamantine. She spun instead toward the boy, now poised for the attack. "Bysshe, I beg of you, stop this madness: don't take arms against your own father!"

Rather than showing remorse as she had hoped, Bysshe swore viciously and blurted, "Father! Devil take you for a fool, Ginnie, are you the only one who doesn't know? He doesn't believe he is my father. He's never believed it!"

Ginevra stared, stunned, as his words pounded into her, shocking and yet almost . . . almost soothing as at last she began to see a reason for the bewildering antagonism between her husband and his heir. With pallid face she turned again to Chadwick. "Richard?" she asked uncertainly.

He glanced at the boy, who still crouched with sword in hand, and he said, "This is hardly the time."

"Tell her!" Bysshe spat, brushing his sandy hair from his eyes. "Why try to wrap it in clean linen? It's common enough knowledge."

"It's common knowledge only in your mind, Bysshe," Chadwick averred. The boy began a halting, sideways circuit of the room, moving awkwardly around the furniture. Chadwick kept a cautious distance, neither retreating nor approaching, and Ginevra marvelled that he could talk and watch so warily at the same time. After a moment, in a voice that betrayed deep spiritual weariness, he said, "I *could* be Bysshe's father, it is not beyond the realm of possibility. My last leave from the Navy coincided with one of Maria's infrequent visits to Queenshaven, and . . ." He shrugged. "Some eight months later, while aboard ship I received a letter from my mother informing me jointly of the birth of my second son and the death of my wife. It was not until after Copenhagen, when I returned to Surrey to recuperate from my wound, that I discovered that Maria had died not in childbed as I thought, but in a carriage accident while absconding with her latest lover."

"And ever since then," Bysshe gritted, "you have treated me not as your son but as the bastard that was foisted off on you!" His fingers tensed on the hilt of the foil.

As Chadwick made ready to parry, he said tightly, "On the contrary, I have dealt with you exactly as I did with your brother."

"Then why—?"

"Oh, stop it!" Ginevra bellowed, her usually quiet voice exploding in the strained atmosphere of the small room. "For God's sake, both of you, just stop it!"

Startled, Bysshe and the marquess paused in their deadly dance to stare at her. Her face was ashen except for two gaudy spots of color painting her cheeks under her sparking eyes, and her breast heaved with annoyance. "Just stop it, both of you," she repeated hoarsely, her throat raw from the force of her cry. Angry tears beaded her lashes, and she scrubbed her aching eyes with hands that quivered as if palsied. She looked first at her husband, then at Bysshe. "I don't know which of you is worse," she declared, "or perhaps it is that you are of a kind, with your violence and your vanity and your overweening pride. What difference does it make whether you share the same blood? In every way that counts, you are exactly alike!"

She turned to the boy and pleaded, "Bysshe, I implore you: put away the sword. You claim to love me; don't make me hate you."

He retreated quickly from her, and his brown eyes were regretful yet defiant. "I can't, Ginnie. It's been all my life . . ."

She pivoted toward her husband, lifting her head to meet his gaze that was made equally of admiration and ironic self-mockery. He said, "You ask much, Ginevra."

She shook her head. "I ask only that you make an end to something that ought never to have begun. Think,

Richard: you and your father, now you and your son—if you will not finish it, how long must this sorry hostility continue?" She took a deep shuddering breath. "Richard, your seed grows inside me. I love you, and I can think of no greater joy than to bear your child, but if that child be doomed to live under a cloud of resentment and jealousy, then . . . then I hope it dies aborning."

He gazed down at her pale, intent face, the wide amber eyes watching him accusingly. "You love me although I am vain, violent, proud?" he asked curiously.

"You are not always thus, my lord," she replied shyly.

Slowly he lifted his free hand to caress her tender cheek, his long fingers brushing gently over the bruise. "Oh, little Ginnie," he sighed wryly, "how you do defeat me." He glanced sidelong at the boy, who still confronted him, weapon in hand, and he made his decision. "I will not fight you, Bysshe," he said, and he threw down his sword.

The foil fell to the floor with a clatter, and its tip caught on the nap of the worn rug. It swung in an arc, rolling on the round guard, the blade flashing as it rotated. When the foil bumped against Bysshe's ankle, he scowled down at it as if he did not recognize it. He shifted his gaze to the sword in his own hand; then deliberately he looked at the distracted couple before him. The tall man was smiling lovingly into the joy-stung features of the girl. Dark angry color suffused Bysshe's face, and he grated, "An apology isn't enough." His voice rose stridently, and he lifted the foil. "Damn you, it's not nearly enough!" With a wild goaded cry he lunged at the marquess.

He moved too quickly for them to react, and his blade might have found its target had he not tripped over the foil that lay at his feet. Unable to catch himself, momentum carrying him forward, his sword turned awry, and as he fell he could only watch with sickened shock as the point of his weapon slashed the muslin skirts of Ginevra's gown and with ghastly ease cut deep into the white flesh of her thigh.

"Ginnie!" Bysshe wailed, picking himself up from the

floor. He flung the foil away from him, and it skittered over the furniture and hit the wall, dislodging one of the framed pictures. Ginevra did not seem to notice. She blinked at her husband and gave a little cough of surprise. Then her legs crumpled beneath her. Instantly Chadwick scooped her into his strong arms and bore her away to the sofa, where he settled her on the worn cushions, trying not to see the blood that smeared in smoky contrast to the faded upholstery. When he eased the shredded fabric of her dress away from the wound, revealing the long raw cut, he heard Bysshe choke sickly. With bleak and terrible eyes the marquess looked up at the boy. They glared at each other, and Ginevra, who watched as if through a dim red haze, waited helplessly for her husband's rage to erupt. She could feel him shake. Tentatively she touched his arm. Her voice came in short, strained gasps. "P-please, darling, it . . . it was an accident—you know it was. I . . . the babe and I . . . will be all right." She tried to chuckle weakly. "With a scar on my h-hip, you . . . you and I will m-make a matched pair." Chadwick's blue eyes were opaque and unreadable in his dark face. "If you care for me . . ." she cried desperately, and at last he nodded. Without looking up, he hissed through clenched teeth, "Go find the caretaker, Bysshe. Go find help—and then never let me see you again."

"Richard," Ginevra protested, her speech dying in a gurgle as she succumbed to the pain that seared her leg and hip, "you can't—"

"Be quiet, Ginnie," he said. His long fingers methodically shaped the muslin of her skirts into a thick pad to stanch the bleeding. "Be quiet, my love." And he said nothing else, not when with an inarticulate moan Bysshe fled from the room, nor a few moments later when the worried cries of women were masked by the receding rattle of the curricle as its matched blacks raced it down the rough drive. Ginevra watched her husband's silent, economical movements, and she wondered desolately if some wounds were simply too deep to heal.

The Lady Kathleen Helena Glover was born just as the

sun rose on the first day of spring, a cold morning bright
with the promise of new life. Her mother, exhausted by
the long labor, raised a bemused finger to stroke lightly
her ruddy cheek, then collapsed into a deep, dreamless
slumber. Her father, who had scandalized almost everyone by remaining at his lady's side all during the birth,
pronounced himself satisfied with his new daughter and
allowed her to be carried away to the nursery. When
Emma Jarvis paused in the doorway with the mewling
bundle in her arms, she glanced back at the dark brooding man still hunched in the chair beside the bed. Dr. Perrin joined her and silently closed the door behind them.
She shook her head in wonder as they walked away together. It was a trick of the light, she decided, or else a
phantasm brought on by her fatigue. Nothing else could
explain what she thought she had just seen: the Marquess
of Chadwick with tears in his eyes.

In the cheery Queenshaven nursery, freshly redecorated, as had been most of the house, Emma handed the
baby over to Susan, who clucked fondly and settled the
infant into her shiny new cradle warmed with hot bricks.
Emma sank into a chair and leaned back wearily, her
green eyes closed. When she opened them again, the doctor was standing in front of her, watching her intently.
She blinked, and he said in his quiet, cultured voice,
"You did very well, Emma. I was grateful for your assistance. It was good of you to take time away from your
school."

She shrugged. "For my Miss Ginevra, how could I do
otherwise?" She glanced in the direction of the cradle and
smiled tenderly. "Such a beautiful baby."

"Oui," he agreed, "but perhaps that is to be expected.
La petite has exceptionally handsome parents." He
paused; then he asked, "Emma, have you never thought
of having children of your own?"

She stared down at the hands suddenly clenched in her
lap. Swallowing hard, she murmured, "Once, a long time
ago. But the war——"

"The war is over, Emma," he declared, and he
swooped down and caught her nervous fingers in his own.

She glanced at him in surprise. When she tried to tug her hand away, he would not release it. "The war is long over," he said again, more quietly, his warm grey eyes intent on her suspicious face. "You know that, don't you?" Reluctantly she nodded. "Just as you know that you and I could be very happy together if you would bury your old bitterness?"

"Yes," she admitted with a sigh.

"*Bon,*" he said. "Now it is time for us to make our own peace." And as she watched him he pried open her tense fist and placed a gentle, seductive kiss in her palm.

When Chadwick returned to Ginevra's room after letting Hobbs shave him, he was astonished to find his wife sitting up in bed, supported by a mound of pillows, her honey-colored hair smoothly brushed and flowing over her shoulders, down the front of a white cambric nightgown delicately embroidered with yellow roses. She looked like a bride, he thought humbly. Only faint violet shadows under her eyes hinted at the agony she had endured, and now she seemed untouched by it all. She smiled at him, but before she could speak, Susan bustled into the room with the baby. She respectfully but firmly brushed the marquess aside while she gave Ginevra whispered instructions on how to feed her daughter. Chadwick watched with hooded eyes as his wife bared her swollen breast and guided the tiny, seeking mouth to the nipple. Susan nodded her approval, readjusted the pillows behind Ginevra's back, and left the room.

Ginevra gazed in wonder at her baby, stroking the black ringlets that covered the small, perfect head. When she looked up at Chadwick, her golden eyes shimmered. "Oh, Richard," she sighed in soft rapture, "is she not beautiful?"

The rings on her slim finger glittered in the bright morning light as she caressed the raven hair of the suckling infant, and the child's curls were brushstrokes of black ink against Ginevra's white breast. "Beautiful," Chadwick whispered huskily. "Like you." With a wave of hungry emotion he dropped to the edge of the bed and gathered Ginevra in his arms, dislodging little Lady Kath-

leen. Tiny fists waved in indignant protest, batting at the
smooth curve of the breast. With gentle fingers he helped
the baby find the nipple again. Ginevra grimaced.

"Does she hurt you?" her husband demanded.

Ginevra shook her head. "She and I are both new to
this. We will learn, I expect."

"I could find you a nurse, some sturdy farmer's wife
who—"

"No," Ginevra said flatly. "She is my daughter, and I
will nourish her as God intended me to."

"I see. I collect you have definite ideas on child rear-
ing." His thin mouth curled up in indulgent amusement.
"Forgive me, my dear. You are right, of course." He grew
serious again, and Ginevra's eyes clouded at the unexpected humility in his voice as he said uncertainly, "It's
just that I know so little about being a father. It is a skill
I have . . . prized too little, to my lasting regret." For a
moment they both thought of Bysshe, who had gone to
live with his grandmother. In her last letter Lady Helena
said the boy was talking about joining the Navy.

"You could learn," Ginevra suggested, reaching up to
stroke the hard line of his jaw. "It is not too late, it is
never too late. If you tried, if the overture came from
you, even now you and Bysshe might . . ."

The Marquess of Chadwick's voice was hoarse as he
pleaded, "Then teach me, little Ginnie. You have taught
me everything I know that is worth knowing: love, trust,
patience. You have given me joy and tenderness, you
have given me a daughter I shall cherish with all my
heart. Now . . ." His voice faltered. "Now I beg of you,
help give me back my son."

She gazed at him, at the dark blue eyes and graven features that she had loved since childhood. She smiled reassuringly. "Soon," she promised, "very soon." She
snuggled against him, and his arms tightened around her
and the infant, now replete, who slept at her breast. His
lips brushed lightly across her temple.

When Susan, carrying a tea tray, opened the door to
her mistress's chamber, she quietly and hastily shut it
again. She shook her head with a grin. Obviously the

master and his wife wanted no intruding on that intimate and emotional scene. She turned to go to the nursery, but then she remembered that the doctor and the schoolmistress seemed to need privacy as well. With a shrug she set the tray on a table and snatched up one of the sesame biscuits from the covered plate. Munching stealthily, she decided to slip up to her quarters for a few minutes. There was bound to be a lively celebration tonight, in honor of the baby's birth, and she wanted to see if her Sunday dress needed pressing.